Disillusioned

A Stan Turner Mystery

Dedication

Disillusioned is dedicated to my brother-in-law, Paul, who has been a Godsend to my sister and who is one of the kindest, unselfish, and most caring persons I know.

Disillusioned

A Stan Turner Mystery
Volume 9

by

William Manchee

Top Publications, Ltd.
Dallas, Texas

Disillusioned, A Stan Turner Mystery
Volume 9

Printed in the United States

Top Publications, Ltd.
12221 Merit Dr. Suite 950
Dallas, Texas 75251

ISBN 978-1-929976-66-9
Library of Congress Control Number 2010921365

This work is a novel and any similarity to actual persons or events is purely coincidental.

Chapter 1

Why is it that some people cannot say no? Stan Turner had this affliction and it damn near cost him his career, his family, and his life. To understand why he felt compelled to take on so many dangerous and impossible pursuits we only have to examine his childhood. Unlike most children who at age fifteen had no idea what career path they wanted to follow, Stan knew he wanted to be a politician. He was fascinated by politics and followed all the state and national elections closely. He quickly realized that anyone hoping for a career in politics needed to have an unblemished record. During his youth, he'd been able to avoid trouble to a large extent because he'd led a sheltered life. He came from a lower-middle class family and his parents had to work so hard to survive they had little time to micro manage his life. In fact, Stan was pretty much left to fend for himself. The only thing his parents insisted upon was that he did his chores, wasn't late for supper, and got passing grades.

Not that Stan was neglected. He never missed a meal nor did his parents ever lay a hand on him. They simply left him to himself and as long as he didn't get in trouble they were happy. This atmosphere resulted in Stan being rather shy, introverted, and more independent than most of his school mates. At school he kept to himself and only had a few friends. Although he envied the popular students, he was more or less comfortable being alone, at least that's what he told himself. His seclusion had its advantages. He didn't feel the social pressures to drink, smoke or experiment with drugs that most teenagers encountered growing up. Not that he didn't try smoking and drinking. He did, but he never found much pleasure in them. In fact, he often wondered why his peers were so obsessed with such unpleasant habits. He particularly couldn't understand why anyone would take drugs when the dire consequences of such behavior were so obvious.

Stan's parents were Republicans so it was only natural that Stan would join the Republican Party too. But Stan didn't think the political system in America made much sense. In his mind there were theoretically four major political classifications: republican, democrat, conservative, and liberal. What confused him was the fact that there were conservative democrats and conservative republicans and liberal republicans and liberal democrats. This made no sense to him until he realized that politics was more about power than philosophical beliefs, so people would pick the party that they thought would give them more advantage and then join either the liberal or conservative wing of the party to satisfy their philosophical leanings.

So at age twenty-two Stan had an unblemished record–eagle scout, number two in his high school class, congressional intern, graduate of UCLA, and the perfect marriage to his soul mate, Rebekah James. But that's when Stan's good fortune came to an end.

When he was fourteen Stan visited the county fair where the new Univac Computer was on display. To demonstrate the new computer's abilities someone had programmed it to tell fortunes, so Stan and his friend, Steve, had their fortunes told. Whereas Steve's fortune was benign Stan's was rather disturbing.

Struggling in a hostile world
Pursuing your destiny
You will stand resolutely against adversity
Undaunted

Stan didn't take the fortune seriously until a year into law school when he was inexplicably drafted into the Marine Corps. The Vietnam War was almost over and he'd drawn #339 in the Draft Lottery, but his draft board got the last laugh by drafting him just days before the lottery took effect. Stan and Rebekah were particularly shocked and bitter about this turn of events because Rebekah was pregnant and Stan was in his first year of law school.

Although he wasn't thrilled about being drafted, he knew it was important to have a successful military tour of duty if he was serious about politics. Unfortunately, fate wasn't in his corner. Just a few days into Officer Candidate School, he found himself in the worst trouble of his life—accused of the murder of his drill sergeant.

Stan was innocent but somehow by a bizarre twist of fate his fingerprints ended up on the murder weapon. When a court martial was convened it didn't look good for him as he'd been disciplined by his drill sergeant the day before the murder and ended up in the hospital. He'd had a few choice words about Sgt. Foster while being treated, of course, which made matters worse. The eventual court martial attracted national media attention and Quantico was besieged with reporters wanting to cover the story.

Fortunately, Stan had friends and allies: the congressman he'd interned for, a nurse who had fallen in love with him, a reporter, Virginia Stone, who wanted his exclusive story, and, of course, his rookie legal counsel who'd never tried a murder case before but was cocky and confident anyway. With all this help he was able to prove his innocence.

After enduring the court martial Stan had no desire to continue his military service, so he requested and was granted a general discharge. Despite his acquittal there were those who still believed he was guilty and he knew he faced a lifetime of suspicion and doubt on that score.

At the time he was drafted, Stan had been in law school in California, but his father-in-law had been transferred to Dallas in the interim. Rebekah wanted to be close to her parents, so after Stan was discharged, he applied for entry into SMU School of Law for the fall semester of 1975. There were a lot of questions about his trial and disastrous military career, but the Dean of Admissions admitted they couldn't legally hold his court martial against him since he'd been acquitted. So, after many interviews and endless paperwork, they reluctantly accepted his application.

Although getting into law school was a big relief for Stan, it also triggered a myriad of problems, not the least of which was how to survive financially, particularly because he was married and had four children. Rebekah was an ER nurse, so her income was good, but it was not enough to pay SMU's steep tuition and the cost of books, along with all the other regular family expenses. Stan had little choice but to get a job to pay for his legal education or mortgage his family's future by taking out student loans. Since he already had unpaid student loans from college, Stan elected to get a job instead of going further in debt.

His job hunting had been difficult, and the best thing he could come up with was selling life insurance for Cosmopolitan Life. He hated the job, but the hours were flexible, so he could work around his schedule at SMU, and the pay was just enough to cover his tuition and books. During his six-week training course, he not only learned about insurance but a lot about business and marketing as well. He found this interesting and figured it would be useful knowledge to have when he started his law practice. They gave him some nifty little gadgets too—calculators, an insurance needs slide rule, and a briefcase with a built-in audio-video player-recorder for making fancy presentations. He also soon discovered that insurance agents often were asked by their clients for referrals to lawyers for needed legal services, so the connections he made in the insurance industry could be very beneficial to him when he started his law practice.

Even though Stan knew a political career wasn't an option for him anymore, he was still keenly interested in politics and couldn't say no when he was asked to join the local Republican Party. In the summer of 1976, the Democrats still controlled almost every political office in north Texas, but that was changing, and for the first time since Reconstruction, Republican candidates in northern Dallas and southern Collin counties actually had a chance of beating their Democratic opponents. This excited Stan as he'd always found himself pulling for the underdog.

When the members of the Republican Executive Committee learned of his legal training and experience as a congressional intern, they asked him to run for county chairman. When he protested that he didn't have the time to take on that kind of responsibility, they assured him the staff would do most of the work and he wouldn't be expected to put that much time into the job.

Rebekah, of course, thought it was a bad idea and told Stan as much, but Stan's was so flattered that the party officials wanted him to run and excited by the prospect of being an elected official, that there was no way he could have turned it down, even though it made no sense to be taking on such a big responsibility. For the first time since his Marine Corps debacle Stan thought maybe he could have a political career after all. So in the June 1976 primary elections he became Collin County's new Republican Party Chairman.

It was Saturday, July 3, 1976 and Stan and Rebekah were attending a barbecue at the home of a wealthy businessman, Brad Thornton. The home was a palace compared to Stan and Rebekah's $18,000 Fox and Jacobs tract home they'd recently purchased. As they strolled past the parade of Cadillacs, Lincoln Town Cars, and Jaguars parked in front of the house, Rebekah spotted their friends Rob and Cindy Shepard coming from the other direction.

"Cindy! Hi," Rebekah said.

"Hi, Rebekah. How are you?"

"Fine. Can you believe this house? It's huge."

Cindy nodded. "Yeah, I love this French country home style. This one's got five bedrooms and seven bathrooms. We looked at it before the Thorntons bought it. It's almost as big as my parent's house."

Cindy Shepard was in her mid-twenties, short, with light brown hair, beautiful green eyes, nice figure and a perfect complexion. She came from a wealthy family that owned a lot of real estate and operated several prosperous businesses in north Texas. Rob's family had been around a long time too, but they hadn't accumulated near as much wealth. Cindy's parents hadn't been thrilled when the two of them announced they were going to get married, but Cindy had a mind of her own and didn't much care what they thought. As a result, there had been a lot of tension between the two families, and that strained Rob and Cindy's marriage.

"Hey, Rob," Stan said, shaking his friend's hand.

Rob was tall and muscular. He'd been the star quarterback on the high school football team and consequently was quite well known and popular in the community. That was why Brad Thornton had recruited him to run for state representative. The Republican Party needed someone well known if they were to have a chance at upsetting the Democratic incumbent, Ron Wells.

"Hi, Stan. Can you believe this heat?" Rob asked.

The temperature in Dallas in July usually hovered around a hundred degrees, and this day was no exception. The girls were dressed in shorts and halter tops since it was an outdoor party. Stan gazed at Cindy's long, sexy legs then smiled at her when she caught him looking.

"Yeah, thank God for air conditioning," Stan replied.

"Look! A waterfall," Rebekah said, pointing to the corner of the courtyard.

"Wow! That's cool," Stan replied enviously.

They entered the courtyard, appreciative of the shade provided by several large cottonwoods. Stopping for a moment, they admired an assortment of exotic plants and a pond full of tropical fish. A small stream ran in front of the house from the waterfall to the pond. They continued to the front door, where they could see guests inside through a stained glass window. Rebekah knocked on the door. A second later Melissa Thornton swung the door open and smiled out at them with her ultra-white teeth and bright blue eyes. She was a dirty blond in her early forties, but with the help of a skillful plastic surgeon, she still looked quite stunning.

"Hello. Come on in," she said.

"Melissa, this is Rebekah and Stan Turner," Cindy said.

"Oh, it's a pleasure to finally meet you," Melissa replied. "Hi, Rob."

"Hi, Mrs. Thornton," Rob said. "How are you?"

"Fine. Go on over to the bar and get yourself a drink. Brad's around here somewhere. I'm sure you'll run into him."

"No doubt," Rob replied.

They went to the bar, got drinks, and then went onto the back patio where most of the guests were mingling. A half dozen children were swimming in the large pool, and a catering company was setting up a buffet. Rebekah spotted an empty table, and they went over and staked a claim to it. After a few minutes they were joined by Brad Thornton.

"You finally made it," Brad said to Rob. "I've been anxious to find out how your meeting with the Chamber of Commerce went."

"Everyone seemed friendly," Rob replied, "but you never know what they are thinking."

Brad Thornton was a tall, thin man with dark hair and a thin mustache. He was never without a Stetson on his head and a grin on his face. Rebekah thought he looked a little like Clark Gable.

"True. A lot will depend on how the presidential race goes. If Reagan gets the nomination, you'll have a good shot at winning."

Ronald Reagan had trounced Ford in the May 1, 1976 Texas primary, winning all 100 Texas delegates, despite the fact that the Republican establishment had been squarely behind Ford. Rob was one of the Reagan delegates scheduled to go to the Republican Convention in August. Stan would have been a delegate had Ford won the primary.

"I hope Reagan gets the nomination," Rob said. "He's a hell of a lot more popular around here than Ford."

"Don't you think the conservatives would prefer Ford over Jimmy Carter?" Stan asked.

"Sure," Brad agreed, "but they won't turn out in the same numbers for Ford as they would for Reagan."

"I don't know," Rob said. "The thought of Jimmy Carter becoming President is pretty scary."

They all laughed.

After a few minutes, Brad left to mingle with his other guests, and Stan and Rob went for more drinks. On his way to the bar, Stan was stopped by Kristina Tenison, one of the volunteers assigned to help Stan with his duties as county chairman. Besides being young and beautiful, Kristina was very well organized and efficient. Stan had been in awe of her from the moment they'd met. In fact, he felt a little guilty because Kristina did most of his work yet he got all of the credit for it.

"Hi, Kristina," Stan said, smiling broadly.

"Oh, Stan, I'm so glad I ran into you."

"Yeah? What's up?"

"I got a call yesterday from Robert Brown, Ford's Dallas Campaign Chairman."

"Oh, really?"

"Yeah. The President's coming to Dallas at the end of the month. There's going to be a reception for local officials and candidates. Robert would like you to pick a dozen people from this area and invite them."

"Really? Why me?"

"Because you're one of only a few who signed up to be a Ford delegate at the convention. Most everyone else is backing Reagan."

"Yeah, but I didn't get picked to be a delegate."

"That doesn't matter. They know where your

allegiances lie."

"Hmm."

"Anyway, he needed an answer right away, so I told him you'd do it."

Stan laughed. "Okay."

"Are you mad at me for accepting the job for you?" Kristina asked. "I didn't want you to miss such a great opportunity."

Stan shook his head. "No, no. It's fine, as long as you're going to help me decide who to invite."

"Of course. Monday's a holiday. Maybe we can get together for a few hours to work on it. "

The thought of spending time with Kristina excited Stan. As a shy teenager he hadn't had many dates. One problem was he looked younger than he was and girls his age were attracted to older boys. It was frustrating for him to be around so many pretty young girls but unable to establish a romantic relationship with any of them. In fact, in high school he'd had only one serious relationship. When he was a senior he went steady with a sophomore girl but that inevitably ended with his graduation.

In college, however, things had changed. He'd grown taller, slimmed down, and girls seemed to see him differently. After a while he found himself hanging around with a number of different women. That's when Rebekah snagged him and hauled him in. Women liked Stan because he was a good listener, actually paid attention to what they had to say and threw out compliments like rice at a wedding. But his compliments were genuine and not followed up by a romantic advance, which some woman found gratifying and others frustrating. So, even after marrying Rebekah, if Stan met a pretty woman, it was a good bet they'd soon be good friends. In fact, most of Stan's friends were women, which made Rebekah very jealous.

"Okay. It will be great meeting the President in person."

"Yeah, that's what I thought."

Stan smiled. "Thanks, Kristina. You're amazing."

Kristina blushed. "Why do you say that?"

"You always seem to know what to do and never hesitate to act. I don't know why they asked me to be County Chairman. They should have asked you."

"They'd never elect a woman County Chairman."

"Why not?" Stan asked surprised by the comment.

"They just wouldn't."

Stan resisted a strong urge to put his arm around Kristina and give her a big hug. So far, he'd managed to resist any show of affection toward her, but it hadn't been easy. Several times they'd been alone at Republican headquarters, and he'd had trouble concentrating on the work they were doing. He wondered if she had similar feelings for him or if it was just her nature to be flirtatious with the men she worked with. But he knew it would be a mistake to try to find out.

When Stan and Rob got back to their table with fresh drinks, Rebekah and Cindy had already filled their plates with barbeque and were starting to eat.

"We got tired of waiting for you," Cindy said to Rob. "What took you so long?"

"It was Stan's fault. Kristina grabbed him the moment we got in the house."

Rebekah's eyes narrowed. "What did she want?"

"Oh, the President's coming to town, and his staff wants me to invite some guests to a reception he's having. I'll put you on the list, Rob, if you're willing to be seen with him."

Rob frowned. "If I thought it would help my campaign, I would, but I'm not sure."

"It couldn't hurt. He is the President."

"Let me give it some thought. I'll let you know on Monday if I want an invitation."

Stan and Rob took their plates and got in the food line. Ten minutes later, they were back and dug in. After dinner, when it got dark, everyone gathered in the back yard to watch the annual fireworks show put on by a church down the street. When it was over, they went inside and caught the end of the big bicentennial celebration in New York on TV.

An hour later, Stan looked at his watch and sighed. "Well, this has been a blast, but we've got to go."

Rebekah nodded in agreement. "Yes, we promised our babysitter we'd be home by ten."

"I'll call you on Monday," Rob said.

"Oh, just put us on the list already," Cindy said. "You're not going to miss a photo op with the President of the United States."

Rob shrugged. "Okay. I guess you're right."

"Good," Rebekah said. "We'll all go together. It should be fun."

Stan and Rebekah said goodbye to Melissa and Brad and then left the party. When they got home, Jenni, Reggie, and Mark were watching the bicentennial celebration on TV. Jenni immediately got up, obviously delighted to see them.

"How were they?" Rebekah asked.

Jenni shrugged. "Okay. Peter went right to sleep at nine, but I had trouble getting Marcia to go down. She just fell asleep a few minutes ago."

"She was probably overtired," Rebekah said. "I have trouble getting her to sleep sometimes."

Stan paid Jenni and she left.

"Alright, it's bedtime," Stan said to Mark and Reggie. "It's after ten o'clock. You guys should already be asleep."

"We were watching the fireworks," Reggie protested.

"Well, if you two don't get in bed in the next two minutes, you'll see some real fireworks."

Mark and Reggie ran up the stairs, and Stan followed them to tuck them in and to check on Peter and Marcia. When he returned, Rebekah was sitting on the sofa watching TV. Stan gazed at her from the top of the stairs for a moment. He loved her long black hair, big brown eyes, and smooth olive skin. He went to her and gave her a long kiss.

"What was that for?" she asked with a sly smile.

"Just celebrating the bicentennial," he said, turning off the lamp next to them.

He kissed her again and then led her to the bedroom. She didn't resist him but the passion she'd shown when they were first married, and she so desperately wanted children, was gone. It seemed to him now that she was simply performing her wifely duty in bed and just as soon be reading a book. Stan never said anything to her but he missed that passion and wished she enjoyed sex as much as he did.

Chapter 2

On Monday, since it was a holiday, Stan took the family out to breakfast. After they'd returned home, he went outside to get the newspaper and was shocked to see Brad Thornton's face on the front page. The headline read:

'Local Businessman Under Investigation"

"FBI agents executed a search warrant at the home of local businessman Brad Thornton. The agent in charge would not comment on the search, but said it was part of an ongoing investigation. Informed sources familiar with the case claim there have been accusations of money laundering against Mr. Thornton in the past and the search today may be related to those accusations."

Stan rushed inside to show Rebekah the article. She was putting a load of clothes in the washer when he found her. "Look at this news report. It looks like Brad Thornton is in some kind of trouble."

"What? You've got to be kidding," Rebekah said, grabbing the newspaper from him. "We were just with him last night."

"I know. Rob's gonna be devastated. Thornton's been bank rolling his campaign."

"You think they'll arrest him?"

Stan shrugged. "I don't know, but if they do, I'm sure Rob's funding will dry up."

"What will he do if that happens?"

"Find new contributors, if he can."

"I should call Cindy," Rebekah said.

"Yeah, do that. I was about to head over to Republican headquarters to meet Kristina. I'm sure she'll know what's going on. Tell Rob I'll call him later."

"Okay. Don't be too long. You promised the kids you'd take them to Penny Whistle Park today."

"Alright. I'll be back by two. That should give us plenty of time."

Rebekah nodded and went to call Cindy. Stan said goodbye to the kids and then left to go downtown to Republican headquarters. It was a hot day, so Stan had dressed casually in jeans and a t-shirt. Kristina was just walking up to the front door when he drove up. She was wearing shorts with a halter top. Her legs were nicely tanned and perfectly shaped. Stan gazed at them a moment before he got out feeling a bit mesmerized.

"Hi, Stan," Kristina said.

Stan smiled and walked up to her. "Hi. Good timing."

"Yes, I was afraid I was going to be late. The phone's been ringing off the wall today."

"Oh? Because of the newspaper article this morning?"

"Right. You saw that?"

Stan nodded. "Yeah. I can't believe it."

Kristina unlocked the door, and they walked in and turned on the lights. It was a small three-room office. In one of the rooms was a small conference table. Stan took a seat at the table and looked up a Kristina expectantly.

"Coffee?" Kristina asked.

"Sure, if you're having some."

She nodded, went over to a kitchen area where there was a coffee pot, and filled it with water.

"So, one of the calls was from my sister Molly. She works as a secretary at the Sheriff's Office and overheard two deputies talking about the investigation. I guess the sheriff has been working with the FBI on the case."

"Really? What are the money laundering allegations they were talking about in the article?"

"Well, a few years ago, Thornton wanted to retire, so he sold his share of an import/export business to his partners for several million dollars. His retirement didn't last long however. Soon, he was investing his money in several new ventures. One of them was Silver Springs Lake, a small lake that had filled up with sediment over the years and become worthless for any recreational purposes. The community around the lake became rundown, and the property values plummeted. Thornton came in and bought up all the property for a tenth of its original value. He drained the water out of the lake and began processing the sediment into commercial mulch. After he'd mined all the mulch, he had the lake dredged to an acceptable depth and then filled it back up with clean water. Once that was done, he started a rehabilitation project for the homes around the lake. Of course, with the lake rejuvenated, the value of the real estate rebounded."

"Okay, but that just sounds like he's a hell of a businessman."

"True, but there were rumors Thornton had teamed up with some Mexican drug dealers and that he was running their drug money through his Silver Springs Ventures and returning it to them in valuable lakefront property."

"Well, I don't know much about money laundering. I understand the concept, but I'm not exactly sure how it works."

"I don't understand it either," Kristina said. "It's very complicated."

"So, I guess that's why Thornton is such a big contributor to all the politicians in the county," Stan reasoned. "He wants to dampen their enthusiasm for any investigation of his businesses."

"That's a possibility. I think that's why the feds got involved. The sheriff and district attorney are Thornton's good friends, so they've protected him."

"I'm worried about Rob," Stan said. "Thornton and Rob's family are friends. Rob may be involved in some of his ventures. I've overheard them talking about Silver Springs Lake before. I know Thornton has somehow contributed a lot of money to his campaign."

Kristina shrugged. "Well, if Thornton is guilty I'm quite sure he wouldn't have left any incriminating evidence around his house, so I doubt they'll be able to prosecute him."

"Well, only time will tell. I guess we won't put Thornton on the President's reception list after all."

Kristina laughed. "No. We probably shouldn't."

"Rob wants to be on the list. I think he's prepared to support President Ford if he gets the nomination. So, with you, Rob, and me, that leaves nine more to pick."

"You're going to put me on the list?" Kristina asked.

Stan frowned. "Of course! You've earned it."

"I'm flattered but—"

"No buts. You're on the list."

Kristina smiled. "I suppose we should put Commissioner Barnes on the list. He's a Democrat, but he's talking about switching parties."

"Yeah, Paul Barnes. I think there'll be a lot of party switching as the county becomes more Republican. Why don't we tell him if he switches, we'll let him come to the reception and announce the switch at the President's news conference? That should provide him a lot of good publicity, and it will demonstrate the President's ability to garner Democratic support."

"Brilliant. I think he'll go for that."

Stan and Kristina worked another hour on the reception list before it was completed. Then they locked up the office and went home. When Stan walked in the door, not only were all his kids waiting anxiously to go to Penny Whistle Park, but Rob and Cindy's kids were there too.

"Daddy! Daddy! You're finally home," Mark said excitedly. "John, Paul, and Jenny are coming too."

"I see that," Stan said.

"Let's go, Dad," Reggie said. "We're all ready."

"What took you so long?" Marcia asked. "We've been waiting for hours."

Rebekah laughed. "I packed you a lunch. I don't imagine you had time to eat."

"No, I didn't. Thanks."

"So, are Rob and Cindy coming?"

"No. I offered to take her kids off her hands for the afternoon. Apparently Rob's not taking the Thornton matter too well."

"Oh, right. They're friends."

"More like family."

They all went out the front door and began piling in the station wagon. Stan locked up the house and then joined them in the car.

"So, what exactly did Cindy have to say about Thornton?" Stan asked as he backed out of the driveway.

"Oh, the FBI is coming by to talk to Rob about

him tomorrow," Rebekah replied.

"What? You've got to be kidding."

"No. He'd like you to be there when they come."

"What? Why me? I don't know anything about Thornton or his involvement with him."

"I know, but you're in law school. He figures you can tell him what to say."

"I can't give him legal advice. I don't have a license, not to mention the fact I have no experience in dealing with the FBI."

"You successfully defended yourself at your court martial, didn't you? You were dealing with the FBI then."

"I had legal counsel and I never actually talked to any of the agents. The reporter I gave my story too did that."

"You told me your lawyer was worthless and had you relied on him, you'd have been convicted."

"He wasn't worthless exactly, just inexperienced. It was legal for me to defend myself, but until I get a license, I can't defend someone else."

"He'll feel better if you're there, even if it's just as a friend. It couldn't hurt."

"The FBI won't allow it. They'll want him alone. But I guess I can go over there ahead of time and prep him."

"Good. Cindy's worried Rob will have to drop out of the race if his campaign funding dries up."

"He can't drop out of the race now. It's too late to get a new Republican candidate."

"I know."

"Did she say whether Rob invested in any of Thornton's business ventures?"

"No, but Cindy says Rob is scared and depressed over the situation."

Stan told her what he had learned from Kristina about Thornton's business ventures.

"Oh, God. I hope he's not involved in anything illegal. Cindy and the kids would be devastated."

"Is Daddy in trouble," Jenny asked from the back seat.

Rebekah turned and looked at Jenny. She was eight, the eldest of the Shepard children. "No, honey. One of his friends is in trouble."

"Uncle Brad. Daddy's scared 'cause he knows too much."

A chill darted through Rebekah. Stan glanced back at Jenny and forced a smile. He wondered what Jenny had overheard.

"He never mentioned any investments to me," Stan finally said, "but that's not something that would necessarily come up. I did hear them talking about the lake project. Thornton was pretty proud of it. All I know is that somehow Thornton is providing the funding for Rob's campaign. I'm not sure how, though. I guess I'll find out tomorrow."

After they'd spent a few hours at Penny Whistle Park, they went to dinner at McDonald's. It was after seven when they finally pulled up in front of the Shepard house to drop off the kids. Rob came out to greet them as they drove up.

"Hi, Rob," Stan said.

"Hey. Thanks for taking the kids this afternoon. It's been a horrible day."

"No problem. Glad we could help."

"Are you going to be able to come over tomorrow?"

"I don't know how much help I'd be. Since I'm not an attorney yet, they probably wouldn't even let me be in the interview with you."

Rob sighed. "Damn it!"

"What I could do is to try to prep you for the interview as a friend, but, honestly, you ought to consider getting a licensed attorney."

"No, I'm sure you'll do fine. I don't need an attorney. When can we do it?"

"If you want, I could come over early tomorrow so we can talk before they arrive."

"No, I won't be able to sleep. Can we talk right now?"

"Now? Well, we need to take the kids home and put them to bed right now."

"Alright. Call me when you get them settled."

"We could talk over the phone, but there's no guarantee of privacy."

"No. Let's meet somewhere later?"

"Yeah. How about Denny's? That's usually a good place to talk."

"That'll work. I'll see you there in thirty minutes."

"Alright."

Stan looked at Rebekah. She nodded, and they got in the car and drove home.

"What was all that about privacy? Do you think his phone is tapped?"

"Possibly—particularly if the FBI sees him as an accomplice."

"How do you know talking at Denny's is safe?"

"I don't, but it's usually pretty noisy, and the FBI won't have had time to bug the place."

Rebekah swallowed hard. Cindy was her best friend, and the thought of Rob being in trouble was unbearable. She'd met Cindy a year earlier at a Republican function, and they'd hit it off immediately. Cindy loved having a nurse for a friend since one of her three kids seemed to be sick all the time. On the other hand, Rebekah loved to have someone to talk to when she'd had a stressful day at the hospital. Cindy was a good listener and loved to hear Rebekah's complaints about rude patients or incompetent doctors. Stan gave her a kiss and left.

Stan was relieved to see that Denny's was pretty crowded. He didn't want anyone overhearing what Rob had to say to him. It was dangerous for Rob to be telling him anything incriminating. There would be no attorney-client privilege, so if the FBI questioned Stan later, theoretically, he'd have to tell them what he knew. Of course, he could claim a bad memory, but that was a dangerous thing for an aspiring attorney to do. Stan parked his car and looked around for Rob. He saw him getting out of his car on the other side of the parking lot and go inside. A few minutes later, Stan went in and joined him in a booth.

"Hey, Rob."

"Hi, Stan. Thanks for coming."

"No problem. What a rotten turn of events, huh?"

The waitress came over and took their order.

"Tell me about it. Everything was going so well. I can't believe this is happening."

"So, what did the FBI say they wanted to talk about?"

"They didn't say. They just said they needed to talk to me."

"Do you know anything about Thornton's businesses?"

"Not really. He's told me about some of them, of course, but I've never actually seen them."

"So, why do you think the FBI wants to talk to you?"

"I don't know. Maybe it's the way he's been financing my campaign."

Stan frowned, fearful of what he was about to

hear. “What do you mean?”

“When he recruited me to run for state representative, he told me I wouldn’t have to worry about financing. He said he’d make sure I had plenty of money. I just assumed he meant he had a lot of contacts and they’d do fund-raising events for me, but that’s not what he had in mind.”

“What was his plan?”

“He said the law wouldn’t allow him to just write me a check for what I needed, but that I could spend my own money and it would be quite legal. I told him I didn’t have any money, and that’s when he told me what he had in mind.”

“Oh, God. What did have you do?”

Rob took a deep breath and let it out slowly. “Well, he had me invest $25,000 in one of his ventures for ninety days. When the ninety days was up, he paid me back $75,000.”

“I thought you didn’t have any money. Where did you come up with $25,000?”

“I just wrote him a check that didn’t get cashed until he paid me the $75,000 return on my investment.”

“Oh, shit!” Stan said. “Why did you go along with that?”

Rob shrugged. “I don’t know. It seemed harmless. I didn’t figure anyone would ever know.”

“Did you report the profit on your income taxes?”

“Huh?”

Stan sighed. The waitress showed up with two cups of coffee and two pieces of pie. Stan smiled at her as she set them down. When she was gone, he continued. “Rob, if you make $50,000 profit, you’ve got to pay taxes on it. Didn’t you report it on last year’s income tax return?”

“Ah. Actually, I haven’t filed it yet.”

"So, if this money wasn't for your campaign, then it was personal income, right?"

"Correct."

"So, you would have declared it as taxable income on your tax return?"

"I would have, except I haven't filed yet. It's on extension."

Agent Adams looked at Rutledge. Rutledge opened a notepad and asked, "Do you know a Tony Rubio?"

Rob pretended to think for a moment. He knew exactly who Rubio was, but he didn't want the FBI to know it. "Um, I've heard the name, but I'm not sure if I've met him or not. He may work out at Silver Springs, so I might have met him while I was out there."

"Did you know he's a convicted felon?"

"I don't know anything about him really."

"How much did you invest with Mr. Thornton?"

"Uh, $25,000 I think."

"And you got $50,000 back?"

"Like I said, I'd have to check the exact numbers. My profit was $50,000, more or less."

"Quite a return on your investment," Agent Rutledge said. "Wish I'd have gotten in on some of that action."

"Like I said, we go way back. He was doing me a favor by letting me in on the deal."

"Yeah. What did he expect in return?" Agent Rutledge asked.

"Nothing—absolutely nothing. He's like an uncle to me."

"You didn't promise him some favors if you got elected?"

"I didn't promise him anything—not a goddamn thing."

Agent Adams sighed. "Okay. I hope you're telling the truth, because if you're not, we'll find out. I promise you."

Rob didn't say anything and just stared at Agent Adams for a moment. Finally, he said, "Is that all?"

"For now," Rutledge said, "but I have a feeling we'll be seeing you again."

"Fine. You know where to find me," Rob said, feeling relieved the interview was over. They all stood up, and Rob showed them out. After shutting the door on them, he went to find Cindy. She was on a lounge chair watching the kids swim. She got up when she saw Rob coming.

"So, what did they say?"

"Nothing unexpected. They saw the money Brad paid me and thought it was a campaign contribution."

"But it was a campaign contribution, wasn't it?"

"Yeah. It's a good thing I met with Stan last night. I would have really blown it had I been questioned without working out my story in advance."

"What do you mean?" Cindy asked.

"It never occurred to me the way Thornton structured the payments they'd be taxable income to me. It's a good thing I haven't filed my return yet."

"You mean we're going to have to pay taxes on an extra $50,000!"

Rob sighed. "Yeah. It's either that or a vacation at a federal country club."

"Oh, Rob, that's gonna be another $15,000 or $20,000, isn't it?"

"That's about right."

"Where are we going to get that kind of money?"

"I don't know. We'll have to find it somewhere."

"Jesus Christ! I can't believe this. I knew you running for state representative was a bad idea. My parents will be livid when they hear about this."

"They won't hear about it. Relax."

"Yes, they will. We'll have to borrow the money from them. Where else could we get it?"

"I don't know. Give me some time to think about it. Maybe Stan will have some ideas."

"You know how embarrassed I am that Stan and Rebekah know about this? It's humiliating," Cindy said as she began to cry.

Rob put his arms around her and held her tightly. "It's gonna be alright, honey. Don't worry. We'll figure this out, I promise."

Rob hated the idea of borrowing money from Cindy's parents. They'd been against the marriage from the get-go and warned Cindy that Rob wouldn't be able to provide for her the way she had grown accustomed. Rob had resented their attitude and vowed to prove them wrong, but now he was afraid they'd been right about him all along.

That night, depression overcame him. He tossed and turned, unable to sleep. He wondered if he should withdraw from the race. How could he possibly finance the campaign on his own? When he did finally fall asleep, he had a nightmare about going to prison and being locked up in solitary confinement. He woke up in a cold sweat.

The next day, Brad Thornton called Rob and asked him to come over to his place so they could talk. Thornton was cool on the phone and wouldn't say anything about the purpose of the meeting. At the appointed hour, Rob went over to their home, and Melissa let him in and offered him coffee. He sat at the kitchen table sipping his coffee, waiting for Brad. Melissa seemed nervous and abnormally quiet. After a few minutes, Brad walked in and sat down. He looked tired and worn down.

"Thanks for coming over, Rob."

"No problem."

"The last few days have been a nightmare."

"I can imagine," Rob replied. "What's it all about?"

"Oh, it's a long story, but the gist of it is that I've been very successful, and in the process I've stepped on a few toes. That happens when you're an aggressive businessman."

"Right."

"When you have enemies, they are always looking for ways to hurt you. Recently, one of them went to the FBI and fed them a bunch of garbage about my operations."

"What's the FBI looking for?"

"A history between me and Tony Rubio."

"Oh, him. Hmm."

"Of course, they won't find the history unless someone points it out to them."

"They asked me about him, but I didn't tell them anything."

"Good. I appreciate that. If they can't find a connection, I'm home free."

"So, what's going to happen now?"

"It will take them months to complete their investigation. In the meantime, we have made an agreement not to make any distributions of funds from any of my ventures."

Rob grimaced. "So, that means you won't be writing me anymore checks for a while, huh?"

"Correct."

"What about John and the ad agency?"

John Savage's ad agency, Pro Media, was responsible for all Brad Thornton's various business ventures, and they'd agreed to manage Rob's campaign for free. Rob paid for the advertising, but out of appreciation for Brad's business, they had waived their fee for handling Rob's campaign.

"You'll have to get a new campaign manager, I'm afraid, for your benefit as well as mine. We can't have any kind of a relationship until this thing blows over."

"That's not acceptable. I wouldn't have gotten into this race had you not recruited me."

"I'm sorry. This was totally unforeseen. There's nothing I can do about it."

Rob stared at Brad angrily but didn't know what to say.

"I'm sorry, Rob. Believe me, I wish things were different. You'll find a new campaign manager."

"How will I pay them?"

"Part of a campaign manager's job is fund raising. Talk to Stan. I bet he'd do it."

"But he's County Chairman."

"You're the Republican candidate, so it wouldn't be a conflict of interest, and there would be a lot of overlap. Talk to him about it."

Rob nodded and left. He knew there was no point in arguing. It was out of Brad's hands. Rob was sick all the way home. He'd hoped Brad would have worked things out with the FBI, but that hadn't happened. Now he was on his own, and things couldn't have been more desperate. When he got home, he told Cindy the bad news and called Stan to let him know the latest.

"You know, Brad had an interesting idea," Rob said.

"What's that?" Stan asked.

"Why don't you be my campaign manager."

"What? Are you kidding? I'm in law school, working full time, and barely able to handle the County Chairman's job."

"It wouldn't be that much more work. A lot of it could be done when you're doing your job as County Chairman."

"Well, to be honest, Kristina does most of that work."

"Come on, Stan. I'm really desperate here."

"I know, but you need someone with the time to do a good job, someone who knows how to raise money. I don't have much experience in fund-raising nor do I have the contacts since I'm new to the area."

"Can you think of anyone who might do it?"

"Actually, there is one person."

"Who?"

"To help you out, I'll talk to Kristina about doing it. If I had to, I could do without her so she could work for you."

"But she's a woman."

"So! She knows everybody, she's a great organizer, and she works harder than anybody I know. I'm sure she'll do a great job for you."

"I don't know. What will people think?"

"If they know Kristina, they'll think you're a smart man."

"Hmm. Okay. Would you ask her for me?"

"Sure, I'll see her tomorrow. I'll talk to her about it then."

"Okay. Thanks, Stan...Oh, and by the way, if I hadn't have met with you before my meeting with the FBI, I'd have been lost when they asked about reporting the $50,000 as income."

"Well, I'm glad I was able to help. Hopefully you won't hear from them again."

"Wouldn't that be nice?"

Rob hung up the phone, feeling better but not as optimistic as Stan. He hadn't told Stan quite everything.

He knew Tony Rubio and Brad Thornton went way back. He hadn't been candid with the FBI on that score. He hoped and prayed they'd never realize he'd lied about not knowing Brad's college buddy at UT, his fraternity's most reliable marijuana supplier.

Chapter 4

Stan wasn't thrilled about giving up Kristina to be Rob's campaign manager, but he knew electing a Republican state representative was his first priority as County Chairman. It wasn't so much the work she was doing for him, but more the companionship he'd be losing. He could figure out how to handle his job without her but he'd miss the time they spent together. Reluctantly he thought about how to replace her. Perhaps she knew someone who could take her place. He pondered that situation while he waited for her in front of Commissioner Barnes' home. They had a meeting with him about switching to the Republican Party and making the announcement at President Ford's reception, which was only a week away. Finally, he saw her driving up in her Mustang convertible. It was a warm but windy day, and she'd worn a short dress that blew up, exposing a lot of skin. Stan watched her, wide-eyed, as she stepped out of her flashy red car. He fumbled with the door a moment and then got out.

"Hi. I like your dress."

She grimaced. "I bet you do. I didn't realize it was so windy."

Stan wondered if she'd worn the sexy dress for the Commissioner or him. He thought about it and couldn't make up his mind. They walked to the front door and rang the bell. A few seconds elapsed, and the door opened. A elderly lady stuck her head out and gave Kristina a hard look.

"What do you want?"

"Uh, we're here to see Commissioner Barnes."

"Who are you?"

"Stan Turner and Kristina Tenison," Kristina said. "He's expecting us."

"Oh, alright. Come in. I'll get him."

She escorted them to a small sitting room and told them to have a seat. Stan and Kristina sat on a small sofa. A few minutes later, Barnes strolled in and greeted them.

"Can I offer you something?" he asked. "A drink, perhaps?"

"Just some water," Kristina said.

"Nothing for me," Stan added.

Barnes nodded to the elderly woman. He didn't introduce her, so Stan assumed she was domestic help. Barnes was a tall man in his mid-fifties. He sat in a chair across from them and stroked his short beard.

"So, what can I do for you?" he finally asked. "You said over the phone that you had something you wanted to discuss with me."

"Well, yes. That's right. Ah. . . We've heard rumors you may be thinking of switching to the Republican Party," Stan said.

Barnes frowned. "Where did you hear that?"

"It's been a topic of discussion around town for some time. I think you know the demographics of the county have changed, and your district is becoming more Republican with each passing election. Fortunately, your term isn't up this year, but in two years, a Democrat could face a difficult time getting elected."

"Yes, and if it is true that you intend to switch parties, we can offer you a prime opportunity to do so," Kristina added.

"Really? How's that?"

Kristina looked at Stan, and he nodded. "Well," Kristina said, "President Ford is coming to Dallas next week, and he's having a reception for some of his supporters. If you were to switch parties now, we could get you an invitation to the reception, and he'd give you a few minutes to announce your plans to the press. It would give you great exposure."

Barnes' face lit up. "Hmm. That's a very interesting proposal, but I'm going to take a lot of heat from my fellow Democrats. They'll call me a traitor and turncoat."

"Well, the influence of the Democratic Party is waning in this county, so I doubt that will have much effect upon your future here."

Barnes nodded. "Probably not, but it's still a hard thing to do."

Stan wondered if Barnes was genuinely concerned for the Democratic Party and his friends there or if he was just putting on a show. In fact, Stan didn't like Barnes or anyone who would forsake their party for expedience. He halfway hoped Barnes would say no, but he doubted that would happen. Stan had gone along with the idea of assisting Barnes with his switch, as he knew it would be good for the party and for President Ford in the short run.

"Can I have some time to think about it?"

Stan shook his head. "No. I'm sorry, we've got to finalize the guest list today. If you haven't made up your mind about switching yet, that's okay. You don't have to make that decision for another year. We just—"

"Okay, okay. I'll do it. I was on the brink anyway. It's good you came, now you've forced my hand and I can get the inevitable over with."

Kristina smiled. "That's great. We'll start working on the arrangements. I'll call you in a few days with the details."

Stan and Kristina stood up. "Thank you, Commissioner. I think you've made the right decision."

"Yes, well, I appreciate the opportunity. It's not too often a politician like myself gets to share the podium with the President of the United States."

"No problem. It should be good for everyone involved."

Barnes showed them out and closed the door.

"You got a minute?" Stan asked. "I need to talk to you about something else."

Kristina looked at Stan expectantly. "Sure. What is it?"

"Let's go get a cup of coffee somewhere. This might take a few minutes. I think I saw a Dunkin' Donuts up the street."

"Yes, I saw it as I was driving up. I'll meet you there."

"Good. Thanks. See you in a minute."

A few minutes later, they were sitting in Dunkin' Donuts, each with a cup of coffee and a donut.

"Brad Thornton pulled his financing for Rob's campaign. He's got to find a new campaign manager too."

"Hmm. I was afraid of that. What's he going to do?"

"He asked me to be his campaign manager."

"That's a good idea," Kristina said excitedly.

"No, it's not. I don't have time to do it, but I told him maybe you would consider it."

"Me?" she said frowning. "But how—"

"I don't want to lose you, but it would be a good move for both you and Rob. He needs you, and I'm sure you'd do a great job. It would be good for your political career as well."

"My political career?" she questioned.

Stan smiled. "Come on. You obviously have political ambition. You're a natural politician. You love this stuff."

Kristina chuckled. "Is it that obvious?"

"To me it is."

"But I'm a woman. There hasn't been a woman elected to anything in this county in decades."

"Maybe so, but times are changing. More and more women are getting elected to political office around the country every year. I have a feeling you'll be one of them sooner or later."

"I hate to leave you in a lurch."

"Don't worry about me. I bet one of your workers could step up and do some of the things you were doing."

Kristina thought about it moment. "Yeah, you're right," she said excitedly. "Glenda Green or Jill Smart could do it. I'll ask them if they'd be willing to put in more time."

"Good. I'll set up a meeting with you and Rob, and then you guys can get started."

"Oh my God! Is this really happening? Am I really going to be Rob Shepard's campaign manager?"

Stan laughed. "Yes. Congratulations!"

"Thank you, Stan. I really appreciate the confidence you have in me. Rob would have never considered me, I'm sure, had you not pushed me for the job."

"Well, Rob's a good friend, so I want him to win. If I were in his shoes, I'd hire you in a flash."

Kristina smiled tenderly. "I'm so happy I could kiss you."

The thought of that excited Stan but he didn't think she was serious, nor could he have let her kiss him if she wanted to, so he just smiled. "I'm glad you're so excited. Just get Rob elected, and that will make my sacrifice worthwhile."

"Don't worry. His election is in the bag."

Stan felt relieved that he'd solved Rob's immediate problem, but now started to worry about being County Chairman without Kristina's help. How could he possibly find the time to do it? Depression and regret quickly washed over him. He knew he had done the right thing, but he also knew his noble gesture was going to cost him dearly.

The next day, Kristina, Stan, Rob, and Cindy met to discuss the campaign. Kristina had already made a list of potential donors and a list of things Rob needed to do. Rob was impressed with Kristina's take-charge approach and approved everything she suggested. Since everything was under control, Stan got up to leave.

"Oh, Stan, I talked to Glenda and Jill, and they said they'd split my duties as vice-chairman of the Republican President. I'm going to meet with them this afternoon to make sure they know what to do."

"Great. I appreciate you getting right on that."

She smiled. "No problem. I'll see you at the Ford reception."

"Right. See you then."

When Stan got home, he was surprised to see a strange car parked in front of his house. When he walked inside, there were a man and a woman talking to Rebekah. The man got up.

"You must be Stan Turner," the man said.

"Right."

"Hi. I'm Special Agent Warren Adams and this is my partner, Special Agent Ruth Rutledge of the Federal Bureau of Investigation."

They both produced their badges, and Stan gave them a cursory look.

"You're not the Stan Turner from Quantico, are

you? Agent Rutledge asked.

Stan looked at her in surprise. "Yeah, as a matter of fact I am."

"Huh. I worked for two years on the Sunday Night Slasher task force. That was nice work you and Ms. Stone did to break the case."

Stan smiled. "Well, I had an advantage since I was forced to spend time with him. It didn't take long to figure out he was insane."

"Have you seen Ms. Stone lately?" Rutledge asked. "We got to know each other pretty well after your court martial."

"No, it's been over a year since I've seen her."

"Listen, we have a few questions for you on another matter."

"Right. Are you talking to everyone that was at Brad's party the other night?"

Agent Adams nodded. "That's one list we're working."

"Hmm. Well, I don't know Mr. Thornton that well. I see him once in a while at party functions, but that's about it."

"Didn't he recruit you as County Chairman?"

"That's right. He did."

"Gave you a big contribution, huh?"

"No. You don't need any money to run for County Chairman. They give the job to the first sucker who'll take it. It's a pretty thankless job."

"You have to get elected, though, and that must have cost some money."

"No. I was unopposed. I didn't spend a dime."

"Just blew a lot precious time," Rebekah interjected.

"Did Mr. Thornton let you in on any of his lucrative investments?"

"No. I'm in law school, so we're pretty much broke. We're barely able to pay our bills and my school expenses each month."

"Oh, that's right—law school," Agent Adams said glancing over at Agent Rutledge.

Stan nodded.

"So, what do you know about Silver Springs Ventures?" Rutledge asked.

"Not a thing really. I've heard people talk about it, but I've never visited the place."

"By 'people' do you mean Rob?"

"Yeah. I overheard he and Brad talking about it once."

"What did they say?"

"Oh, I don't remember. I wasn't paying that much attention."

"Do you know a man by the name of Tony Rubio?"

"No. Never met him."

Agent Rutledge nodded. "Okay, that's all the questions I have."

"Sorry I couldn't be more helpful."

"Actually, there is something you could do for us," Agent Adams said.

"Oh?. . . What's that?" Stan asked.

"Rob's your best friend, I understand?"

Stan nodded. "You could say that?"

"Do you know what a CI is?"

"A CI?"

"Yes, a confidential informant."

"Oh, right. A snitch."

"No. Not necessarily a snitch. If you were mixed up in criminal activity and you provided information to the FBI you'd be a snitch, but if you are not part of the criminal enterprise but are in a unique position to acquire information about it for the FBI, that is something entirely different."

"Okay," Stan said skeptically.

"What I'm trying to say, is because you are close friends with Rob and have an inside position in the Republican Party you could acquire evidence that would be difficult or impossible for us to get."

Stan took a deep breath not liking the way this conversation was going. He didn't want to do anything to hurt Rob, his family or the Republican Party.

"You want Stan to be a spy for you?" Rebekah asked mortified.

"That's not what we call it, but the concept is the same," Agent Adams acknowledged.

"If there is money laundering going on," Stan said, "I'm sure Rob knows nothing about it. At worst he's an unwitting accomplice."

"You may be right," Adams agreed. "In fact, if it makes you feel better one of our objectives would be to get Rob to agree to an immunity deal. He testifies to what he knows with full immunity from prosecution."

Stan nodded. "That sounds good, but I don't know if Rob would testify against the Thorntons. They're like family."

"Well, if he is going to be a State Representative he's going to have to show that his integrity is more important than friendships."

Stan sighed. "I suppose."

"So, will you do it?" Adams pressed.

"Ah. Won't this be dangerous?" Rebekah asked.

Agent Adams shrugged. "It could be but we'll have you under surveillance at all times and if you ever feel threatened you can alert us and we'll be on top of the situation immediately."

"I don't know," Rebekah said. "I don't like it. Can we think about it? Stan really doesn't have time for this."

Stan looked at Rebekah. "What's the objective here? The article in the newspaper was a little sketchy. You're after some drug cartel?"

Adams nodded. "Yes, for years we have been after the Burilo Drug Cartel. They are involved in drugs, arms sales, and human trafficking all over Texas. There organization is very sophisticated and well run. Every time we think we are close to coming down on them they thwart us one way or another. Recently we got a lead that they were laundering their money through Brad Thornton, so that's why the investigation landed here."

Stan nodded and looked at Rebekah. "We really don't have a choice, honey. If I'm going to be an attorney how can I turn down an opportunity to help bring down a bunch of murdering thugs."

"Stan. It's too dangerous."

"The FBI will protect me, right," Stan said looking at Agent Adams.

"Yes. Like I said we'll have someone watching you at all times. It's not like you will be in the thick of things. You'll just be in a position to snoop around because of your position as County Chairman and a friend of Rob's."

"And CI's can get paid," Agent Rutledge interjected.

"Really?" Rebekah said. "How much?"

"It depends on how much you are able to help."

Stan shook his head. "No. That wouldn't be right."

Rebekah glared at Stan but didn't say anything.

"It's my duty as a citizens to help. Just tell me what I need to do."

Rebekah sighed deeply. "Stan!"

Stan shrugged. "I'm sorry, honey, but I don't really have a choice."

Rebekah shook her head angrily at Stan and

stomped off.

Shan smiled. "Sorry. Rebekah's a worrier. This will be hard on her."

"Well, I appreciate you doing this, Stan," Agent Rutledge said. "We'll be in touch with more details in a few days. Sorry we upset your wife."

Adams and Rutledge departed, leaving Stan feeling sick. He felt like he was doing the right thing, but fear and dread suddenly washed over him. Not only was he about to embark on a very dangerous endeavor, despite the FBI's promise of protection, but Rebekah wouldn't forgive him for it. In fact, she didn't talk to him the rest of the evening and locked the bedroom door when she went to bed forcing him to sleep on the couch. That night he had trouble sleeping, not because of his makeshift bed, but because all he could think about was what Rob might know that he hadn't shared with him and the FBI. He wondered what his reaction would be to an offer of immunity for help in prosecuting Brad Thornton and if he'd hate Stan for what he was doing.

Chapter 5

Stan and Rebekah were excited when they got to the Fairmont Hotel for the fund-raising dinner for President Ford. The enormous dining room was festively decorated and packed with hundreds of tables, all set for the feast that was about to be served. Stan handed his ticket to the doorman, and he motioned for them to go inside. The tables were numbered, so Stan and Rebekah searched for their assigned number, 256. When they found it, Rob, Cindy, Kristina, and Commissioner Barnes were already seated.

"Hi, Cindy," Rebekah said as she took a seat. "Isn't this great!"

Cindy nodded excitedly. "Yes. This is the place to be tonight, huh? Having dinner with the President."

Stan smiled. "I wish you two could come in with us and meet him. I asked if I could sneak you in, but they said I'd have to clear it with the Secret Service, and that would take several weeks."

"Oh, well," Cindy said. "Thanks for trying."

"It's alright," Rebekah said. "I saw a great dress shop on the first floor. We can do a little shopping while they're rubbing elbows with the President."

Cindy's eyes lit up. "Hey, now that's an idea!"

"You can come to the press conference after the reception," Kristina said. "Go to the press area when we go into the reception, and you'll get a good seat. I doubt the reception will last twenty minutes."

"I don't know. We could spend a lot of money in twenty minutes," Rebekah teased.

"Hmm. You can't spend money we don't have," Stan reminded her.

"Sure you can," Cindy said. "That's why they invented credit cards."

"Yes, Cindy's got the art of spending money we don't have down to a science," Rob noted.

Everyone laughed. As they were talking, waiters began serving salads and rolls to the tables. Waitresses came around and poured coffee and iced tea. Before they began eating, the Mayor, acting as Master of Ceremonies, welcomed everyone and then advised them a local minister would give the invocation. Soon, the auditorium was abuzz with lively conversation as people ate each course of the meal that had cost most of them $1,000 a plate. Fortunately, Stan and Rebekah had only had to pay $100 since they had helped organize the event. After they'd eaten, the Mayor gave a brief address and then introduced President Ford. The President spoke for forty minutes about Jimmy Carter's misguided liberal philosophy, the state of the nation, and his vision of America's future. By the time he was done, he had the crowd standing and screaming for his election.

When the President had left the podium and the crowd began to disburse, Stan, Rob, Kristina, and Commissioner Barnes headed for the private reception. When they got to the small conference room set up for the event, a Secret Service Agent checked their invitations and then let them in one by one. Stan was surprised they hadn't been searched, as any one of them could have been carrying a knife or a gun. He figured the Secret Service must have checked out all the guests carefully prior to the event.

"This is exciting," Kristina said. "I've never met a President in person."

"I shook hands with President Nixon once," Stan said. "What a disappointment he turned out to be."

"Yeah. I think the job got to him and he got a little paranoid."

"You want a drink?"

"Sure," Kristina replied. "Gin and tonic."

Stan and Rob went to the bar and got everyone drinks. Just as they returned, the door opened, and two Secret Service Agents stepped through, followed by President Ford. People started to drift over to him, shaking his hand and talking to him briefly. When he got to Kristina, he held her hand and smiled broadly.

"Hi. Kristina, isn't it?"

"Yes."

"You're Shepard's new campaign manager."

"Yes."

"Good luck with his campaign. It's so nice to meet you," the President said.

"We're thrilled to have you here," Kristina replied.

President Ford let go of Kristina's hand and moved to Stan. "Mr. Turner, thanks for helping to put this event together. We raised a lot of money here today. It's really going to help down the home stretch."

"Well, I was honored to help, Mr. President."

The President moved past Stan to Rob. "So, Rob, how's the campaign coming? I heard you have a shot at taking the seat away from the Democrats."

"Yes, I think we do."

"Well, if I can help out in any way, let me know."

"I will. Thank you, Mr. President."

The President stopped and gave Commissioner

Barnes a hard look. "Commissioner Barnes. So, you've finally come to your senses and joined the Grand Old Party, eh?"

Barnes smiled broadly. "Yes, Mr. President. The Democratic Party has gotten a little too liberal for me. I support your more moderate philosophy."

"Good. I'll see you later at the press conference."

"Yes, sir, I'll be there."

The President continued to work the room until he had talked to everyone, and then he and his entourage left to go to the conference. Stan and his friends followed him to the press room to meet up with the girls and sit in on the press conference. The room was packed with media and supporters. Stan and Rob were glad to see the girls had saved them a place and squeezed through the crowd to join them. After a moment, the press conference began, and the President gave a short statement before answering question. As the press conference came to a conclusion, the President said he'd invited Commissioner Barnes to give a statement and say a few words.

Commissioner Barnes nodded and took the podium. "Thank you, Mr. President, ladies and gentlemen. As you know, I'm the incumbent Democratic County Commissioner for Precinct Three. I've been a lifelong Democrat, but recently, I've seen my party drifting further and further to the left. Now, with Jimmy Carter as the likely Democratic nominee for president, I can no longer tolerate the direction the party is going. Therefore, I have decided to become a Republican."

There was an outcry of support from the crowd, cameras flashed, and people began clapping. The President shook Mr. Barnes' hand and went back up to the podium.

"As you know, Commissioner Barnes' conversion

to the Republican Party is not an isolated event. People all over the country are turning away from the liberal Democratic Party to become Republicans. Commissioner Barnes, I commend you for your courage and conviction and welcome you to the Grand Old Party."

When the press conference was over and the President on his way to his next campaign stop, the crowd began to disburse. After Stan and Rebekah had said goodbye to everyone they headed for the parking garage. While they'd been in the hotel, a storm system had moved in, and it was beginning to rain. Lightning could be seen in the distance, and the wind was picking up. Stan was tired and had a little buzz from drinking too much, so Rebekah drove. She hated driving at night, and the rain made it doubly difficult for her.

When they finally made it home, the babysitter was glad to see them, as she hated thunderstorms and had been very nervous during the storm. Stan paid her, and she left. While Stan was undressing, Rebekah went upstairs and checked on their sleeping children. She found them all fast asleep and breathing normally. Stan was asleep when she came back downstairs, but Rebekah felt uneasy and didn't think she could sleep. So, she made herself a cup of tea and watched the lightning show from their kitchen window.

After a while, she looked up at the clock and saw it was almost 3:00 a.m. Alarmed at how late it was, she shut the light and started toward the bedroom, but just as she got to there she saw headlights shining through the front window. She went over to it, peered outside, and saw two men in trench coats getting out of a white Chevy Impala. When they started up the front walkway, she ran into the bedroom and woke Stan up.

"Wake up, Stan! There are two men here!"

"Huh?" Stan said sleepily.

"There's two men coming to the door. They look like cops or FBI."

The doorbell rang, and Stan sat up. "What do they want?"

"How should I know? Put some pants on and go to the door."

"Okay, okay. I'm going."

Stan slipped on a pair of jeans and headed for the front door. He looked through the peephole and saw one of the men holding up a badge. He assumed someone must have died and the police were coming to notify them. Oh, God, is it one of their parents? Fear shot through him, and his stomach tightened. He took a deep breath and opened the door.

Chapter 6

Rob and Cindy stopped for a cup of coffee at IHOP on the way home from the President's press conference. It was raining, so they dashed from their car to the door. Rob felt a little hungry when he sat down at their table, so he ordered breakfast. Cindy objected since they had a babysitter to relieve, but Rob was determined to eat, and there was nothing Cindy could do but urge him to do it quickly.

"What's wrong with you?" Cindy asked. "You haven't said a word since we left the hotel."

"You know, I'm going to bust my butt getting elected state representative, and then the shit's gonna hit the fan over the Thornton mess."

"You didn't do anything wrong. They can't do anything to you."

"Yeah, but they can destroy me by just trying to pin something on me. You know what criminal lawyers cost. That's one reason I talked to the FBI without a lawyer. The one my dad recommended wanted a $2,000 retainer just to represent me during any preliminary investigation. If I'm charged, they'd want $10,000 more. It's going to be a damn nightmare being a political candidate with an FBI investigation in progress. Maybe I should withdraw."

"No. Everything will work out. You'll see," Cindy assured him.

Rob looked at Cindy and just shook his head. He

was as tired and depressed as he'd ever been in his life. They ate their breakfast silently and then left. Thirty minutes later, they made it home and parked in the driveway, but when they walked up to the front door, they noticed it was ajar. Fear and dread of what they'd find inside shot through them. They rushed inside, and Cindy screamed. On the floor, Maureen Peters, a sixteen-year-old neighbor who had been babysitting was lying on her side in a pool of blood. Rob ran over to her, knelt down, and felt her wrist for a pulse.

"She's dead," Rob announced grimly.

Cindy gasped and started running up the stairs to the children's bedrooms, but before she got there, a man stepped out of the shadows and grabbed her. He put his gloved hand over her mouth, but she still emitted a muffled scream that Rob heard just as clearly as a church bell ringing a block away. He ran up the stairs to defend the wife he loved so dearly, but just as he reached the landing, another man stuck out his foot and tripped him. He hit the ground hard, and while he was down, the man pounced on top of him and pinned him to the carpet.

The first man hit Cindy with the butt of his revolver, and she collapsed to the floor unconscious. He immediately shot her in the head. Her body jumped from the impact of the point-blank shot and then fell limp. The man walked over to where his accomplice had Rob pinned down and positioned the gun just above Rob's ear so that it would look like Rob had killed himself. Without a second of hesitation, he pulled the trigger, and Rob's head exploded against the interior wall. A second later, he placed the gun in Rob's hand, pointed it in Cindy's direction, and pulled the trigger again.

The two men got up quickly, looked around to be sure the crime scene was staged the way they wanted, and left out one of the upstairs bedroom windows. A neighbor, John Rogers, had heard the shots from his home next door, and he came over to investigate. He gasped when he saw the babysitter lying on the tile floor in a pool of blood. His wife, Molly Rogers, was close behind and began screaming and wailing when she saw her husband hovering over Maureen's dead body.

Soon sirens could be heard in the distance, and more people from the neighborhood began to gather around the Shepard's front door. After a few minutes, a police car drove up, and Officers Lynn Jenkins and Sheila Sands jumped out and told the crowd to back away. They went inside, guns drawn, to investigate the situation. They looked at Mr. Rogers kneeling over Maureen's body.

"Is she dead?" Officer Jenkins asked.

Mr. Rogers nodded.

The two officers went past them into the dining room, the kitchen, and the master bedroom. Finding nobody else on the first floor, they began to climb the stairs.

Two paramedics rushed in and started to examine Maureen. One of them escorted the Rogers out of the house to be questioned. Two more officers came in and scanned the scene.

"Oh, my God!" Officer Sands moaned from upstairs. "What kind of a bastard would murder his own children!"

"Shit!" Jenkins gasped.

Hearing this the two officers' distress they ran upstairs. Detective Wallace Moore walked in the front door an instant later. He took a hard look at Maureen Peters' body before he too headed upstairs.

"Hi, Detective," Jenkins said looking up. "There are five of them up here—three young children. I'm pretty sure they're all dead. The paramedics are making sure."

"God have mercy!" Detective Moore said.

"Looks like a murder-suicide," officer Sands advised.

"Who are these people?" Detective Moore asked.

"The Shepard family," officer Sands said. "You know…Rob Shepard, candidate for state representative."

"Oh, right. Wasn't he connected to Brad Thornton?"

"Right. Shepard was a close friend and investor."

"Huh. I guess he knew what was coming down the pike and decided he didn't want his family to go through it."

"Looks that way," Officer Sands agreed.

"I don't know," Jenkins said. "I knew Rob Shepard. I can't see him committing suicide. I know he couldn't have murdered his wife and children. He always been a good guy."

"Well, we'll let the medical examiner decide," Detective Moore said. "It's not our call."

Detective Adam Albright walked in and grimaced at the grizzly sight. "I can't believe he'd kill the babysitter too. You'd think he'd let her go home before he started executing his family. It doesn't make any sense."

"None of this makes any sense," Jenkins said.

"Jenkins," Detective Moore said, "there's nothing for you to do up here. You and Sands go outside and start interviewing the neighbors. See if anybody saw anything."

"Yes, sir," Jenkins said, and he and Sands left.

Several members of the Crime Scene Unit came up the stairs and started taking photographs and bagging evidence. Moore and Albright went into the other rooms to look at the children's bodies. They just stared at the children with identical gunshot wounds to the head.

"How could someone do that to a child, let alone his own flesh and blood?" Detective Albright asked angrily.

"God only knows," Detective Moore replied. "Let's go see if we can find out where the Shepards went tonight. Whoever saw them last might be able to give us some clue as to why this happened."

Detective Albright nodded. "I'll search his car. Maybe there will be something in there that will tell us something. You go ask the Peters if they know. Maybe Maureen told them where the Shepards were going."

"Right," Moore said and left.

A few minutes later, Moore found Albright in the Shepards' garage. "I found out where they went tonight," he said.

Detective Albright looked up. "President Ford's fundraiser," Albright said, handing Moore an envelope. "I found this invitation sitting on the front seat."

"Right. Mr. Peters thinks they were meeting Stan Turner and his wife and some other friends there."

"Alright. I guess we better go talk to Mr. Turner and see if he knows anything."

"It's 2:00 a.m.," Moore said. "Shouldn't we wait until morning?"

"No. If it were my friend who'd died, I'd want to know right away. Wouldn't you?"

"I suppose."

Moore and Albright left the garage and went back into the house. As they walked into the kitchen, the Medical Examiner spotted them and came over.

"What do you think happened here, Detectives?" he asked.

"Well, it's hard to say," Detective Moore said," but I think when the Shepards got home, Mr. Shepard went upstairs and shot the children. His wife heard the shots and came running up the stairs. He probably let her go by and went downstairs and shot the babysitter. Then he went upstairs and shot his wife and then himself."

"Why would he kill the babysitter? What did she have to do with anything?"

"Sometimes when you're depressed or angry, you just want to take down as many people with you as you can," Detective Albright replied.

"What about an intruder? Did Mr. Shepard have any enemies?"

"There's no evidence of a forced entry, and none of the neighbors saw any strangers in the neighborhood," Detective Albright replied.

"That's true. We'll have to see if any unidentified fingerprints, fibers, or other evidence shows up. If not, it looks like it's a murder-suicide."

"Kind of looks that way," Detective Moore agreed. "We're going to go talk to Stan Turner. He and his wife were with the Shepards before all of this went down."

"Okay. Let me know if you find out anything enlightening."

"Will do. See you later," Detective Moore said.

Detectives Moore and Albright left and drove to Stan Turner's house. It was nearly 3:00 a.m when they rang the doorbell and held their badges in front of the peephole so anyone who looked out would see them. After a few minutes, Stan opened the door wearing a t-shirt and jeans he'd hastily put on.

"Yes, what's wrong?" Stan asked.

"We've got some news you're going to want to hear," Detective Moore said. "Can we come in?"

"Okay," Stan replied and motioned them into a small living room just inside the door.

The two detectives sat on opposite ends of a sofa,

and Stan sat across from them in a stuffed chair. A minute later, Rebekah walked in wearing a robe.

"This is my wife Rebekah," Stan said.

"Hello, Mrs. Turner. I'm Detective Moore, and this is Detective Albright from the Richardson police Department. Sorry to come by at such an early hour."

"What's going on?" Stan asked.

"We understand you and your wife went out with Rob and Cindy Shepard last evening."

"Yes, that's correct."

"Well, we just came from their home, and I'm sorry to report they are both dead, along with their children."

"Dead!" Rebekah gasped "Oh, my God! . . . No! . . . That can't be."

"Yes, I'm afraid it is."

"But, how?" Stan asked, incredulous. "We were just with them a few hours ago, and they were fine. What happened?"

"It looks like a murder-suicide, but the Medical Examiner hasn't made a final determination yet."

"Murder-suicide? That's impossible. Who are you saying was the murderer?"

"The evidence points to Rob," Detective Albright replied.

Stan shook his head. Rebekah became pale and started to wobble. Stan stood up and grabbed her arm to steady her. He sat her down in the stuffed chair he'd been sitting in.

"What was Rob and Cindy's mood when you saw them last?" Detective Moore asked.

"They were happy and upbeat. We just went to a reception and met President Ford, for godsakes. Rob's running for state representative and has a good chance of winning."

"Ah. We heard he's been tied into the Brad Thornton money laundering investigation," Detective Albright noted.

"True, but only indirectly. He wasn't involved in Thornton's business operations. He was just an investor."

"That's not what we've been told," Albright replied. "It kind of looks like he was afraid of the investigation and couldn't face the truth coming out."

"You think murdering your family and committing suicide is easier to face than being convicted as a money launderer?" Stan asked. "That doesn't make sense. There must be another explanation for what happened."

"Well, like we said, the Medical Examiner hasn't made a determination yet."

"I hope not. Someone else murdered the Shepard family, and you should find out who it was."

"You know anybody who would want to hurt Mr. Shepard?" Detective Albright asked.

"Well, the obvious ones are Brad Thornton and his alleged business associate—what's his name?"

"Rubio. Tony Rubio," Detective Albright replied.

"That's right. If Rob did know something that could have connected those two, either would have had ample motive to kill him."

"That's a nice theory and one I personally hope is true, but unfortunately, we have no evidence to support it."

"I'm sure that was the killer's plan. He wanted to make it look like a murder-suicide, so you wouldn't come looking for him."

"How long have you known the Shepards?" Detective Albright asked.

"Just about a year. We only moved to Texas the

summer before last."

"So, there's a lot about Rob Shepard you probably don't know, don't you think?"

"True. He probably didn't tell me all his secrets, but we were pretty open and frank with each other."

"Well, we'll let you get back to bed," Detective Moore said.

"Yeah, like we'll be able to sleep," Stan replied bitterly.

"Have you told Cindy's and Rob's parents?" Rebekah asked.

"No. Do you have their numbers?"

"Sure. I'll get them," Rebekah said and left the room. She returned a moment later and handed Detective Moore a piece of paper with the numbers written on them. He thanked her, and then the two detectives left.

Stan and Rebekah sat silently for a long time, trying to grasp what had happened. Rebekah was crying softly when Reggie came in.

"What's wrong, Mommie?" Reggie asked. "Did you have a bad dream?"

Rebekah looked at Reggie and sighed. "Oh God! I wish that were the case."

Chapter 7

The next morning, Stan received a call from Dick Stuart, Chairman of the Republican State Executive Committee. He wanted to give his condolences about Rob's death and find out more about what had happened. Stan told him everything he knew, and Stuart asked if Stan would consider running for the state legislature in Rob's place.

The idea excited Stan as his dream had always been to go into politics, but he knew if he ran for public office now his disastrous military career would surely come up and be intensely scrutinized. He couldn't put his family through that again nor would the party nominate him if they knew he had a skeleton like that in the closet.

"No. I'm still in law school, and I want to get my degree before I get serious about politics."

"You sure? We've heard some great things about what you've done up there."

"Well, that's good to hear, but I still need to finish up my law degree and get a practice going."

"Okay. The Committee's going to meet the day after tomorrow at 10:00 a.m. in Austin to vote on a candidate. Will you be able to attend?"

"I don't know. It depends on when the funerals are scheduled. You know, you might want to consider Kristina Tenison. She was Rob's campaign manager and my assistant before that. She comes from a well established family from this area and would probably have good financial backing."

"Okay. You can nominate her at the meeting. What about Commissioner Barnes?"

"Well, I don't know him very well. Frankly, I'm a little suspicious of anyone who switches parties."

"I agree, but he'd pick up a lot of Democratic support, which would enhance his chances of victory in November."

"That's probably true."

"Alright, Stan. Hopefully, I'll see you tomorrow."

Stan hung up and then went looking for Rebekah. When he found her he told her about his conversation with Dick Stuart. She couldn't believe they were already looking for a replacement for him.

"His body's not even cold yet," she complained.

"True, but whoever takes his place has a lot of catching up to do to be competitive in the election."

"I suppose. Do you think Kristina will want to run?"

"I don't know. I'm going to call her and see."

Rebekah nodded. Stan picked up the telephone, dialed her number, and waited.

"Hello," Kristina said softly.

"Did you hear the news?" Stan asked.

"Yes. I can't believe it. Rob seemed just fine last night. I didn't think he was depressed."

"He was a little depressed but not suicidal. There is no way he killed his family."

"I agree. He'd never do that. What do the police think?"

"The two detectives on the case think it was a murder-suicide, but there's been no official word from the medical examiner."

"I can't believe they're all dead. It just seems

surreal."

"I know. It's hard to accept."

"I was really looking forward to the campaign."

"I know. I'm so sorry. I already got a call from Dick Stuart."

"Really? That's right...they need to replace Rob quickly."

"They wanted to know if I was interested."

"What did you say?"

"No, of course, but I told him he ought to consider you."

"Me? Don't be silly. You should do it."

"No, I can't. I need to finish law school plus I have a full time job. You'd be a perfect candidate."

She laughed. "I could never get elected."

"I don't know about that."

"It's okay. I'm happy as your assistant. They'll find somebody else."

"Yeah. They're talking about Barnes."

"Right. He could probably win. He's the obvious choice, thanks to us."

Stan laughed. "That's right. He's going to owe us, big time."

They talked a while longer then Stan hung up and looked at Rebekah. "I think I'm going to go over to the crime scene and look around. Something's not right about all of this."

"They won't let you, will they?"

"I don't know. Probably not, but I can talk to some of the neighbors and get a feel for what happened. I'd like to try to clear Rob's name. I know he didn't do this."

"That's not your job," Rebekah said. "Let the police handle it."

"Yeah, right. You heard Moore and Albright. They've already decided it was a murder-suicide. You want me to trust them to find the truth?"

"No. But you don't have time to get involved, honey. You're stretched too thin as it is."

"I just want to look around."

"Right. But I know you. Once you start something it will become a crusade and ultimately the kids and I will suffer."

"Oh, come on. It's not that bad."

Rebekah shook her head. She knew it was useless to argue with Stan once he got an idea in his head. "Be careful. If someone else did do it, they won't like you snooping around."

"I'll be careful. Don't worry."

Stan left and drove over to Rob's house. There were still a police van and two squad cars parked in front of the house. Stan parked behind one of the squad cars and got out. Crime scene tape had been placed around the front of the house to keep out unauthorized personnel, but otherwise, the house looked like it always did. When an officer came out the front door, Stan approached him.

"Officer, hi. I'm Stan Turner, a friend of the Shepards."

"Oh, right," the officer replied. "I'm Lynn Jenkins. Sorry for your loss."

"Thanks. Has the medical examiner made a determination as to the cause of death yet?"

"No, but unless he finds some evidence to the contrary, I've been told he'll rule it a murder-suicide."

"Hmm. That's not right."

"Why do you say that?" Officer Jenkins asked.

"Rob was my best friend," Stan said. "He loved his wife and children. He'd never kill them."

"That's my take on it too. I've known Rob since high school. He loved living too much to take his own life, and I know he'd never hurt his family."

Stan nodded. "What can we do to set this straight?"

Jenkins shrugged. "I'm not a detective, and I've already given them my opinion. So, I don't know if there's anything else I can do."

"There's always something that can be done. We just have to figure out what it is."

"Well, if someone else is responsible for this atrocity, then I agree they need to be brought to justice."

"Right. That's what we need to make happen."

"Wait a minute. What's this we business?"

"Well, as a police officer you have a duty to uphold the law, right?"

"True."

"And as a law student, I'm dedicating my life to the pursuit of justice, so if we both know Rob didn't kill his family and someone is getting away with murder, we have a responsibility to find the murderer and clear his name."

"That sounds good, but it's not very practical. You've got to go to school, I have to work all day, and neither one of us is a detective."

"I know, but do we really have a choice? I mean, can you just walk away an let this travesty of justice stand. I don't think I can. There are still a few weeks before school starts up again, so I've got some time I can devote to the investigation. What I don't have is the resources of the police department. That's why you need to help me."

"I don't know. I could get in a lot of trouble if I'm discovered."

"There is no reason for you to get discovered. Just be careful, and even if you get caught, your superiors will not be too upset that you're trying to clear the name of a friend. In fact, they'll probably be impressed by your loyalty and initiative."

"Okay. You're probably right. Just let me think about it a day or two."

"Sure. I'll get in touch with you when I need your help."

"How do you even know where to begin?"

"Oh, I've had a little experience in a murder case—my own, in fact."

Stan told him about his court martial for allegedly murdering his drill sergeant.

"Jeeze. What a nightmare that must have been."

"Detective work is pretty much just common sense. You just keep asking questions until you get the right answers. The key is not to give up. I'm stubborn by nature, so it's comes natural for me. "

"I see."

"So, do you have a card?"

Officer Jenkins pulled out a card and handed it to Stan. Stan looked at it carefully and then smiled. "Thanks, Lynn. Do you mind if I call you Lynn?"

"When we're alone, it's okay. In front of other officers, you better keep it formal. I don't want to raise any eyebrows."

"No. We wouldn't want that. . . . Were you on the football team with Rob?"

"Yes. I was a receiver, and Rob had a great arm."

"So I've heard. I bet people around here will be anxious to help us clear his name."

Officer Jenkins nodded. "Yes, a lot of them will be."

"Good. That will make it easier."

Jenkins didn't say anything.

"Is Detective Moore here?" Stan asked.

"Yes, he's inside."

"Would you go in and tell him I'd like to have a word with him?"

"Sure. I'll be right back."

While Officer Jenkins went inside, Stan examined the front flower bed and area around the front porch. Something's not right. He'd remembered a small sign indicating the Shepards were members of the neighborhood Homeowners Association. The sign seemed to be missing. Looking around, he finally spotted it on the ground behind a bush.

"What are you looking at?" Detective Moore asked.

Stan turned around and smiled at the detective. "Oh, hi, Detective. I was just noticing that the Homeowners Association sign has been kicked over behind that bush."

"How do you know it hasn't been there for months?"

"Well, it was right here in the ground the day before yesterday when I was here last," he said, pointing to a hole. "See? The hole impression is still there."

"Okay. Jenkins, bag that sign and get one of the crew inside to look for footprints."

"Yes, sir," Officer Jenkins said.

"So, what can I do for you, Mr. Turner?" Detective Moore asked.

"I'd like to see the crime scene. I know you don't usually let civilians in a crime scene, but I've been in the Shepard's house many times, so I might see something out of place that your crime scene people wouldn't notice."

Officer Jenkins came out the front door with two crime scene crew members. He pointed to the flowerbed, and they went over to it and started working.

Detective Moore studied Stan for a moment and

then shrugged. "Okay. We're almost done with the place anyway. Jenkins, take Mr. Turner through the house, but make sure he doesn't touch anything."

"Yes, sir," Officer Jenkins said and motioned for Stan to go on in.

Stan stepped into the house, and his stomach twisted as he observed the outline of Maureen Peter's body on the tile floor. She was facing away from the staircase like she'd been running for the front door and was tackled from behind.

"How'd Maureen die?" Stan asked.

Jenkins pointed to the fireplace in the den. She was hit with a fire poker the perp got from over there. Stan walked over to the fireplace and looked around the large room. There was a large TV cabinet on one wall and two blue leather sofas facing it.

"I wonder why she wasn't shot in the head like the others," Stan asked.

Jenkins looked around the room and then said thoughtfully, "Maybe she ran to the fireplace, got a poker to use as a weapon, but the perp caught her and wrestled it away from her."

"And then used the poker on her?" Stan added.

"Right."

Stan shrugged. "That's possible. . . . Okay, let's go upstairs."

Jenkins turned and started up the staircase.

"Don't touch the banister. I'm not sure if they're finished dusting for prints yet."

"Right," Stan said, putting his hands in his pockets.

When they got to the top of the stairs there was a strong odor of blood and chemicals. Stan felt sick as he saw the blood-soaked carpeting where Rob had been found.

"So, did they recover the gun?"

"Yes. It was in Rob's hand."

"How many rounds were fired?"

"Six."

Stan frowned. "Six? Five killed by gunshot but six rounds missing? That doesn't add up."

"Right. Detective Moore thinks maybe Cindy was struggling and Rob missed the first time he shot at her."

"Hmm. Or, a third party wanted to make sure Rob had powder burns on his hand and forced Rob to fire a wild round after he was already dead."

Jenkins shrugged. "I don't know. That's a possibility, I guess, but you could never prove it."

"Maybe, maybe not," Stan said, moving on to where Cindy's body had been lying.

Stan felt nauseous and struggled to keep from vomiting as he didn't want to be kicked out of the crime scene before he'd had a good look around.

"What was the order of the killings?" Stan asked.

"They were all killed about the same time. I doubt you could conclusively determine the exact order."

"What was the murder weapon?"

"Rob's .38 special," Jenkins replied.

"Rob kept that gun in his car," Stan said. "He's shown it to me before. The killer probably waited until Rob and Cindy came home and went into the house, and then he went into the garage, got the gun, and entered the house."

"That also means the killer knew Rob had a gun in his car, so Rob must have known his killer."

"Or the killer was hired by someone who knew Rob pretty well."

"Are you thinking Brad Thornton?"

"He would have known about Rob's gun, that's for sure," Stan said, "but, he doesn't strike me as someone who would be capable of ordering a hit like that. He really comes across as a decent man."

"It could be all show," Jenkins said.

"Maybe. Was anything missing?" Stan asked.

"His parents are coming by this afternoon to inventory the house, so we don't know for sure. It doesn't look like anyone was searching for anything."

"They wouldn't need to search if they knew what they were looking for and where to find it."

"True. Do you know of something a thief might want?"

"Cindy's parents were well off, so she had a lot of valuable jewelry. I remember her wearing a diamond necklace that was supposedly worth $25,000. In fact, she wore it to the President's fundraiser."

"Really? Let's go find out if it's missing."

Jenkins walked over to one of the crime scene technicians. "Hey, Walt, did they find a diamond necklace on the wife?"

Walt looked back at Jenkins thoughtfully. "No. She wasn't wearing a necklace."

"Well, look around for it. She was wearing it earlier in the evening at President Ford's fundraiser. If it's not around here, this could be a robbery-murder rather than a murder-suicide."

Detective Moore came up the stairs and walked over to Stan and Jenkins. "What's this about a robbery?" he asked.

"It seems Cindy Shepard was wearing an expensive diamond necklace last night when she came home, but it's nowhere to be found right now."

"Shit!" Detective Moore said. "Thanks a lot, Stan. Now you've really complicated things."

"I'm sorry, but if this was a robbery, then Rob's not a murderer."

"Well, more likely someone ripped it off her neck after she was killed. Now I'm going to have to call in internal affairs."

While Detective Moore was lamenting this turn of events, Stan wandered into Jenny's room. From the appearance of the room, Stan figured Jenny must have been asleep and never knew her life was about to be snuffed out. Anger and rage welled up inside him at the thought of someone putting a gun to her head and pulling the trigger. He knew Rob couldn't have done that. A few minutes later, Jenkins walked in.

"Jenny was asleep when she was murdered, huh?" Stan asked.

"Right. That's what it looks like."

"So, the babysitter had put all the kids to bed and was downstairs watching TV when all this went down?"

"That's probably true," Officer Jenkins agreed.

"If Rob intended to kill his family, he'd just pay the babysitter and get rid of her. Then he'd kill his wife since she'd be the only one who could upset his plans. There would be no reason to make her witness her children's murder unless he was a heartless bastard, which we both know he wasn't. And I'm pretty sure Cindy would have told Rebekah if there had been any animosity between them that could have fueled such a horrific act. This murder-suicide theory is a load of crap!"

"I agree," Jenkins said. "Maybe this necklace thing will make everyone re-think the investigation.

Stan thanked Detective Moore for allowing him to look at the crime scene and went home to tell Rebekah what he'd found out. He hoped the missing necklace would delay the Medical Examiner's determination as to what had happened at the Shepard house, but somehow he doubted that would be the case.

Chapter 8

Even the suspicion that Rob had murdered his family and then committed suicide didn't deter many from coming to the funeral to grieve the tragic loss of the Shepard family. Even the big Baptist church in downtown Plano, couldn't accommodate all the family, friends, and supporters who showed up to pay tribute to the Shepard family. Many of them were forced into the church's recreational building to watch the service on video.

As Stan feared the service was held at the same time as the Republican State Executive Committee meeting to replace Rob, so Stan missed the meeting. After the ceremony, Stan and Rebekah went up to Rob's parents to give them their condolences. They'd met Marge and Tom Shepard once or twice at various functions and had hit it off quite well. Tom Shepard was a retired airline pilot, and Marge had been a ticket agent for the same airline. Currently, Tom helped Marge run a flower shop in downtown Plano.

"We are so sorry," Rebekah said to Marge. "This whole thing is such a shock."

"Yes, it is," Marge agreed. "I still don't understand any of it."

"Don't believe what the papers or the police are saying," Stan advised. "It's all a bunch of crap. I know Rob didn't kill anyone."

"Thank you, Stan," Tom said. "I understand

you've been doing your own investigation of the murders."

"Where did you hear that?" Stan asked.

"Oh, I have my sources," Tom replied.

"Well, the police and the medical examiner seem a bit too anxious to wrap up the investigation, and I can understand that. It's nice when a case is simple and nobody has to work too hard."

"Yeah. That's typical for lazy government bureaucrats."

"Anyway, I'm going to get to the bottom of this. I'm not going to let them drag Rob's name through the dirt. He was a good man and he loved his family. I know that for a fact, so how could I stand by and do nothing."

"Thank you," Stan. "If I can help in any way, let me know. If you need any money—"

"I don't want any money for me, but there might be some expenses that come up."

"No problem. Just let me know how much you need."

"What I do need now is some information from you."

"What kind of information?"

"I understand Brad Thornton has been a longtime family friend," Stan said.

"Yes, damn near part of the family. His dad and I have been good friends for years."

"So, you know a lot about Brad?"

"Yes, I suppose I do."

"Well, I need to find out as much about him and his business operations as possible. I think he may be the key to discovering the truth about what happened."

"Okay. Why don't you come over to the hose this afternoon, and we'll answer any questions we can."

"Good. I'll do that."

Stan and Rebekah said goodbye and then went to the reception to mingle. They talked to Kristina and some other friends and then ran into Officer Jenkins. Stan hardly recognized him garbed in a suit instead of his typical police uniform.

"Hey, Lynn," Stan said. "This is my wife, Rebekah."

"Hi, Rebekah."

"I'm glad I ran into you. I'm meeting with the Shepards this afternoon to get background information on the Thorntons and wondered if you wanted to come too."

"Okay. That could prove useful, and it will be nice to talk with Tom and Marge. I haven't seen them in a while."

"Good. I'll see you at their place at three-thirty."

"Okay. See you then."

As they were about to leave the reception, Stan noticed Commissioner Barnes talking to a reporter. He wondered if the Commissioner had heard anything from the Republican State Executive Committee. Stan led Rebekah over to where they were talking. Barnes spotted Stan and perked up.

"Oh, here's the man who made it all possible," Barnes said to the reporter.

"Hi, Commissioner," Stan said. "I'd like you to meet my wife, Rebekah."

He bowed slightly and shook her hand lightly. "I was just telling Jim Bowers here that the State Republican Executive Committee's decision to have me take Rob Shepard's spot on the ballot wouldn't have happened had it not been for you, Stan."

"Oh, so they've made the decision? Congratulations!"

"Thank you. In fact, I was looking for your friend Kristina. I'd like her to be my campaign manager. I understand she's a dynamo."

Stan laughed. "She is that...and that's great. She'll be thrilled. I saw her earlier. She should be around here somewhere."

"I'll go find her," Rebekah said, "and send her over this way."

"Would you?" Barnes asked. "That would be most kind."

"So, Mr. Turner," Bowers asked. "I understand you don't agree with the Medical Examiner's determination that the Shepard family's demise was the result of Rob Shepard's actions."

Stan raised his eyebrows. "Jeeze. Word spreads fast around this town."

"I've got eyes and ears everywhere, my friend. I heard you shook up the detectives at the crime scene the other night."

"I guess. . . . So the Medical Examiner has made a final determination?" Stan asked dejectedly.

"Yes. The official report was posted at noon–murder-suicide."

"Jesus! . . . . I can't believe this. He's dead wrong. Rob would never have killed his family. He didn't do it."

"I don't know. The crime scene looked pretty clear."

"Not really," Stan said bitterly. "I can't believe he's made a decision already. He hasn't had time to do a proper investigation." Stan sighed deeply. "Now I'm going to have to find out who the killer is myself to clear Rob's name. . . . Like I have time for this."

"You feel pretty strongly about it, I see."

"Yes, I do, and I'm extremely disappointed with the police department and the medical examiner for taking the easy way out in this investigation."

"Do you have any evidence to refute the Medical Examiner's conclusion?"

"Yes, but I should probably read his report before I comment further. Perhaps there's something in it that I haven't heard about yet."

"Mr. Turner, if someone else is responsible for these gruesome murders, aren't you worried about your and your family's safety if you continue to investigate this crime?"

"Yes, of course, and I'll take whatever precautions are necessary to protect my myself and my family."

"Good, because I don't think anyone wants to ever see a tragedy like this again."

Rebekah returned with Kristina, and Stan was glad she'd missed the last question Jim Bowers had thrown at him. She would have come unglued, he was sure of it.

"Did Rebekah tell you what I wanted?" Barnes asked Kristina.

"Yes. She said you want me to be your campaign manager."

"Yes, and I understand you already have a campaign all mapped out."

"I do. This is wonderful. And here I thought all my hard work was going to go to waste."

"No. We should get together tomorrow and rework your plan so it fits me."

"Absolutely," Kristina said, smiling broadly.

Bowers directed his attention to Kristina. "So, Ms. Tenison, do you think the Commissioner can win, getting in the race at this late date?"

"Oh, absolutely. He's the perfect candidate to step in at the last minute. Everybody knows him and he has an impressive track record."

Stan and Rebekah slipped away while Kristina was being interviewed, as they had to get home and relieve the babysitter. On the way home Stan thought about what Bowers had said about protecting his family. He wondered if the FBI would keep Rebekah and the kids under surveillance too. He vowed to bring that up with Agent Rutledge the next time he talked to her.

On the way to the Shepard's place Stan wondered what questions he should ask them. He didn't know exactly what he or the FBI was looking for, so he finally decided to just start asking whatever came to mind and hope something would turn out to be useful.

He told Rebekah he'd only be a few hours and then left. The Shepards lived in a restored mansion in Central Plano. It was a beautiful yellow Queen Ann styled home with fish-scale shingles, a circular two-and-a-half-story tower, large wrap-around porch, and two-panel glass windows.

"You have a beautiful home," Stan said as he stepped into the house.

"Thank you," Marge said. "We've put a lot of work into the restoration, and it's turned out quite nice."

"When was it first built?" Stan asked.

"Around the turn of the century," Marge said. "Go on into the den. Can I bring you coffee or a cold drink?"

"Coke would be good if you have it."

Stan walked into the den where Officer Jenkins and Tom Shepard were already talking. He smiled when they looked over at him.

"Hi."

"Hey, Stan! Come on in and have a seat."

Stan sat in a big stuffed chair, and a second later, Marge brought him a glass of Coke.

"Lynn and I have been doing a little catching up. It's been a while since we've talked."

Stan nodded. "Right."

"So, you wanted to know about Brad Thornton?" Tom asked.

"Yes. I understand he recently sold his business?"

"Uh huh. He had a string of lumber yards with a partner, Brett Townsend. They got at odds, so Townsend bought Brad out for a nice chunk of change, or so the rumors go."

"Do you think the rumors are accurate?" Stan asked.

"I kind of doubt it. The lumber yards were close to bankruptcy, I was told. That's one of the reasons they got at odds. They had different philosophies about how to turn things around. So, I seriously doubt Brad got all that much money when he was bought out."

"Is Brad the type to exaggerate things, or is he a straight shooter?"

"Exaggerates is a nice way to put it. Actually, you can't believe anything Brad tells you. He likes to impress people—you know, dazzle them with brilliance or buffalo them with bullshit."

Stan laughed. "Okay. I understand he has a home in Maui."

"That's true. We stayed there a week last year. Don't ask me how he can afford something like that. It must have cost him a mint, and the upkeep must be incredible."

"What can you tell me about his recent investment, Silver Springs?"

"That was a pretty slick little development. He told me one day he had a client who was looking for an investment project. The guy had lots of cash and wasn't afraid to dump a lot of it into a project if it would pay off at the other end. Brad spent a lot of time scouring north Texas to find something appropriate, and Silver Springs was what he came up with."

"So, Brad didn't use any of his own money on that project?"

"Nah. I don't think he had any, if you want my opinion."

"Was this investor Tony Rubio?" Officer Jenkins asked.

"I don't know. I never met the investor. I met Carlos Morales, his CFO, but he never really said who he worked for."

"Do you know how much he invested in Silver Springs?" Jenkins asked.

"Ten million was a number I heard once or twice. You've got to understand I just heard bits and pieces of conversations. Brad didn't confide in me that much."

"Can you check on Carlos Morales?" Stan asked Jenkins.

Jenkins shifted uncomfortably in his chair. "Not officially. I might be able to sneak onto the computer while nobody is looking and run a search."

"Does Carlos Morales have an office in Texas, or does he just show up from time to time?"

"He used to have an office out at Silver Springs, but I'm not sure if he still does, particularly with the feds investigating the venture. He's probably back in Mexico by now."

"Does Brad have anybody who works for him that might be capable of murder—someone who does his dirty work, perhaps?" Stan asked.

"That would be Todd Watson," Tom replied. "He's a thug Brad met in the army when he served in Vietnam. Brad hired him on for security out at Silver Springs, but he's also Brad's driver and bodyguard."

"Can you check him out too, Lynn?" Stan asked.

"I'll add him to the list, but I can't spend a lot of

time on the computer without getting caught."

"I understand. Just do what you can without getting in trouble," Stan said, looking at Jenkins. He turned back to Tom, "Do you know anybody Watson hangs around with, a girlfriend perhaps?"

"Why?" Tom asked.

"Oh, I'd like to find out if he has an alibi. I'm sure he won't tell me anything, but I might be able to get the information from his girlfriend if I knew who she was and how to find her."

"I've seen him with a blond a time or two. I'll see if I can find out her name and get her address," Marge replied.

"What about Brad's wife Melissa? Is she involved in Brad's businesses?"

"No. She's active in the community—Junior League, her kid's school, and the Baptist church," Marge replied.

"How's the marriage? Is it stable, or have there been rifts?" Stan asked.

"It's been stable. I don't see Melissa providing any information against her husband," Marge said.

The meeting continued on a while as one question led to another. When it was over, Stan thanked them and left. While he and Officer Jenkins were walking to their cars, Stan asked him about security. He knew the FBI had promised to keep an eye on him, but they hadn't said anything about his family.

"You know, that newspaper reporter had a good point. What's going to stop the lunatic who killed Rob and his family from coming after me and my family once he finds out I'm on his trail."

Jenkins nodded. "That's been worrying me too. I know a guy who can install a good security system for you. You'll have to punch in a code when you come and go from your house. It's a pain in the ass, but it's worthwhile. He can also set you up a panic alarm that will alert the police if you push a button. I've already put your house on the list for extra patrols."

"Oh, great. That makes me feel a lot better."

"You better have Rebekah take your kids to school and pick them up—no buses, and definitely don't let them walk to school."

"She does that already," Stan said.

"Okay. That takes care of your family. I don't know what to do about you. I guess you could carry a gun."

"Right, so they can set me up for a murder-suicide too."

Jenkins chuckled. "Yeah, you're probably right. You'd be no match for a professional hit man from one of the cartels anyway. You better let me do the snooping around. They won't mess with a police officer, but a civilian they'll have no qualms about wasting."

Stan thanked Lynn for his help and left. On the way home he stopped at a pay phone and reported to Agent Rutledge what he had learned so far.

"You probably already knew all of this," Stan said. "I didn't know precisely what to ask."

"No. You did fine. Thornton lawyered up so we don't know a whole lot about him right now. Just keep asking questions."

"Oh, I'm having a security system put in at the house, since I doubt you're going to be able to watch both me and Rebekah."

"No. We don't have that kind of manpower. That's a good idea."

"So, is there anything in particular you'd like me to do right now? Anybody I should be talking to?"

"Yes, why don't you take your family out to Silver

Springs Lake. Just act like your are a potential customer. The manager out there hasn't been particularly candid, but she might open up to you."

"Sure, I've actually been anxious to see the place. It will be a fun outing for the family."

"Okay. Let me know what you learn," Agent Rutledge said.

"I will," Stan replied and hung up.

The next morning, Rebekah dug through the newspaper to find the article about the Shepard funeral. She was surprised to see another article about Stan's investigation into the Shepard murders. She brought the article to him at the breakfast table.

"Stan, why did you talk to this Bowers guy? Look at this article! Now whoever killed Rob and his family will be watching you like a hawk."

"I know. I'm sorry. The guy caught me off guard. I've already talked to Lynn, and he's sending a guy out to install a security system. They also have our house on a special police watch list. I don't think anyone will bother us."

"What about you? I don't want you getting hurt."

"The FBI will be watching me."

"Only if you're doing something specific for them on the Thornton case. They're not going to be watching you when you're out looking for Rob and Cindy's killer."

"I'll be careful. Don't worry. I'm going to let Jenkins handle all the sensitive stuff. I'll just do the background investigation and help on the periphery."

Rebekah rolled her eyes. "Uh huh. I'll believe that when donkeys sing. Why don't you just stay out of it? You don't have to make this thing right. It's not your responsibility."

"Do you want the Shepard family's murderer to get away scot free?"

"No, of course not, but I don't want to lose you or my family."

Stan sighed. "Seriously, I won't do anything too dangerous."

"You better not," Rebekah said sternly. "It's your children's lives you're messing with."

Stan swallowed hard. He knew he should just back off and let it alone. After all, he couldn't bring Rob and his family back. But the thought of people thinking of his friend as a murderer mortified him. He couldn't let that perception stand. The record had to be set straight.

Chapter 9

Unfortunately, Stan couldn't devote all his time to finding the Shepard family's killers and helping the FBI take down the Burilo Cartel. In addition to law school he had a full-time job selling insurance for Cosmopolitan Life. Fortunately, being a salesman, he managed his own time and only had to show up at the office once a week to turn in applications and talk briefly to his sales manager. He wasn't the greatest salesman in the world and didn't really have his heart in the insurance game, but he soon discovered being an agent was good cover for his investigative work.

It was a week after the murders had taken place when Rob's mother, Marge Shepard, called Stan and gave him the contact information for Todd Watson's girlfriend. Her name was Tina Small, and she worked in the cosmetics department of Neiman Marcus in Northpark Mall. While Stan was at his office, he looked her name up in the company database and discovered her mother had taken a policy out for her when she was a child. According to the records, the policy had never been turned over to her, so Stan gave her a call.

"Hello, Miss Small. This is Stan Turner from Cosmopolitan Life."

"Okay."

"Uh, our records show that you are one of our policyholders, so I just wanted to sit down with you and review your policy."

"Really? I don't remember a policy with

Cosmopolitan Life."

"Apparently your mother, Kathy Small, took it out."

"Oh, that's right. She mentioned that. So, what do you want to talk about?" she asked.

"There are conversion options I need to explain to you, and it's always good to review your current situation. You may want to change your beneficiary or something."

"Hmm. Okay. When do you want to meet?"

"Just as soon as it's convenient for you. How about tomorrow?"

"Okay. I could do it during my lunch break."

"Where should I meet you?" Stan asked.

"Well, come to the cosmetics section at Nieman's at noon, and you can buy me lunch," Miss Small replied.

Stan laughed. "Okay. It's a deal. See you at noon."

The next day, Stan met up with Tina Small and took her to an Italian restaurant in the mall. She was a blue-eyed blond in her early twenties and wore a ruffled front knit dress that matched her eyes. After they'd eaten and he'd reviewed her insurance policy with her, he eased the conversation to her boyfriend.

"Did you know your dress matches your eyes?" Stan said.

She smiled. "Is that right?"

"Yeah. What color is that anyway? I love it."

"Prussian blue," she said warily.

"Oh? Are you German?"

"Yes. My grandparents immigrated to the US from Berlin after World War I."

"Oh, that's cool. So, do you have a boyfriend?"

"Well, more or less."

Stan laughed. "What does that mean?"

"It means he hasn't asked me to marry him yet."

Stan felt guilty flirting with Tina, but in his mind, it was for a good reason. He didn't want Tina telling her boyfriend about meeting Stan. If Todd Watson learned about their meeting and recognized the name, he might realize Stan was investigating him. Stan figured that if he flirted with Tina, her boyfriend would be the last person to ever hear of it.

"Hmm," Stan said. "Doesn't sound like he's a very smart guy. What kind of business is he in?"

"He's kind of a troubleshooter for a businessman up in Richardson. You may have heard about him. He's being investigated by the FBI."

"Oh, do you mean Brad Thornton?"

"Yes. He's the one."

"So, your boyfriend works for Mr. Thornton, huh?"

"Unfortunately. I haven't seen much of him since the shit hit the fan."

"Oh, so you're not busy then—if I wanted to see you again?"

Tina's eyes narrowed. "I thought you just wanted to sell me some more life insurance?"

"Well, initially that was true, but you're beautiful Prussian eyes have mesmerized me. I'd like to study them some more."

"Hmm," she said, blushing slightly. "That's quite a line."

"So, were you out with Todd the night Rob Shepard murdered his family?"

"No. He got busy the day before when the FBI decided to search Thornton's place."

"What do you think he's doing for Thornton?"

She shrugged. "Who knows. Cleaning up one of his messes, I guess. The guy's always got some kind of problem. That's why he needs a troubleshooter."

"So, how does someone train to become a

troubleshooter like that?" Stan asked.

"Tom's always been tough. He joined the Marines when he was seventeen. He had nine kills to his credit in 'Nam, and he loves to talk about each and every one of them."

"You probably know them by heart, I bet?"

"Oh, yeah."

"Do you think Rob Shepard really killed his family?" Stan asked. "I mean, how could a father kill his children like that?"

"I don't know. They said he was very depressed."

"Right. Did Todd know Rob?"

"Yeah, I think they knew each other."

"But you haven't talked to Todd since it happened?"

"No."

"What an idiot, ignoring a woman like you," Stan said with a sly smile.

Tina studied Stan a moment like she was considering something. He met her eyes and smiled warmly. "You know," she said. "I could call my boss and tell her I'm not feeling well. Then we could go to my apartment and you could make me forget about my lousy boyfriend."

Stan's heart quickened. The idea excited him, but he knew it could never happen for many reasons. "Yeah, now that's a plan," Stan said treading carefully, "but I don't want to get you in trouble, and I've got to meet my manager at two-thirty. I'll call you, though. I've got your number."

"You sure? My boss won't say anything."

"You're lucky. My boss is a real asshole. He'd give me hell if I didn't show up for our meeting."

"Well, don't take too long to call. You've gone and got me stirred up. You shouldn't do that to a woman if you're not serious."

"I'll call you, I promise, "Stan lied and then made a hasty exit. It had been fun flirting with Tina, but he realized he'd gone a little too far and things could have gotten out of hand. He felt relieved that the encounter was over.

While he was driving back home, he ran what he'd learned through his mind. First, Todd was working for Brad Thornton when the murders took place, and since he was Brad's troubleshooter, he'd be the most likely one ordered to do the Shepard hit. Secondly, Todd was a Vietnam vet who'd killed plenty of times before and wouldn't have had any qualms about killing the family. Finally, Brad Thornton still had his men working overtime. Stan wondered what they were doing. Were they really trying to tie up more loose ends before the FBI discovered them, or was something else going on?

Later that afternoon, Stan met up with Officer Jenkins at Denny's in Plano. The waitress served them a cup of coffee, and then Jenkins told Stan what he'd found out from the police database.

"Okay. Carlos Morales is an accountant who used to work for a prominent Mexico City accounting firm until he suddenly quit two years ago. The feds apparently believe he has been recruited by the Burilo cartel. The story is that he had been caught embezzling from his firm, and when the Burilo cartel heard about it, they paid off his employer on the condition that he come to work for them. Apparently, the cartel felt he had to be a pretty talented thief to steal from a national accounting firm, so they wanted some of that talent for their organization."

"Interesting," Stan said. "Any arrests or convictions?"

"No, but he's been questioned several times by the

FBI in conjunction with the cartel's activities. So far, he's been loyal and hasn't said much about their operations. It does appear he was the front man for Silver Springs Ventures, though. In fact, according to the Texas Secretary of State's records, he was the incorporator and one of the initial members of the Board of Directors."

"Okay, Were you able to get any financial information on Silver Springs?"

"No. There wasn't anything in the database about it. I think the FBI has locked everybody out of the Silver Springs file. Unfortunately, since I'm not working the case, I can't go ask them for it. I did find out, however, that his loan officer at First National Bank was Don Karnes."

"Don Karnes? He's on the Republican Executive Committee. I bet he'll talk to me," Stan said.

"Good. He probably has copies of all the financial records. Legally he can't give them to you, but he might bend the rules if he believes in what you're doing."

"Rob referred me to him, so I'm sure he's as upset about Rob's death as anybody. He'll help out, I bet."

"Good. What did you find out from Tina Small?" Officer Jenkins asked.

Stan told him about the lunch and what he'd learned about Todd Watson. Then he told Jenkins he was thinking of taking the family to Silver Springs Lake to look around and get the lay of the land.

"I don't know if that's wise. Do you really want to drag your family out there amongst the criminals?"

"I'd rather have them with me than be worrying about them back at home. Besides, nobody will know we're going out there, so it's unlikely they'll know we ever made the trip. I'll just tell anyone we run into that we're thinking of buying a lakefront condo."

"Be careful."

"I will."

The next day, Stan took his family on a picnic to Silver Springs Lake. He called Agent Rutledge before they left to update her on his meeting with Todd Watson's girlfriend and to alert her of the trip to Silver Springs Lake. She thanked him for the update and promised she would assign someone to follow him out there in case there was trouble.

It was about a ninety-minute drive East on I30, deep into beautiful East Texas. It was a hot, dry day, and Rebekah had brought a picnic basket, hoping to find a park near the lake where they could eat and enjoy the view. When they arrived, they were not disappointed. Adjacent to the information center was a small park with picnic tables overlooking the lake. A playground complete with swings, teeter totters, and lots of sand adjoined the park. Stan parked the station wagon in the parking lot and then claimed a picnic bench. Since it was the middle of the week, there weren't too many people around. After lunch, the kids went to the playground, and Rebekah watched them while Stan walked up to the information office. A middle-aged lady was manning the desk.

"Hi," Stan said casually as he walked in.

"Good afternoon. Welcome to Silver Springs Lake," the woman said. "I'm Ruth Snowden."

"Hi. Nice to meet you," Stan said. "Pretty nice place you have here."

"Yes. Isn't it beautiful? Are you up from Tyler?"

"No. Dallas."

"Oh, that's a nice drive this time of year."

"Yes, it is. . . . So, how's business?"

"Oh, a little slow, as you can see."

"Yes, I was expecting a little more activity."

"Well, it's late in the year. Spring and early

summer are our best seasons. Nobody wants to move after school starts in the fall. It will be dead the rest of the year."

"How many units do you have up here?"

"I think around 440."

"That many? Wow. How many have you sold?"

"Seventy-nine by my last count."

"So, you have 361 units still available?"

"Something like that."

"That's a lot. How long have you been operational?"

"About nine months."

"What do these babies go for?"

"Uh, they range from $80,000 to $120,000. Would you like to see one?"

Stan thought about that for a moment and then decided that might not be a bad idea. On a tour, he could ask a lot of questions without creating any suspicion. He also might get a sales packet that might contain some useful information. "Sure. Let me get my wife and kids. I left them at the park."

"Okay. I'll meet you at Unit 139," she said and pointed to a map on the wall. Stan looked where she was pointing and nodded.

"Alright. We'll meet you there."

Ten minutes later, Ruth Snowden was unlocking the door to Unit 139. She held the door open and Rebekah, Stan, and the kids walked inside and stood in the entryway looking down into a sunken living room. Off to the left was a big dining room, and beyond it was the kitchen. Stan walked into the living room and saw a large window that over looked the lake.

"Wow! I could get used to this view."

"Oh, I know. Isn't it gorgeous?" Ruth said.

"I heard this place was a dried-up swamp just a

few years back. Is that true?" Stan asked.

"Actually, it is. Brad Thornton, the founder of Silver Springs Ventures, discovered this place three years ago when it was pretty much a swamp. Fortunately, he was a man of vision and saw not what it was, but what it could be."

"He must have been one gutsy guy to put all his money into swampland."

"Actually, I don't think he had to put much of his money into it. I doubt he'd have had enough. Fortunately, there are a lot of people looking for tax write-offs, so finding investors isn't that difficult if you're a good salesman like Brad."

"Is this the same Brad Thornton we've been reading about in the newspaper?" Stan asked.

Ruth nodded. "Yes, I'm afraid so, but I wouldn't worry about that. Brad assured me they've dotted all the i's and crossed all the t's on this project, so the FBI is just spinning their wheels."

"That's good to hear. Did they come out here?"

"Yes, the same day the article came out in the newspaper."

"What did they do when they came out?"

"They hauled off all the records we keep here. Luckily, I had backup copies. Otherwise, I would have had to shut down this place. You can't run a business without your records."

"Yeah," Stan said. "I don't understand how the FBI can just saunter in and take all your records. I could understand it if they just went through them, but to take them away? That's ridiculous."

"I know. They acted like Brad was guilty already."

"I think in the paper they mentioned a guy Tony...Tony—"

"Oh, Tony Rubio?"

"Yeah, that's him. Was he one of the investors?"

"Uh huh, but I can't believe he's a criminal like they say. He's been by many times, and he's a real gentleman."

"Really? Have you seen him lately?"

"No, not since the investigation."

"Has the FBI been able to track him down yet?"

"I doubt it, unless they've chased him down to Costa Rica."

"Costa Rica? Is that where's he from?"

"I don't know where he's from, but he spends a lot of time at his beach property there."

"Did you tell the FBI that?"

"No. They were nasty to me, so I just answered their questions and didn't volunteer anything."

Stan chuckled. "How were they nasty to you?"

"They came in and stuck their badges in front of me and started bossing me around. I didn't appreciate their arrogant attitude."

"Yeah, you give a badge to some people, and it goes to their head."

"Boy, ain't that the truth?"

"Where in Costa Rica is his beach property located?"

"Playa Langosta. I'm not sure what the address is, but it's a Mediterranean style villa in a gated community. He told me that much."

"Sounds expensive."

"A little under a million according to the local listings. I checked it out when he told me about it. I was curious."

Rebekah and the kids had finished their inspection of the condo, and they were getting bored, so Stan thanked Ruth, and they went back to their car. As they were leaving, Ruth handed Stan an application packet. When they got back in the car, Stan inspected it and found it contained a sales contract, brochure, and confidential prospectus. Stan wondered why she'd stuck the prospectus in the packet since he hadn't expressed any interest in becoming an investor. Then he realized Ruth must have known who he was and decided to help out. He opened the prospectus and smiled broadly. Inside were the names and addresses of all the investors in the Silver Springs Ventures. Stan went down the list looking for anybody he knew. He saw Rob's name, referencing his $25,000 investment, but he didn't expect to find Commissioner Paul Barnes on the list, indicating he'd invested $100,000!

Chapter 10

Stan dreaded the start of the new semester. He'd enjoyed having some spare time to spend with the family, time for a little politics, and lately, time to try to clear Rob Shepard's name. Now, with law school starting up, he'd barely have time to breathe. Not only would there be three or four hours of classes each day, but also the endless reading and preparation for them. He'd been told each year of law school would get easier, but he hadn't found that to be the case. He figured it was because of the interruption of his legal education by service in the Marine Corps that had made his second year just as difficult as the first. He prayed that was it and this final year would be a tad easier.

It was the first Thursday of September, and he'd just picked up his schedule. He noticed his first class was advanced criminal procedure with Professor Harry Hertel, aka "Snake." No one knew why he was called Snake, but apparently it was a name he'd earned in private practice before he became a professor. There was a lot of speculation as to what he'd done to deserve such a nickname, but no one dared ask him about it.

This wasn't Stan's first class with Professor Hertel. He'd been Stan's professor for basic criminal law during his first semester at SMU. Stan liked him because he often told stories of actual cases he'd been involved in. His class was a welcome change from the Socratic teaching style most of the professors imposed upon their students. As he was walking up to the classroom, he saw a friend coming the other way.

"Paula," Stan said. "Hi!"

Paula looked up at Stan and smiled. "Stan? Oh, do we have criminal procedure together?"

"It looks that way."

"Good. It will be nice to sit with someone who has practical knowledge of the subject matter."

Stan laughed. "I doubt the Uniform Code of Military Justice is much like the Texas Penal Code."

On Stan's first day at SMU, Paula had sought him out to see if he was the Stan Turner she'd read about in the newspapers. When he told her he was, she became his best friend on campus. Paula wanted to be a high-profile criminal defense attorney, and hanging around with someone who'd beaten a murder rap was exciting to her. Stan liked Paula because of her honesty and propensity to say exactly what was on her mind. Because of that, Stan had no reservations about speaking freely to her, something he couldn't do with Rebekah, who was defensive and often critical. She was a worrier too and would drive Stan nuts if he shared his concerns with her.

Paula took Stan's arm, and they entered the classroom together. It was one of the smaller, more intimate classrooms in the old wing. Professor Hertel was at his desk talking on the telephone. The room was about three-quarters full, and Paula led Stan to two empty seats.

"So, I've been reading about you, as usual," Paula said. "You seem to attract publicity."

"Yes. It seems that way. I certainly didn't expect to be involved in another murder case."

"Hmm. So, why are you so convinced Rob Shepard didn't kill his family?"

"I knew him. He wouldn't have done something like that, no matter how bad things got. He was obviously set up."

The bell rang, and Professor Hertel got up from his desk and went to the lectern in front of the room. He brushed back his long black hair and addressed the students. "Good morning. This is Criminal Procedure 301. My name is Professor Harry Hertel. You may have heard that my nickname is Snake. If anyone here calls me by that name, I will flunk them."

Everyone laughed.

"He's cute," Paula whispered.

"You think so?" Stan replied.

"Yeah. Look at those sexy eyes. I wonder if he's married."

Stan shook his head. "I believe he's divorced. He mentioned his ex-wife in a disparaging manner a few times last year."

"Hmm. I think I'm going to get an A in this class."

Stan rolled his eyes.

Professor Hertel noticed Stan and Paula whispering to each other. He looked at them and said, "So, Mr. Turner, I see we have you back for another semester. I'm kind of surprised. From what I've been reading in the newspaper, you've already started practicing law."

"No, sir," Stan replied, "just a little informal investigation."

"Well, you've got guts. I'll say that for you. But you may be letting your personal feelings cloud your judgment. That's something you've got to watch out for as an attorney. You've got to maintain your objectivity."

"Yes, sir. It's just that the police and the Medical Examiner are wrong, and if I don't keep digging, a killer will go free and my friend will go down in the record book as a murderer. You're not the first person that's told me to let it go, and perhaps I should, but I can't."

"Well, there's nothing like tenacity when you are in the pursuit of justice. So, I hope you're right and wish you well. In fact, if there is anything I can do to help, let me know. Perhaps we'll make it a class project. Criminal investigation is part of our curriculum, and it's always more interesting and meaningful to work on an actual case. This could be a unique opportunity for all of us."

"That would be awesome!" Stan said. "I can use all the help I can get."

"Why don't you tell us where you are in the investigation?"

Stan spent the rest of the class time explaining everything that had happened and telling his classmates what he had done so far in the investigation. Everyone seemed mesmerized by the tale and excited about helping out. After class, Stan and Paula went across the street to Dairy Queen to get an early lunch.

"Jesus Christ, Turner! No matter where you go, you're the center of attention."

Stan laughed. "That was totally unexpected. I'm surprised Professor Hertel even remembered my name."

"It's alright. I'm just jealous, I guess. I'll just have to be satisfied with being your sidekick for now. Someday, I'll get my day in the sun."

"This isn't about me. I'm just doing it because nobody else is. Believe me, I wish it weren't necessary."

"I know. So, what do you want me to do?"

"Huh?"

"Well, you can't have all the fun. Give me an assignment. I want to help."

Stan looked at Paula and then thought a minute. He liked Paula and she was a pleasant companion, but Rebekah would be upset if she found out he was hanging out with yet another female friend. He knew he should decline the offer but heard himself say, "Well, okay. You took Business Organizations, didn't you?"

"Sure, it's a required class."

"Well, you know the prospectus I mentioned I got from the realtor up at Silver Springs Lake?"

"Right."

"Well, it details a rather complex structure of corporations, partnerships, and trusts. I need someone to find out as much about each of these entities as possible. We need to know how the money flows through this maze of legal entities."

"Okay. I can run down to Austin and check the records at the Secretary of State and State Comptroller's office. If any of them are public companies, I can check with the SEC in Ft. Worth to see if they have anything on them."

"That's great, but that's a lot of work."

"That's okay. If I need help I'll get some volunteers from class to pitch in. I need an excuse to talk to Snake anyway."

"Snake? You better not let him hear you call him that."

Paula smiled. "Why not. You think he'd seriously flunk someone for calling that?"

Stan shrugged. "He'd flunk me, but he probably wouldn't flunk you."

"My thinking as well," Paula agreed as they parted company.

After lunch, Stan went to his torts class and then to the library to study. While he was there, he ran into another friend, Lamar Jones.

"Hey, Stan. How was your summer?"

"Pretty wild," Stan said.

"Yeah, that's what I understand. I heard you were

elected County Chairman."

"That's right. I kinda got roped into it."

"That's unbelievable—just a law student and already County Chairman."

A tall, thin man in his mid-twenties, Lamar was from a wealthy Austin family, and when he'd found out Stan was a member of the Republican Executive Committee he sought him out to discuss politics. Stan liked Lamar, and they usually sat together in the classes they had in common.

"It's no big deal, really. If you volunteer down in Austin, they'll probably run you for Congress before you know it."

They continued to talk, and Stan filled him in on the President's reception, Rob Shepard's death, and the connection he'd found between Commissioner Barnes and Brad Thornton.

"It sounds like a can of worms," Lamar said. "What are you going to do?"

"I don't know, but if our candidate for the state legislature is a crook, I sure have an obligation to report it to the appropriate authorities."

When Stan got home that night, he was startled by a buzzing noise as he opened the door. Rebekah rushed over when she heard it and punched in some numbers on a keypad. The buzzing immediately stopped.

"I see they installed our new security system," Stan noted.

"Yes. It took them all morning. The code is Marcia's birth date."

"Oh, okay. That should be easy to remember."

"You have thirty seconds to punch it in or the alarm will sound. If the alarm sounds, besides waking up the whole neighborhood, you'll get a call from the monitoring service. Your password is Quantico."

"Quantico? Thanks for digging up bad memories." Stan said, remember his court martial at the Marine Corps base at Quantico, Virginia.

Rebekah shrugged. "Sorry. It just came to mind when they asked for a safe word."

"Hmm. Well, I'm glad we're secured now."

"Yeah. Just don't forget to disarm it when you come in, or it will go off. If the monitor service calls and you don't respond with the safe word, they'll send the police."

"Oh, wonderful."

"And they charge fifty dollars for a false alarm, if they don't accidentally shoot you while they're here."

Stan laughed. "Thank you. Now I'm going to be a nervous wreck in my own home."

Rebekah smiled and put her arms around him. He held her tightly for a moment, and then Rebekah went back into the kitchen to finish supper. Stan heard Marcia starting to cry.

"Stan, change Marcia and then round everyone up for dinner."

"Okay," Stan replied as he walked into Marcia's room. He looked down at her and smiled. "Hey, little lady. How are you today?"

After he'd changed her, he brought her into the kitchen and held her on his knee with one hand while he ate his dinner.

"So, how was school?" Rebekah asked.

"Interesting. It seems Professor Hertel has been following the Shepard case. He offered to help out."

"Really? That's surprising. Why would he do that?"

"I don't know. He says it will be a good learning experience for the class."

"That makes sense."

"But they call him Snake, so he may have ulterior motives."

"Like what?"

"I don't know. He's only a part-time professor, so maybe he thinks he'll have an inside track on defending the real killer if we find him."

"Wow. He is a snake."

"Maybe, but most snakes are harmless."

"Daddy, can we get a snake as a pet?" Mark asked.

"No! Absolutely not," Rebekah said. "You don't take care of your parakeets as it is. The last thing I need is a snake slithering around the house."

"Maybe we'll get a fish tank," Stan said. "I've always wanted one of those big ones with a hundred brightly colored fish swimming around."

"Can we, Daddy?" Mark asked. "That would be cool."

"Maybe. We'll go to the pet store and check them out this weekend."

Rebekah shook her head. "Thanks a lot."

Stan laughed. "We'll take care of them. You won't have to do anything."

Rebekah rolled her eyes.

"I think I'm going to stop by and see Don Karnes tomorrow at the bank. I don't have class until eleven."

"Hmm. You think he'll tell you anything?"

"Probably not, but I need to discuss some Republican business with him anyway."

The next morning, Stan stopped by the First National Bank and asked Don's secretary if he had a moment to talk. She said he had a director's meeting at ten, but she'd check and see if he had five or ten minutes to spare. A few minutes later, she showed Stan into his office. Don pulled his rotund body up from his chair and stepped around his desk to shake Stan's hand. He wore a $1,000 suit, a red silk power tie, and shoes so shiny you could use them as a mirror in a pinch.

"So, to what do I owe the pleasure of a visit from Stan the man?" Don asked.

Stan smiled. "Oh, a couple things came up that I wanted to talk to you about."

"Well, my secretary tells me we have ten minutes, so fire away."

"Well, I understand Brad Thornton does his banking here."

"That's right," Don replied warily.

"Does he have all his accounts with you, including Silver Springs Ventures?"

"As far as I know. Why?"

"I'm trying to clear Rob Shepard's name. I know he didn't kill his family. What I'm looking for is a large sum of money being paid from one of Brad's accounts to someone about the time of the murders—probably the next day."

"The FBI took all Shepard's records. Why don't you talk to them?"

"They don't care about Rob Shepard. All they care about is Brad Thornton and his alleged money laundering. I know you just gave the feds copies. You still have the original records."

"True, but it is illegal for me to give you access to those records."

"I know, but if you happen to be looking through his records for any reason and come across a large payment to Todd Watson or anybody else about the time of Rob's death, I'd appreciate a heads up. It could be a check, wire transfer, or maybe a large cash withdrawal."

"Who is Todd Watson?"

"Brad's driver-body guard. As I understand it, if

he needs some dirty work done, Todd's the go-to man."

"Okay. What's the second thing on your mind?" Don asked.

"Well, in my investigation, I have discovered our new candidate for state representative was an investor in the Silver Springs Lake venture."

"Oh, my God!" Don moaned.

"Yes. It seems Mr. Thornton was trying to ingratiate himself to everyone with any political clout in the county. Unfortunately, he wasn't able to buy off the FBI."

"Damn. What are we going to do?"

"Well, we could confront him and ask him to resign. If he does, then we could just let the feds worry about him. Or, we could go to the feds and blow the whistle, have a big scandal, and lose the election."

Don shook his head. "No, I like the first option. It's not perfect, but if we can get Barnes to resign, that will save the party a lot of grief. Who could we get to replace Barnes?"

"That's the State Executive Committee's problem."

"Why didn't you discover this before you talked Barnes into becoming a Republican?"

Stan sighed. "Yeah. I wish I had, believe me."

"So, how do we go about doing this?"

"You check with the other members of the committee and, if they agree, I'll talk to Barnes. Either way, I've got to take this evidence I have to the FBI."

"Right. Good luck with that."

"Call me just as soon as you've talked with the rest of the Committee," Stan said as he stood up to leave.

"I will. Thanks for bringing me such wonderful news."

Stan smiled and left. He wondered what Barnes

would do when he confronted him. He could claim he thought it was a legitimate investment, in which case he wouldn't need to withdraw from the race. If he did withdraw, that would be a good indication of his guilt, albeit not necessarily conclusive. Forty-five minutes later when Stan got to class, Paula was standing in front of the classroom. He walked up to her.

"There you are," she said anxiously. "Wait 'til you see what I found out."

"You've already gone to Austin?" Stan replied, incredulous.

"I sure did. Professor Hertel took me yesterday afternoon. We got there just before the Secretary of State's office closed. They let us stay an hour past closing time to do our research."

Stan laughed. "Boy, you don't waste any time."

"It wasn't me. After you left yesterday, Professor Hertel asked me what your next move was, so I told him my assignment to go to Austin. He thought a moment and then asked if I wanted some help. I said I was hoping to get a couple of students to volunteer, but he said he wanted to go with me. What could I say?"

"So he drove?" Stan asked suspiciously.

"Uh huh."

"And when did you get home?"

"Early this morning."

Stan shook his head. "Hmm. What did you find out?"

Paula grinned triumphantly. "I found out Professor Hertel is very athletic."

"No. . . . I mean, what did you find out about Silver Springs Ventures?"

"Oh. Well, Silver Springs Ventures, Ltd. is owned 9 percent by Thornton Enterprises, Inc. and 51 percent by Calidad Intereses, Ltd.—both Texas limited partnerships—and the rest by eleven individual investors, including Rob Shepard and Commissioner Barnes."

"Right. I knew about Barnes."

"Now, the interesting thing is that Calidad Interests, Ltd. is 98 percent owned by a Mexican corporation called Baja Explotaciones, Inc. and 2 percent by Carlos Morales, who is also the General Partner. He's a notario from Mexico City."

"What's a notario?" Stan asked.

"It's a very powerful person, kind of a cross between a notary and an attorney. If you want something done in Mexico, you have to have a notario do it for you. If you can arrange to become a notario, you'll soon be a millionaire, or so they say."

"Really?"

"Uh huh."

"So, who owns Baja Explotaciones?" Stan asked.

"I don't know. You'd have to go to Mexico to find that out, if it's even possible."

"Well, we can assume the Burilo cartel owns it in some fashion."

"Probably," Paula agreed.

"And Carlos Morales is calling the shots for Calidad as GP and has a controlling interest in Silver Springs, so effectively, he controls it as well."

"Does any of this get us closer to our killer?"

"It's hard to say, but if we get enough information, I think everything will come into focus."

After lunch, Stan called Don Karnes to see if he'd had a chance to talk to the other members of the county Republican Party Executive Committee. He said he had and that they all agreed with his approach to the problem, so Stan went to see Commissioner Barnes at the courthouse. Barnes was in a meeting, so Stan waited in his reception area. Thirty minutes later, he walked in the door.

"Stan? What are you doing here?"

Stan stood up. "Hi. We need to talk."

Barnes' eyes narrowed . "Okay. Come into my office."

Stan followed Barnes into his office and took a seat across from his desk.

"Hey, your gal, Kristina is doing a great job. She's got me so busy I don't have time to breathe."

Stan smiled. "Yeah, that sounds like Kristina."

"So, what's up?"

"You know I've been investigating the Shepard family murders."

"Right," Barnes chuckled. "Don't worry. I have an alibi."

Stan forced a laugh. "Anyway, in the course of my investigation, I came across a list of investors of Silver Springs Ventures, and I found Rob's name. He was in for $25,000. I was surprised to see you were in for $100,000."

Barnes' smiled disappeared, and his body stiffened. For a moment, he said nothing, and then he turned and shrugged. "So. I had no idea Thornton was in bed with a bunch of thugs. He came to me as a friend offering to let me in on a very lucrative investment. When he showed me the numbers, I couldn't resist."

"Well, I'm sure in your mind it was a legitimate deal, but I think you can see it's going to be a problem in your campaign when word of this gets out."

"Are you going to turn me in?"

"If I've discovered your involvement, the FBI must already know, so it's just a matter of time before they drag you in for questioning. As soon as that happens, the press will be all over it, and your chance of becoming a state representative goes down the toilet."

Barnes sighed. "Damn Thornton. I should have known it was too good to be true."

"If you want to ride it out, I can't stop you, but it's not likely you'll be able to clear yourself before election day."

"You're right. So, you want me to withdraw?"

Stan nodded. "I've discussed it with the Executive Committee, and that is our recommendation. That way you can come up with whatever explanation you feel comfortable with and step out of the limelight. You should probably get a criminal attorney, though, as soon as possible."

"Do you know anybody?"

"Actually, I do. My criminal law professor has been following the case. He might consider representing you."

Stan gave Barnes Professor Hertel's phone number and then went home. When he opened the front door, the alarm started buzzing.

"What was that code number?" he muttered to himself.

As he was trying to remember it, Rebekah flew around the corner and punched in the code, and the buzzing stopped.

"What's the code number?"

"Your daughter's birthday."

"Oh, right."

Rebekah rolled her eyes. "Where have you been? Everyone's been calling here for you."

"Who's everyone?"

"Professor Hertel, Don Karnes, and some guy named Todd."

Stan felt his stomach twist. "Todd? Todd who?"

"Uh, Todd Watson. Why?"

"Todd Watson?" Stan repeated.

"Right. That's it."

Stan hadn't told Rebekah about Watson or his encounter with Watson's girlfriend. He wondered how he'd found out. He called Watson's number, but there was no answer. Stan went to the front door to be sure it was locked. Then he put on the alarm. After a while, he tried Watson again. This time a recorder picked up, so he left a message. While he was waiting, he decided to call Special Agent Ruth Rutledge.

"Hey. You said to call if I felt threatened."

"Right."

"Todd Watson may be on the war path. I kind of hit on his girlfriend to get some info out her and he's called looking for me." He explained the situation to her. "I've got some evidence I picked up at Silver Springs too that might be helpful to you."

"Okay. I'll swing by and pick it up? If Watson shows up stay inside and don't open the door."

"Thanks. See you soon."

Stan hung up the phone and looked out the front window again. Everything seemed quiet.

Rebekah walked in and gave Stan a hard look. "What's going on? Who's coming over?"

"Oh, I'm going to give that prospectus we got up at Silver Springs Lake to the FBI."

"Why now?"

Stan told Rebekah the situation but didn't mention he was expecting trouble from Todd Watson. Rebekah sensed Stan wasn't telling her everything. Suddenly, there was a knock at the door. Stan froze.

"Take the kids upstairs and lock yourselves in the bathroom."

"What?"

"Just do as I say!"

Rebekah just stared at Stan and then turned and headed upstairs. Stan went to the front door and looked out the peephole. A tall man dressed in jeans and a t-shirt was standing there flexing his fingers. Stan guessed it was Todd Watson. He wondered if he should open the door or not. Agent Rutledge had said not to, but he figured since he'd come alone and had bothered to knock, perhaps all he wanted to do was talk. Cautiously, Stan opened the front door. As the door opened, the alarm buzzed. Stan quickly closed the door and punched in the code. Then he opened it again and played innocent.

"These alarms are a pain in the ass," Stan said, forcing a smile.

"Are you Stan Turner?"

"Yeah."

"I understand you've been asking a lot of questions about me?"

"Who told you that?"

"I know you talked to my girlfriend."

"Did she tell you that?"

"If there's something you want to know, you ought to be man enough to face me one on one."

"That's not it. I just didn't think you'd talk to me."

"You're right. I wouldn't have talked to you because what I do is none of your damn business!"

"Where were you the night the Shepards were murdered?"

"Who do you think you are, a cop? I don't have to tell you shit!"

"That's true, but if you have an alibi, just tell me, and I'll leave you alone."

Watson grabbed Stan's shirt and yanked him forward. "Listen, you little twerp, I'm not telling you anything, and you better stay out of my business."

Watson pushed Stan, and he fell to the ground. Just then, a blue Buick pulled up, and Agent Rutledge got out of her car. She looked over at Stan getting up off the ground and dusting himself off.

"What's going on here?" she asked sternly.

Stan smiled at Todd. "Oh, Todd, I'd like you to meet Special Agent Ruth Rutledge of the FBI."

Watson looked at Rutledge then glared at Stan. "Just mind your own business," Watson spat and walked off.

Agent Rutledge frowned. "I thought I told you not to open the door?"

Stan shrugged. "I know, but he knew I was inside so he would have just got more agitated had I not opened the door."

Agent Rutledge shook her head. "He's not someone you should be messing with, Stan," she advised. "You need to try and avoid confrontation, particularly when there isn't any backup around."

"Yeah. I know, but he was the most likely person to have murdered the Shepard family. Unfortunately, now I know he didn't do it."

"How do you know that?"

"He wouldn't have come over here in broad daylight and knocked on my door if he was the killer. He'd have come at night and slit our throats."

"And what if he had turned out to be the killer?"

"Well, we've got a good security system. We'd have heard him coming and called the police."

"Listen, these security systems are nice, but I wouldn't bet my life on them. I've seen seasoned criminals disarm a security system inside a minute."

A wave of apprehension ran over Stan. He suddenly realized how foolish he'd been. "I guess I'll have to re-think my security."

Agent Rutledge nodded. "I think that would be wise. Now, you said you had some evidence?"

"Yes, come on inside. Give me a minute to give the all-clear to the family."

Stan went upstairs and knocked on the bathroom door. "He's gone," Stan announced. "You can come out now."

The door opened, and Peter looked up at his father, rather bewildered. Reggie pushed on past him and ran down the stairs. Mark nudged Peter out of the bathroom and then led him back to their bedroom. Rebekah shifted Marcia from one hip to the other and walked out of the bathroom.

"What happened?" Rebekah asked.

"He's gone. Agent Rutledge showed up right on cue."

Rebekah shook her head angrily. "This is ridiculous, Stan."

"I know. I'm sorry. I've got to talk to Agent Rutledge right now. I'll make this up to you. I promise."

Rebekah's eyes narrowed. "Yeah, you owe me big time for this."

Stan smiled tentatively and then went downstairs, where he found Reggie talking to Agent Rutledge.

"Reggie!" Stan exclaimed. "Are you bothering Agent Rutledge?"

"No, no," Agent Rutledge said. "He was just telling me he wants to be an FBI agent."

"Oh, really? You must have impressed him."

"I don't know about that," she said, looking at her watch, "but I don't have much time, so—"

"Sorry," Stan said and then began explaining how Ruth Snowden must have slipped the prospectus in with sales materials she'd given them. Then he went into his study and returned with the document. She took it and started leafing through it. Her eyes widened when she saw the list of investors with the amount each had contributed.

"So, I take it by your reaction that you haven't seen this yet?"

"No. This is very interesting. I wonder how Ruth got it. She didn't mention it when we interviewed her. Why did she give it to you and not us?"

"I don't know. She seemed a little upset with the way the FBI showed up unannounced and started ordering her around."

"Yes, some people are a bit sensitive to our procedures, but we have to go by the book."

"I understand."

"This isn't a typical prospectus that you'd give to the SEC."

"No. It's clearly meant for investor eyes only. There's a lot of confidential information in there. That's why I thought you'd want to see it."

"Yes, thank you. So, is that it?"

"Well, did you look at the list of investors over carefully?"

Agent Rutledge frowned. "Not yet."

"When you do, you'll find the name of Paul Barnes, our state representative candidate."

Agent Rutledge opened the prospectus, found the list, and looked at it more closely. "Right. I see him on the list," she said, giving Stan a hard look. "It must have been difficult for you to turn this over to us."

"Yes, very difficult, but what else could I do?"

"Nothing. You did the right thing."

"I confronted Barnes, and he's agreed to withdraw from the race due to the inevitable investigation and adverse publicity."

"Boy, you tackle every problem head on."

"This is our first real opportunity to elect a state representative. I don't want to blow that opportunity by having a candidate embroiled in a scandal."

"Do you think you can put up another viable candidate at this late date?"

"I don't know, but anything's possible."

"Well, I really appreciate this, Stan. Keep up the good work."

"Of course," Stan said, smiling broadly. "And thank you for showing up at the right moment."

"Right, but next time wait for your backup."

Stan laughed. "I'll do that."

Stan breathed a sigh of relief as Agent Rutledge drove away. He turned and went back into the house. Now all he had to do was calm Rebekah down and explain to his kids why they'd been locked in the bathroom for twenty minutes.

Chapter 11

The next morning Commissioner Barnes withdrew as the Republican candidate for state representative. Within minutes of the withdrawal, Stan got a call from Dick Stuart, Chairman of the State Republican Executive Committee. He wanted to give Stan notice of an emergency meeting of the Committee he had called for the following day and to be sure Stan was going to be there.

"We need you to explain what the hell is going on. Barnes was very secretive about his reasons for withdrawing, and he said I should ask you about it."

"Right. Okay, I'll have to cut a couple classes, but I guess this is more important."

"Why don't you bring Kristina Tenison with you? There are some people who would like to meet her."

"Sure, that's a good idea. She knows the district better than anyone."

Stan hung up and immediately called Kristina to pass on the invitation.

"Barnes said you forced him to withdraw," Kristina said. "Is that true?"

"No. The Executive Committee just recommended it. It was his call."

Stan explained the situation to her without getting in to any great detail. "I don't want to compromise his case by being very specific."

"This is getting ridiculous," Kristina said. "Has this ever happened before—having to replace two candidates in one year?"

"I haven't researched it, but I kind of doubt it."

"So, what time are you going to pick me up tomorrow?"

"Six o'clock. It's a three-and-a-half-hour drive to Austin, and going that early, I'll need a coffee stop along the way."

"Great. I better go to bed early tonight."

"Good idea," Stan said. "See you bright and early."

Stan hung up and took a deep breath. He wondered who they could possibly find to run at this late date. As he was contemplating this, the phone rang. It was Don Karnes.

"Hey, have you checked your mail yet today?"

Stan looked at his watch. "No. Our mailman usually comes about noon."

"Well, I ran across an article that might interest you, and I made a copy and dropped it in the mail."

Stan wondered what he was talking about and then remembered the banking records he'd requested. He couldn't wait to see what he'd found.

"Okay. Thanks."

"So, are you going to Austin tomorrow?"

"Right. They want me to bring Kristina too. I guess whoever they pick won't have time to be organizing a campaign. They'll just adopt Kristina's plan and move forward."

"Makes sense. The election is only six weeks off."

Stan talked a few more minutes with Don and then hung up. He looked at his watch and saw it was eleven thirty. While he was waiting for the mailman, he called Officer Jenkins.

"Hey, you got any new info for me?" Stan asked.

"A few items," Jenkins replied.

"Good. I may have something big here in a minute. I need to update you on a couple other items as well. Why don't you drop by for lunch?"

"Alright. I'll see you at twelve thirty."

"Good. See you then."

Stan went into the kitchen where Rebekah was working on lunch. "Hey, you got enough for a guest? I invited Lynn over."

Rebekah turned and nodded. "Sure. Does he like peanut butter and jelly? That's what we're having."

Stan laughed. "He's a cop. He'll eat anything if it's free. Any donuts left over from breakfast?"

"No. Reggie ate the last of them."

"Hmm. Too bad."

Stan walked over to Rebekah and put his arms around her. Nothing felt better than being in Rebekah's arms, he thought. He bent down and kissed her.

"We don't have time for a quickie, if that's what you're thinking," she said when their lips parted.

"You read my mind."

"Forget about it. I've got peanut butter and jelly sandwiches to make," she said, pushing him away.

"Oh, alright. I'm going to check and see if the mail came."

As Stan walked out the front door, the mailman was driving up. He said "hi" to the mailman and when he pulled away took the mail out of the box. The big manila envelope from the First National Bank sat prominently on top of the pile. He stuck the rest of the mail under his arm and opened the envelope. Inside was the bank statement for Silver Springs Ventures, Ltd. There were three red checkmarks next to three entries dated within three days of the Shepard massacre. The withdrawals were for $7,500, $8,500, and $9,000 for a total of $25,000.00. On three separate sheets were copies of the withdrawal slips showing that Carlos Morales had signed for each withdrawal.

When Jenkins showed up, Stan showed him the bank statement.

"Interesting," Jenkins said. "I wonder who got the $25,000."

"I don't think it was Todd Watson. He paid me a visit today."

"Oh, really? How did that go?"

"He was really pissed off and was going to beat the crap out of me had Agent Rutledge not showed up."

Stan described the altercation and told Jenkins about the evidence he'd turned over to the FBI.

"Well, if it wasn't Todd Watson, it must have been someone who worked for Carlos Morales and the cartel."

"Or," Stan added, "a contract assassin. The way the massacre was set up, I'm inclined to think it was a professional job."

"Or a team of assassins," Jenkins replied. "It would almost take two killers to handle six victims and make it look like a murder-suicide."

"I hadn't thought about that, but you may be right. I'll check with the FBI and see if I can find out who Carlos Morales uses for muscle. I figure they owe me a favor or two."

"Oh, I've got something for you," Jenkins said.

"What's that."

"We found the necklace Cindy Shepard was wearing the night of the President's reception."

"Where did you find it?"

"At A+ Pawn Shop. One of our informants spotted it on display and recognized it from a description we'd given the press."

"Did they have a record of who brought it in?"

"Yes, but the name and address and personal information turned out to be bogus."

"Great. Did the owner of the pawn shop give you a description?"

"Only that it was a woman in her thirties, brown hair, darkly tanned, a little overweight."

"I doubt the killer is a woman," Stan said, "so the real killer must have paid her to fence the necklace. How much did the pawn broker pay for it?"

"He said $5,000, but it was worth $25,000 apparently," Jenkins said. "The pawn broker said he'd have given her $10,000, but she wasn't very good at bartering."

"Hmm. That doesn't fit. A professional would have held out for more money."

"You would think so."

Stan and Jenkins talked a while longer, and then Rebekah told them lunch was ready. Stan wondered if they were getting peanut butter and jelly sandwiches but was relieved to see a stack of hamburger patties, buns, and condiments on the kitchen table.

"Oh, those smell good," Jenkins said as he picked up a plate.

"I got a beer in the fridge if you want it," Stan said.

"No. I'm on duty. A Coke or iced tea would be fine."

Rebekah poured a glass of iced tea and handed it to him. Reggie and Mark walked in, went directly to the table, and sat down. Rebekah fixed them each a plate and got them something to drink.

"Where's Peter?" Rebekah asked.

"He's hiding in his room," Reggie said.

Rebekah frowned. "Why is he hiding?"

"Mark told him a policeman was here to haul him off to jail for stealing his dump truck."

Stan rolled his eyes. Officer Jenkins laughed.

Rebekah shook her head in disgust. "Mark! Get up there and tell Peter you were joking."

Mark scrambled to his feet and ran out of the kitchen. A few minutes later, Peter walked in and looked around warily. When he saw Officer Jenkins, he stiffened.

"Peter, this if Officer Jenkins," Stan said "You've met him before. He's a friend."

"Oh," Peter said as he walked slowly to the table.

Rebekah stifled a laugh. "Sit down. I'll get you a hamburger."

After Jenkins left, Stan sat down to study for his oil and gas class, but he was having trouble concentrating. He kept thinking about the woman who'd pawned Cindy Shepard's necklace. He wondered if perhaps someone other than the killer had stolen it. Who else would have had the opportunity to do it?

Since he couldn't study, he decided to go visit some of the neighbors who'd been at the crime scene shortly after the murders. The first one he visited was John Rogers, the neighbor directly south of the Shepard house. John Rogers was a tall, stout, partially-bald man in his late fifties. Stan introduced himself.

"You knew Rob Shepard pretty well. Do you think he could have killed Maureen Peters and the Shepard family?"

"If you'd have asked me that before it happened, I would have said no."

"But now you think he might have?" Stan asked.

"I don't know. The evidence seems to suggest it."

"I understand you discovered the body?"

"Yes. I was watching the Johnny Carson Show,

and it had just ended, so I was about to go to bed. That's when I heard the gunshots."

"How many did you hear?"

"The first one just startled me. I thought maybe it was a backfire or kids shooting off a firecracker. But when I heard a second and a third, I got up and went outside to investigate. After I was outside, I heard a fourth shot, and I could tell it came from the Shepard house, so I ran over there."

"What did you find?"

"The front door was ajar, so I ran inside and saw Maureen on the floor."

"Did you hear anymore shots?"

"Yes, two more. One right away and a second about twenty seconds later."

"Did you go upstairs?"

"No. I was busy trying to get Maureen to breathe."

"Who was next on the scene?"

"My wife Molly came in right after me. She screamed seeing Maureen in a pool of blood. I told her to calm down and go call the police, so she went into the kitchen to call, but the phone had been ripped out of the wall. Before I knew it she was running up the stairs to use the bedroom phone. I yelled after her not to go up there, but I guess she didn't hear me."

"Did she tell you what happened upstairs?"

"Yes. She found Rob's and Cindy's bodies in the hall, but they were both already dead, so she went around them carefully and into the bedroom to use the telephone but it had been disabled as well. When she came back downstairs, I sent her home to make the call."

"Who was next on the scene?" Stan asked.

"A couple policemen. I don't know their names."

"Before the police showed up, did you see anyone

else there besides your wife?"

"No."

"Did you hear any strange voices?"

"No."

"Had you seen any strange cars in the neighborhood?"

"Not that I recall."

"Had you heard the Shepards when they drove into their driveway earlier?"

"No, but I saw headlight beams coming through the side window, so I knew they were home."

"Did you happen to look out the window after that?"

"No. I was tired, so I didn't move."

"Had you seen the Shepards when they left for the evening?"

"No. I hadn't gotten home from work yet."

"Okay. Well, that's all I can think of right now."

The front door opened, and Molly Rogers walked in. Stan smiled and stood up. She was a middle-aged brunette, darkly tanned, and wearing a black dress under a tweed coat with black gloves.

"Well, that was good timing," Mr. Rogers said. "You remember Stan Turner."

Mrs. Rogers didn't smile. In fact, she looked upset.

"Stan would like to ask you a few questions, honey."

Mrs. Rogers forced a smile. "What about?"

"Just what you remember the night of the killings."

"I've already told the police everything I know."

"He knows that. He doesn't think Rob killed anybody, and I think he may be right. I've told you all along it didn't make any sense.

"But he did kill them. I don't know why you can't accept that. You saw the crime scene. Did you see anyone else there?"

"No," Mr. Rogers admitted.

"Then leave it alone," Molly said, turning to Stan. "You should quit playing detective too. You're just prolonging the agony of this tragedy and giving people false hope."

Stan and Tom just stared at Molly as she slowly climbed the stairs and didn't look back.

"I'm sorry, Stan. This whole thing has been very traumatic for Molly. She hasn't had a good night's sleep since it happened."

Stan nodded. "I understand. I'm sorry I bothered you."

"I'll talk to Molly. If she feels like talking later, I'll call you."

Stan thanked Tom and left. As he walked back to his car, he thought back to the description of the woman who'd pawned Cindy's necklace. The description fit Molly Rogers, and he thought she'd acted very strangely. Stan wondered if she was trying to hide something.

As he got in his car, he looked at the Shepard house, which stood quiet and dark. The crime scene tape was still across the door, but Stan suddenly felt an urge to go inside and look around. Having been Rob's best friend, he knew where the Shepard's kept a spare key to the back door, so he went around the back of the house, retrieved the key, and slipped in the back door.

What he wanted to check out was how hard it would be for someone to sneak out of an upstairs window and climb down to the ground. Reggie had confessed to him that he and Paul Shepard had done it one time and that Paul did it all the time. Stan climbed the stairs, being careful not to disturb any of the markings the police crime scene crew had left behind. When he got to Paul's room, he slowly opened the door and was startled when he heard a screech.

The Shepards' cat rushed past Stan, nearly giving him a heart attack. Stan stopped and breathed deeply, trying to let his heart rate slow. Then he eased over to the window and inspected it. He noticed it was locked but could easily be unlocked from the inside, so he unlocked it and slid it open. There was no screen, which seemed odd to Stan unless Paul had taken it off the window to make it easier to get in and out. Slipping over to Paul's closet, he peered inside. Sure enough, the screen was tucked in between two long coats.

Stan returned to the window, slid it open, and peered out. Directly under the window were shingles that covered the first-story roof. Stan could see it would be quite easy to climb out the window, drop to the roof, crawl over to one of the drains, and climb to the ground. Feeling satisfied with what he'd discovered, Stan closed the window and left Paul's bedroom. After looking around for another ten minutes, he slipped out the backdoor and went home.

Rebekah was cooking dinner when Stan walked in. "Something smells good," he said.

"Oh, you're back. Good. I made spaghetti and meatballs."

"Mmm. That sounds good."

"So, did you find out anything?"

"Yes. Reggie was right. It is easy to climb out of Paul's window and down to the ground."

"You think the killer might have done that?"

"Killer or killers. I'm starting to think there was more than one of them."

"Did the crime scene crew dust for prints in Paul's room?" Rebekah asked.

"I don't know. We'll have to ask Lynn about that. If they did, they may have the killer's prints."

"Unless they wore gloves, which I imagine they did."

"True."

"I talked to Tom Rogers, and as I was leaving Molly came home. I wanted to talk to her, but she refused and was rather nasty about it."

"Really? That's odd."

"I thought so. Molly actually fits the description of the woman who pawned Cindy's necklace."

Rebekah frowned. "You think Molly stole the necklace?"

"She could have. She went upstairs before anyone else. Maybe she thought Cindy didn't need it anymore."

Rebekah shook her head. "She'd just witnessed a murder. The last thing she'd be thinking about was Cindy's necklace."

"True. I guess it could have simply been a robbery gone bad—the thieves thinking it would be an easy heist with just a babysitter and three kids at home, but then Rob and Cindy coming home at the wrong time."

"Maybe, but why wouldn't they wait until nobody was home? Burglars usually don't try to steal from an occupied house."

"I don't know. Let's eat. I'm famished, and I've got to study my oil and gas or I'll be in trouble if I get called on in class."

"You have to go to bed early tonight," Rebekah reminded Stan.

"True. I wish I didn't have to go. I hate to skip class. I can't afford to get behind."

After dinner, Stan studied for a couple hours, laid out everything he'd need the next morning, and then went to bed. He was a night person, so getting up at five in the morning was extremely unpleasant. Rebekah offered to get up and fix him breakfast, but he told her he'd get some donuts on the way to Kristina's house for them to eat on the road. Rebekah didn't like the fact that Stan would be spending all day with Kristina, but she hadn't said anything because she knew it wasn't something Stan had planned and, that early in the morning, Stan needed someone with him to keep him awake.

When the alarm went off, Stan shut if off quickly, not wanting to wake Rebekah up. He got up, dressed quickly, and soon was on his way. After stopping at Dunkin' Donuts, getting a half-dozen donuts and two cups of coffee, he pulled up in front of Kristina's house. She was waiting at the front door and came out immediately.

It was still dark, as Dallas was still on Daylight Savings Time for another few weeks. Stan took Kristina's coat and briefcase and opened the door for her. She was wearing a short red knit dress and matching high heels. He inhaled a hint of perfume as she stepped by him and sat down in the passenger seat. His heart rate quickened as he glanced at her shapely legs. As he closed her door, he felt a slight adrenaline buzz just being near her. After putting her things in the back seat, he climbed in the driver's seat and smiled at her.

"I brought donuts," Stan said as he started the car and they took off.

"Good. I didn't get up early enough to eat. I was up late last night working on the campaign."

"Really? It's kind of hard to work on a campaign when you don't know who the candidate is, isn't it?"

"Yeah, but they are going to expect me to dazzle them with a game plan, so I thought I'd better prepare something."

Stan smiled. "That's my girl—always on top of things."

"Who do you think they'll pick to run?" Kristina asked.

"Isn't that obvious?"

"Huh? What do you mean?"

"They're going ask me again, and if I refuse, they're going to ask you."

"Me! What are you talking about?"

"I recommended you last time, so they know you'd do it, right?"

"I suppose."

"I'm sure the general consensus is that whoever they pick is going to lose, so I doubt they have many potential candidates. If they nominate a woman, it looks good for the party, even if you don't win."

"You don't think I could win?" Kristina asked.

"They don't think you can win, but I think you could."

Kristina laughed. "How do you figure I could win?"

"In spite of what they think, whoever they nominate is likely to win."

"How do you know that?" Kristina questioned.

"Let's just say I've got inside information."

"Really? Hmm. So, why don't you run if it's a sure thing?" Kristina asked.

"I'm tempted, but my disastrous military record would no doubt come up and I'd be on the defensive from day one. I couldn't put Rebekah through that again. You, on the other hand, don't have any skeletons in your closet, do you."

"No."

"And, if you do lose it won't destroy your political future because you weren't expected to win and showed great courage in even running."

"Well, I'm not as optimistic as you are about getting elected, no matter what inside information you have."

"Good. That's the attitude you need to have to win. You can't take anything for granted, but in case you haven't noticed, the county has a Republican majority now."

"Yes, but Ron Wells has been in office a long time. He'll get some Republican votes."

"Not if I do my job."

"You mean your job as County Chairman?"

"No, I mean my job as your campaign manager. That is, if you want to hire me."

Kristina felt so happy tears welled in her eyes. "Are you serious?"

"I don't know if you can afford my price though."

"Really? What's your price?"

"You've got to promise me you'll keep your independence and not sell out to any special interest groups the moment you get to Austin."

"I've already made that promise to myself, so that's not a problem."

"Good. Then it's settled."

When they got to the meeting, Kristina was amazed at how Stan had accurately predicted the committee's actions. They first tried to convince Stan to run, and when he refused, they started discussing how it might not be a bad idea to appoint a female candidate. Stan agreed and suggested they nominate Kristina since she was well liked in the district and had a campaign organization already set up. They debated Stan's suggestion for a while, but some of the members were still reluctant to appoint a woman until Stan announced he'd be Kristina's campaign manager and knew how to make sure she would win.

"But how can you make sure she will win?" Dick Stuart asked skeptically.

"I've discovered that the incumbent has a serious vulnerability. All I have to do is figure out how to exploit it."

"What vulnerability?"

"I'm not a liberty to say right now, but it's enough to totally discredit him in the eyes of the public."

"Well, even without an ace up your sleeve, I like Kristina's positive attitude and courage in wanting to take on this most difficult challenge, so I place in nomination Kristina Tenison to be the Republican candidate to replace Commissioner Barnes in the state representative race."

There was a second, a vote was taken, and the vote for Kristina was unanimous. After the meeting was over, there was a press conference and then a lavish luncheon to kick off the campaign. Late in the afternoon, Stan and Kristina said their goodbyes and left for home. As they drove along I35 they were both happy and full of anticipation. Kristina couldn't thank Stan enough for what he had done and would be doing for her as her campaign manager. Stan sensed he could have stopped at a motel and Kristina would have willingly given herself to him.

Although Stan wanted to stop, somehow he managed to keep driving past motel after motel until he noticed he needed gas. They were coming up to Hillsboro, so he exited the freeway and drove into a gas station.

"Are you hungry? There's a Chili's up the road a few blocks."

"Yes. I'm famished. That would be great."

Stan filled up the tank and then drove them to the restaurant. They passed two more motels along the way and Kristina gave them both a hard look but Stan managed to keep his eyes on the road.

"Here we are," he said as they drove into the parking lot.

They got out and went inside. A hostess seated them and took their drink orders. Kristina looked longingly at Stan but finally sighed picked up a menu.

"So, you really think I can beat Ron Wells?" she asked.

Stan nodded, and they began planning in earnest Kristina's campaign for state representative.

When Stan got home, Rebekah was glad to see him. She hated when Stan traveled, as she always imagined the worst. After Stan had filled her in on the day's events, they went to bed and made love. Stan was more passionate than usual, and Rebekah wondered why that was but didn't complain. She felt happy and secure when he was passionate, and her only fear was that his passion would some day fade or be directed to another woman.

Chapter 12

Stan's investigation into the Shepard murders took a nosedive after he realized Brad Thornton and his bodyguard, Todd Watson, were probably not behind it. It was looking more like Carlos Morales and the Burilo cartel were behind the massacre. Since the FBI was anxious to get information that would advance their investigation of the cartel anyway, Stan adjusted his focus in that direction.

But it was a much more dangerous and challenging proposition to dig into the operation of a drug cartel rather than a simple businessman. Since Stan didn't have a death wish, he didn't have any intention of going to Mexico City to continue his investigation. This left him dead in his tracts with no idea where to look next. About a week later, he unexpectedly caught a break when Paula informed him Commissioner Paul Barnes had retained Professor Harry Hertel to represent him in the FBI investigation of the Silver Springs Ventures.

"Professor Hertel tells me you recommended him to Barnes," Paula said.

"Yes, I did. I figured he was already up to speed on the case."

"Uh huh," she said wryly. "So now we're both going to get an A in Criminal Procedure."

Stan shrugged, stifling a smile. "More importantly than a good grade will be the fact that I will have access to some good intel that may be helpful in my investigation of the Shepard murders."

"What makes you think the professor will share what he uncovers? He's got attorney-client privilege to worry about."

"He can hire me as a volunteer law clerk so anything I learn will be protected. And, should I uncover any evidence that will help in Barnes' defense, I'll share it."

"Sounds like a fair trade. I'll talk to him about it."

"So, you two are still—"

"Yes. I'm not about to break it off until semester break, and my 'A' is in the books."

"Right," Stan said, shaking his head.

"Don't give me that sanctimonious look," Paula spat. "You're no angel!"

"No, I'm not. Did I say I was?"

"You use women just like I use men."

"How do you mean?" Stan protested.

"You cozy up to every good-looking woman you meet—flirting with them, patiently listening to every word that comes out of their mouths, making them feel like you really care about them until they'd do anything for you."

Stan looked at Paula, shocked by her outburst. "I do care about them, even if I can't take them to bed. Sure, it may be partially a sexual attraction, I don't deny that, but I have a lot of respect for them too and I'm always up front about being married and just wanting to be friends. Fortunately, honesty doesn't seem to drive them away."

"You're right. I'm sorry. Forget I ever said anything," Paula said quickly, wiping a tear from her eye.

"I'm not trying to hurt anybody," Stan added.

Paula nodded. "We better get to class."

A few days later, Professor Hertel caught Stan after class and thanked him for the Barnes referral. He said Paula had told him about trading information and it sounded like a good idea. Stan worried for a moment about the possibility of a conflict of interest in that he was giving information to the FBI and also to a potential defendant who may be charged with a crime the FBI was investigating. He finally decided both the prosecution and the defense were entitled to know the facts, so as long as he wasn't privy to trial strategy he wouldn't have any ethical concerns. Later that afternoon, Stan and Professor Hertel met in his office to discuss their respective investigations.

"I've got an investigator looking into Brad Thornton, Calidad Interests, Ltd., and Carlos Morales," Professor Hertel said. "Barnes claims he didn't know anything about Morales' connection to the Burilo crime family. He thought it was a legitimate investment."

"Did he actually invest $100,000, or was that a sham?" Stan asked.

"Not initially. He signed a note for the hundred grand and then paid it back from profits."

"That's a hell of a deal. Didn't he think that was kind of odd?"

"No. It's like trading on margin in the stock market. You buy stock on credit hoping the price will go up. If it goes up, you make a nice profit without any additional money invested. If the stock goes down, you still have to pay the loan off, even if you didn't make any money. Many fortunes have been lost trading on margin."

"Right," Stan said. "Leveraging your investment.

I studied it in economics at UCLA."

"So, in this case, had the venture not been profitable, Barnes would have had to pay back the $100,000 loan."

"Right," Stan said, "except everybody knew this venture couldn't lose money because the cartel was pumping so much cash into it."

"Maybe, but that's going to be awfully hard for the feds to prove. Barnes may have simply been an unwitting pawn of Brad Thornton's criminal venture."

"Sounds like a good defense to me," Stan said. "Rob claimed it was a legitimate investment too."

"He told you that?"

"Un huh—before the FBI questioned him."

"Good. I may have to call you as a witness."

"Whatever helps."

"Okay. I've told you what I have. What do you have for me?"

Stan told Professor Hertel everything he'd learned since their last conversation, in particular what he'd given the FBI.

"That prospectus could be helpful. I'll have to request a copy from the FBI."

"Yeah. It would be interesting to know if Barnes had ever seen it. Hopefully he hasn't."

"Yes. Fortunately, he doesn't have to testify, so the feds won't ever find out the answer to that question."

After his meeting with Professor Hertel, Stan went to Cosmopolitan Life to turn in his applications for the week and talk to his boss. The offices were downtown, across the street from Neiman Marcus. Stan had to park in the nearest parking garage and then walk several blocks to the Cosmopolitan Towers. Their offices occupied the eighth through eleventh floors, but the agents' cubicles were on the ninth. The elevator attendant looked expectantly at Stan when he stepped in. Stan told him he needed to go to the ninth floor. The man closed the gate and pushed a lever. The elevator creaked and moaned as it climbed upward.

The seasoned agents at Cosmopolitan Life had cubicles or small offices, but the debit agents were lucky to get a desk. Stan's desk was one of eight in a small, stark room called "the bull pen." A tall, skinny man with glasses looked up at Stan as he sat down at his desk.

"Stan. Haven't seen you in a while."

"Hi, Ned. Yeah, I've been busy."

"Read about you in the paper. You're going to be Kristina Tenison's campaign manager. huh? She's hot!"

"Yeah. She does look good, doesn't she?"

"If you're such a hotshot politician, why are you selling insurance for Cosmopolitan Life?"

"I'm a poor hotshot politician with a family that likes to eat," Stan replied.

"There was a woman around here looking for you," Ned said.

Stan looked at Ned, startled by the revelation. It would be unusual for anyone to come to his office. Agents almost always went to their prospects' homes or places of business.

"Who was it?" Stan asked.

"I don't know. I never saw her before. She was good looking, but a little old—thirty-five, I'd say."

"Did she leave a number?"

"Check with Becky at reception. I saw her talking to her."

"Okay, thanks."

Stan went to the receptionist and asked if there were any messages for him. Becky looked through a stack of pink message slips and handed one to Stan. He looked at it and was surprised to see that it was from

Melissa Thornton. Stan put the message in his pocket and went back to his desk.

"So, what's her name?"

"Melissa Thornton."

"Oh, the mobster's wife?" Ned said.

"Why do you say he's a mobster? He hasn't even been indicted yet."

"It's just a matter of time."

"Even if he is indicted, there's still a presumption of innocence."

"Just a technicality."

"Well, I hope you don't ever show up on one of my jury panels."

Ned laughed. "So, what does she want from you?"

"I don't know. I guess I'll have to call her to find out."

Stan picked up the phone and dialed the number. The phone rang several times before Melissa picked up. "Hello."

"Mrs. Thornton? This is Stan Turner."

"Hi. Stan. How are you?"

"Fine. Hey, we really enjoyed your party. I'm sorry about all the hassle with the FBI."

"Thank you. It has been a rather nasty affair."

"I bet. So, what can I do for you?"

"I need to buy some life insurance."

"Really? For you or for Brad."

"For both of us. I suddenly realized that if something happened to Brad, I'd be destitute."

"What about all your property—your home and the house on Maui?"

"Oh, none of that's in our name."

Stan didn't know what to make of Melissa's sudden interest in buying life insurance. He didn't want to turn down a legitimate sale, but the thought occurred to him that maybe she knew Brad was about to get whacked and wanted to be sure she cashed in on his death. He finally decided it wouldn't hurt to talk to her if he took precautions.

"Okay. We should meet. Can I come by your house? Brad will have to sign the application."

"He's out of town. We can work out all the details, and then he can sign the application when he gets back."

"Okay," Stan said. "When should I come by?"

"Tonight. Say seven?"

"Alright. I'll see you then."

Stan looked at Ned and shrugged. "She wants to buy life insurance."

"You lucky son of a bitch," Ned moaned. "I don't think in ten years I've had one lousy call-in. She'll probably want a big policy too. Be sure and tell her if she murders her husband, the company won't pay."

Stan laughed. "Of course. That's the first thing I'll tell her."

"She doesn't really want to buy a policy, does she?" Ned questioned.

"I don't know. She may just want to talk to me."

"Well, I hope she does buy a big policy, for your sake. Either way, be careful."

"I will," Stan said thoughtfully.

When Stan got home, he told Rebekah about Melissa's call. He knew if he was going over to Melissa's house, Rebekah needed to know about it so she wouldn't be upset if she somehow heard about it later. She didn't like the idea.

"Can you get life insurance when the FBI is investigating you?"

"Well, there hasn't been an indictment yet, but it could get held up in underwriting pending the outcome of the investigation. I'm inclined to think she just wants to talk."

"You should call the FBI and tell them you're meeting with her."

"Yeah. I should."

Stan went to the telephone and dialed Agent Rutledge's number. "Yes," Agent Rutledge said.

"Hi. This is Stan Turner."

"Oh. Hi, Stan."

"You said to call you if I needed backup."

Agent Rutledge laughed.

"Who'd you piss off now?"

"Nobody yet. I got a call from Melissa Thornton. She says she wants to buy some life insurance, but I kind of doubt that's why she wants to see me."

"That is rather odd. Why don't you come by? We'll put a wire on you in case she says something incriminating."

"I don't need a wire. I've got a recorder in my briefcase that we use for sales training."

"You sure it's reliable?"

"Oh, yeah. It works great, and the customer never knows they're been taped. I didn't call you really for backup. I doubt Melissa Thornton is going to try to hurt me. I just wanted to give you a heads up so you wouldn't be surprised if you saw us together or heard us on one of your wires."

"When are you meeting?" Agent Rutledge asked.

"Tonight at seven at her home. Her husband's out of town apparently."

"He is? I wasn't informed he'd left the city."

Stan chuckled. "Maybe he gave you the slip."

"Or Melissa is lying."

"Right."

"Okay. We'll be close by if you need us. I want that tape when the meeting is over."

"Not a problem. Just come by the house later, and I'll give it to you."

Stan hung up the telephone and looked at Rebekah. She shook her head and went back into the kitchen to finish cooking supper. Stan heard the kids playing in the back yard and went out to join in the fun. After supper, Stan got his briefcase, put in fresh batteries in the recorder, and made sure he had applications and the right rate book in case she was serious about life insurance. He kissed Rebekah goodbye and left.

When he got to the Thornton residence, he looked around to see if he could see any FBI agents lurking about. He didn't see anybody. There were a few cars on the street, but they all seemed unoccupied. After a minute, he got out, went to his trunk, and pulled out the briefcase. The house seemed dark, which he thought was unusual, but he figured Mrs. Thornton was just in a back room. It was a big house. He knocked on the door and waited. After a moment, the door opened a crack, and Stan heard Melissa say to come in. Stan stepped inside and closed the door. He heard footsteps walking quickly away, and when he glanced that way he saw Melissa, half naked, slipping into her bedroom. He looked away embarrassed.

"I'm not dressed yet!" Melissa yelled from her bedroom. "Have a seat. I'll be right with you.

He went into the study, took a seat, and set his briefcase down where he could stealthily engage the record button on the audio recorder. When she appeared fully dressed ten minutes later, Stan stood up and engaged the recorder. He wondered if she knew he'd seen her naked breasts. She seemed at ease, so he guessed she hadn't realized it or had wanted him to see them. Either way, he knew it was going to be an interesting evening.

"We can't talk here, Stan. I'm sure they have the place bugged."

"Oh, really?" Stan said, trying to act surprised.

"Yes. Let's go up the street to IHOP and have a cup of coffee."

"Okay," Stan said tentatively.

She got up, and Stan followed her into the garage. A red Corvette Stingray sat majestically in the big garage that was as clean and organized as her study. She opened the door, and Stan ran around to the other side and climbed in. There wasn't much room, so he held the briefcase in his lap. After they'd shut the doors and buckled up, the garage door opened, she started the engine and backed quickly out of the garage. Stan looked in his rearview mirror but didn't see anyone following them.

"So, Kristina's running for state representative?"

"Right?" Stan replied, wondering if IHOP was really their destination. Much to his relief, Melissa turned into the IHOP parking lot and found a parking spot. They went inside and were seated immediately. After they'd been served, Melissa got to the point.

"Listen, Stan," Melissa said softly so no one around them could hear. "You've got to stop your investigation."

Stan frowned. "Why?"

She swallowed hard. "You're upsetting some very powerful people. I know you're just trying to clear Rob's name, but in the process, you're giving the FBI some damaging evidence against them."

"Who are we talking about? Carlos Morales?"

"He and others more powerful. You need to call off your investigators."

"I don't have any investigators," Stan protested.

"Well, there is some professor at SMU who's hired investigators. I was told you and he are working together."

"Who told you that?"

"I don't know."

"Well, Professor Hertel is representing Commissioner Barnes. He's got some investigators working the case."

"They must be the ones. Stop them or the consequences will be most tragic."

A cold chill washed over Stan. He stared at Melissa for a moment and then said, "Who told you to give me this warning?"

"Nobody. I'm doing it because I don't want any more bloodshed."

"Do you know who killed Rob and his family?"

She turned away. "That's all I have to say. Get out an application. I want to buy an insurance policy on my life."

"Are you serious?"

"Yes. This meeting must look like business. Make my daughter the beneficiary—Amanda Sue Thornton. She's a sophomore at A&M. She wants to be a doctor, and I promised her I'd help her get through medical school."

Stan reluctantly opened his briefcase slightly and pulled out an application. He closed it quickly so she wouldn't see the recorder and then started filling it out.

"How much do you want?"

"Give me $500,000."

"Whole life or term?"

"What's the difference?"

"Whole life is more expensive, but the premiums won't go up. It's got an investment aspect to it."

"Give me term if it's cheaper."

Stan nodded and completed the application. When he was done, he had her sign it and got a check for the first month's premium.

"This isn't effective until the company issues the policy. You'll have to have a physical for a policy this size."

"How long will that take?"

"I can have a doctor come by tomorrow."

"Good. Have him call to make sure I'm here."

"Right," Stan said and returned the application to his briefcase.

"Thank you for meeting me, Stan. Please quit worrying about Rob. He's dead. Think about the living."

Stan nodded but didn't reply. Shortly thereafter, they drove back to her house and parked the Corvette back in the garage. Stan admired the vehicle as he got out and wondered if he'd ever be able to afford one for himself. Melissa noticed Stan admiring the car and smiled.

"Pretty nice ride, huh?"

Stan nodded and followed Melissa back into the house. As she stepped into the kitchen, a man came out of the shadows and grabbed her. He put one hand over her mouth and the other one around her waist. Seeing the attack, Stan rushed in to help her. Just as he cleared the door, another man grabbed Stan and wrestled him to the ground. Stan smelled a strong odor before he felt lightheaded and became limp.

Chapter 13

When Stan awoke, he found himself lying in the back of a panel truck with his hands and legs tied. He felt pressure against his back and soon realized Melissa was lying next to him. He struggled a moment, trying to get loose, but the knots wouldn't budge. A sharp pain shot though his back from the effort. He became still hoping the pain would stop.

"Melissa," Stan whispered. "Are you awake?"

"Yes," Melissa replied softly.

"Are you okay?"

"I'll live. How about you?"

"Other than a horrible pain in my back, I guess I'm okay. Where are they taking us?"

"I don't know. I just woke up a minute ago."

"Who are these people?"

"Some of Morales' men, I think. I got a glimpse of one of them before he drugged me."

A sick feeling came over Stan. He knew where they were going—a secluded spot in the country to kill them. He didn't say anything, not wanting to upset Melissa. He felt certain the FBI was following them, probably hoping they'd lead them to a hideout or to people higher up in the organization.

"How did you get mixed up with these people?" Stan asked.

Melissa sighed. "We got into financial trouble, and were on the verge of bankruptcy. Brad was desperately looking for a way out when he remembered an old college friend that he'd heard was doing quite well. He thought maybe he could get a loan from him. He called him and told him his predicament, and a few weeks, later Carlos Morales contacted us. He said Tony Rubio had sent him to deliver a very lucrative business proposition. Brad listened to the proposal and jumped at it since there was enough cash up front to get us out of the hole we were in."

"So, he knew he was dealing with Rubio?"

"Uh huh."

"Did he know Rubio was connected to a Mexican drug cartel?"

"No. He just thought Rubio was a shrewd businessman. The proposal seemed legitimate. Nobody ever mentioned breaking the law. It was only later, after it was too late, that Brad realized he was laundering money for Rubio."

"How about Rob? Did he know what he was getting into?"

"No. Brad told him Silver Springs was a good deal, that he could use the profit in his campaign and he should get into it. You know Rob. He was very trusting and never questioned the propriety of the venture, particularly since he'd known Brad for so long."

"Why was Rob killed?"

"He was the only one who knew about Brad's college connection to Rubio. If that connection were to come out, it would be just what the feds needed to get a conviction of Brad and Morales."

"So Morales ordered the hit?"

"He must have, because Brad wouldn't do something like that. He's a businessman, not a murderer."

"The FBI should be following us. I told them about our meeting."

"You did?" Melissa gasped.

"Yes. I didn't want the feds to get the wrong idea about our get together," he lied.

"Well, that may have saved our lives."

"Hopefully."

The truck stopped abruptly, and the front doors opened and shut. A moment later, the back latch rattled, and the back doors flung open. One of the men grabbed Stan's legs and dragged him out of the van until he was sitting on the back bumper. He was a Hispanic male, medium height, with dark hair and a mustache. Another man, a few inches shorter and without a mustache, did the same thing to Melissa. They yanked them up and started pulling them along a path that led into the woods.

Stan looked back, searching for some sign of the FBI, but he saw nothing. His heart began to quicken as he realized the FBI may not have followed them after all. His mind raced, wondering what could have gone wrong. Had their kidnappers somehow eluded the FBI stake out? He imagined them carrying Melissa and he out the back door and through a neighbor's yard to a truck parked a block or two away. He regretted getting involved in Rob's investigation. Now he was going to die, and his children would grow up without a father.

"Where are you taking us?" Stan demanded.

The shorter man following behind Stan gave him a hard shove, knocking him to the ground. Stan rolled over and glared up at the man. The man kicked him hard in the ribs, and Stan doubled over.

"Get up and get moving—NOW!" the man ordered.

Stan stumbled to his feet and started walking. After they'd walked about ten minutes, they came to a clearing where they left Stan and Melissa standing helplessly. Stan's heart nearly stopped as he realized the men were about to shoot them. They raised their guns and were about to pull the triggers when Stan heard a helicopter swooping down on them. A shot was fired, and the shorter man went down. Stan ran toward Melissa and knocked her to the ground. The taller man returned the fire and took cover. The short man recovered and began firing as well.

A moment later, the sound of heavy footsteps reverberated from the woods behind them. Suddenly, an FBI SWAT team emerged from the woods and surrounded the men. They dropped their weapons and stuck their hands in the air.

Stan breathed a sign of relief as someone jerked him up and started untying his hands. Soon, he and Melissa were being escorted to a waiting car. Before they got to it, Special Agent Rutledge intercepted them.

"You two alright?" Agent Rutledge asked.

"I think so," Stan said. "Just a few bruises and emotional scars."

Agent Rutledge laughed. She looked at one of the SWAT team members and said, "Take Mrs. Thornton to the your vehicle. We need to question them separately."

The man nodded and led Melissa away.

"I bet you weren't expecting a ride in the country," Agent Rutledge said.

"No. That was a surprise," Stan replied.

"We found your briefcase. Quite an interesting conversation."

"Oh, you haven't heard the half of it. I got a complete confession on the way here. I didn't tell Melissa you were following us until the very end."

"That was pretty clever."

"Rob didn't kill anybody. Melissa said it was Morales' men."

"Good. Hopefully she won't have a memory lapse when we get her back to the office."

"Well, you've got my testimony. Isn't that good enough?"

"Not necessarily. You've made it clear you think Rob is innocent, so I'm not sure you'd be a credible witness without corroboration."

Stan sighed. "Well, she'll probably back me up."

"Don't count on it."

Stan looked at his watch and suddenly remembered Rebekah and the kids.

"Has somebody told Rebekah I'm safe?" Stan asked urgently.

Agent Rutledge nodded. "Yes. I sent an agent over there. She's been advised that you're safe and not to expect you home anytime soon."

"Oh, thank God. She's probably a nervous wreck."

"I'm going to need your statement, and if you like, you can watch the interrogation of Mrs. Thornton and your abductors."

"Yes. Definitely. That ought to be interesting."

"I hope so. You want to stop by the emergency room on the way home to get checked out?"

"No, I'm fine."

"Okay, I'm going to let you ride with Mrs. Thornton. See if you can get any more information out of her. She seems to like you."

"She's a good woman. She feels guilty about Rob and his family."

Agent Rutledge nodded. "I'll see you later."

Stan was escorted to an FBI vehicle and put in the back seat next to Melissa. She smiled at him when he sat down.

"You alright?" Stan asked.

Melissa nodded. "Yeah, I guess."

"So, where did your husband go? Did he tell you?"

"He didn't say. He just told me he'd back in a few days and while he was gone, I was to talk to you and get you off his back."

"Really? Do you think he just wanted to get us together so Morales' thugs could get rid of both of us all at once—kill two birds with one stone?"

Melissa burst into tears. Stan put his arm around her. "I'm sorry. I don't mean to be cruel, but that's what it kind of looks like."

"I know," she said, wiping the tears from her eyes with her sleeve. "I'm sure he had no part in it. He's not a bad man."

"I'm sure he's not," Stan said, squeezing her tightly.

Stan couldn't think of much else to ask her, so he just held her while they were taken to FBI headquarters. It was nearly midnight when they pulled into the parking garage adjacent to their offices. Melissa was escorted upstairs for processing by a female agent, and Stan was taken to Agent Rutledge's office to wait. While he was waiting, he used Rutledge's phone to call Rebekah.

"Oh, Stan, I was so worried."

"I'm okay. I'm sorry you had to go through all of this."

"It's not your fault. I'm just glad you're okay."

"It's a good thing I called the FBI. If they hadn't come—"

"I'd have been a widow," Rebekah interrupted.

"Mrs. Thornton told me Morales was responsible for killing Rob and the family."

"Oh, my God! That's good news. Now you're done with all this, right?"

"Maybe. I hope so. If she doesn't change her

story."

"Oh, I hope so. I am really getting sick of this."

"I know. It will be over soon, hopefully."

"It better be."

"Well, I've got to go. I just wanted to hear your voice."

"Thank you for calling. I love you."

"Me too. Bye."

Stan went back to his chair and thought about his family and how close he'd come to losing them. He wondered if he'd done the right thing in trying to clear Rob's name. A half hour later, a receptionist came in and told Stan that Agent Rutledge had been delayed. She showed him to the break room, where he bought a Coke and a sandwich and continued to wait. Ten minutes later, Agent Rutledge finally showed up.

"Okay. I've got some good news and some bad news," agent Rutledge said.

"What's the bad news?" Stan asked warily.

"Mrs. Thornton has a fancy lawyer already, and he's advised her to keep her mouth shut."

"You've got to be kidding," Stan said dejectedly.

"No, I'm afraid not. The good news is one of your abductors, Pablo Gomez, wants to cut a deal."

"Really? What kind of deal?"

"He'll tell us everything he knows and testify against Morales if we'll drop all charges against him."

"But he may be a murderer!" Stan protested.

"I know that, but don't you think it's better to bring down Morales and maybe even the Burilo cartel?"

"I know, but I hate to let the sleaze ball get away with murder."

"Well, I don't know if I can sell it to the US Attorney anyway. I just wanted to let you know we may have caught a break in the case on account of your stubborn persistence."

Stan laughed. "If that's a compliment, thanks."

"Come on. We're about to interrogate the less cooperative of our two suspects."

Stan followed Agent Rutledge to the viewing area adjacent to the interrogation room. There was a one-way window and hidden speakers so observers could watch and listen. Stan stood in front of the window and watched Special Agent Adams as he interrogated the suspect, Manuel Rubicardo.

"Mr. Rubicardo, my name is Special Agent Adams of the FBI. Before we start, I want to advise you that you have the right to remain silent and anything you say can and will be used against you in a court of law. You have the right to obtain an attorney of your own choosing. Should you be unable to afford an attorney, one will be provided for you. If you are an illegal alien, you have the right to consult with someone at your consulate before you talk to us should you so desire. If you decide to talk to us, you can terminate the interview at any time and request legal counsel."

A translator repeated the Miranda Rights in Spanish. When he was done, Agent Adams continued, "Do you understand these rights?" he asked.

"I guess so," he said. "You'll get me an attorney if I can't afford one."

"Right. Are you willing to talk to us then without counsel?"

He shrugged. "I don't know, man. Should I?" Rubicardo asked.

"If you cooperate, we'll put a good word in for you with the judge at the time of sentencing," Agent Adams promised. "He might be more lenient with you if you cooperate."

"What if I refuse to talk?"

"Then the judge will probably give you the maximum sentence."

"I would like to talk, but Carlos will kill me if I do."

"Carlos Morales?"

"Si."

"Did he tell you he'd kill you if you spoke to the police?"

"Many times."

"Well, we can protect you from him," Adams said without conviction.

"Maybe, maybe not."

"We can…don't worry. Did Carlos Morales tell you to kidnap Stan Turner and Melissa Thornton?"

"I didn't talk to him."

"Who did you talk to about the kidnapping."

"I don't want to get him in trouble."

"But somebody told you to kidnap them?"

"Si."

"You don't personally have anything against Stan Turner or Mrs. Thornton, do you?"

"No, sir. I don't know them."

"Okay, so this person—we'll call him 'Mr. X---told you to kidnap Mr. Turner and Mrs. Thornton?"

"Right."

"What exactly were you supposed to do?"

"He said for us to go to the house and wait in the alley. When they came home, we were s'posed to grab them and take them to the dump."

"The dump?"

"Right, the dump—a place to bury people you don't want found."

A cold chill washed over Stan. He thought how close he'd come to dying at the dump.

"Have you taken people there to be killed and

buried before?"

"No. Not me, but others have."

"These others have been killed there?"

"That's what I'm told."

"Did Tony Rubio order you to kidnap Stan Turner and Melissa Thornton?"

"No. I haven't seen him for months."

"So, you won't tell us who Mr. X is?"

"I'm not stupid. I tell you, I'm a dead man."

"Have you ever killed for Mr. X before? I know this time you were stopped before you killed anybody, but on previous jobs for Mr. X, has anyone been killed?"

"I didn't kill anyone."

"But you were prepared to kill Mr. Turner and Melissa Thornton, weren't you?"

"If I didn't, Rubio would send someone to kill me."

"Oh, so you're saying you acted under duress?"

"I not sure what you call it, but I was ordered to kill them, and if I didn't, they'd kill me."

"Ah. So, Mr. X threatened harm to you if you didn't do as you were told?"

"It was understood. They'd kill me, then my family in Mexico."

"How long have you been working for Mr. X?"

"Many years."

"Have you ever been to Rob Shepard's house?"

"Who is he?"

"Rob Shepard. Do you remember going to his house, killing him, his wife, three children, and the babysitter?"

"No, not me. I don't know Shepard. I didn't kill him or his family. "

"Five people were brutally murdered, and I think you and your amigo were responsible. I bet you were going to take them all to the dump but something went wrong, so you staged the murder-suicide, isn't that right?"

He shook his head vigorously. "No! That's all I have to say. I want a lawyer."

"A lawyer? You want a lawyer now?"

"Yes! You caught me with Mr. Turner and Mrs. Thornton. How can I deny we kidnapped them? But now you accuse me of murder. I want a lawyer. I'm done talking."

"You were going to murder Mr. Turner and Mrs. Thornton. It's not much of a stretch to pin the Shepard murders on you."

Rubicardo just shook his head and turned away.

Agent Adams sighed and then reluctantly got up. "Alright, but I think you're making a mistake. The judge is going to throw the book at you since you're not cooperating.

"I cooperated, but you weren't satisfied with the truth. I want the lawyer."

Agent Adams left the interrogation room and closed the door behind him. "He's not going to tell us anything we don't already know. We're wasting our time," he spat.

"He's scared to death of Mr. X, whoever he is," Agent Rutledge said.

"Do you think they'll really kill his family if he talks?"

"Yes, they will. Once you go to work for a cartel, you belong to them, and if you don't follow orders, they'll kill you and your family in the blink of an eye."

"Do you think there are bodies buried up at this so-called dump?" Stan asked.

"Maybe. I guess we better send a canine team up there to check it out."

Stan yawned. "I'm exhausted. Are we done here

tonight?"

"Yes," Agent Rutledge replied. "Go on home. I'll call you tomorrow when I find out what the US Attorney says about the immunity request."

"Okay. Thanks for everything," Stan said and headed to the elevator.

On the way home, his mind raced over everything that had happened. He wondered if the US Attorney would approve the immunity deal and what they'd find out if the suspect talked. He prayed he'd confess to the Shepard murders so he could wash his hand of the whole thing, but deep down, he didn't think he'd be that lucky.

Chapter 14

Several days later after Stan had recovered from his kidnapping ordeal, he picked up Kristina to take her to a talk show interview on NBC Channel 5. They took LBJ Freeway to I-35 and went south to the Dallas/Ft. Worth Turnpike. When they got to the studio, they were directed to a green room where several guests were already there waiting for their scheduled appearances. Stan looked at his watch.

"Forty-five minutes until you go on," Stan advised. "I don't know why they insist we get here so early."

"They want their guests to suffer, I guess," Kristina replied.

Stan smiled. "You're not nervous, are you?"

"No, of course not. I'm terrified. This is the first time I've been on TV."

"You'll do fine, don't worry. Just be yourself."

"What if I puke?"

"Oh, give me a break. You're going to knock 'em dead."

Kristina smiled warmly at Stan. "Thanks for coming with me, Stan. I feel much better with you here."

Ten minutes before the scheduled interview, the producer came out, introduced herself, and then took Kristina to her place on the set. Stan sat and watched from a monitor in the waiting room. Ten minutes, later

The Veronica Brooks Show came on the air, and Stan watched with great anticipation.

"Today, as our first guest, we have Kristina Tenison, candidate for state representative in District 67. Hi, Kristina. It's nice to see you."

"Thank you, Veronica. It's a pleasure being here."

"So, how does it feel to be suddenly cast into the ring? Did you ever in your wildest dreams think you'd be running for state representative?"

"No, I didn't. It's all been such a shock."

"Shock is a good word. First, there was the Shepard tragedy, and then Commissioner Barnes' unexpected withdrawal from the race on account of the FBI investigation of Silver Springs Ventures."

"Right."

"So, do you think you have any chance at all of beating your opponent, Ron Wells? Beating an entrenched incumbent isn't easy when you have six months to campaign, but with less than six weeks that's almost impossible, isn't it?"

"No. Nothing is impossible. It's definitely an uphill battle, but the Republican Party is growing rapidly in this district, so Ron Wells may be in for a surprise."

"Well, I like your confidence, but I saw a poll today that showed you're ten points behind Wells. Do you think you can close that large of a gap in the four weeks remaining before election day?"

"Well, Veronica, I've only been the Republican candidate for less than two weeks, so the people don't know me yet. I plan to make a lot of appearances and talk to a lot of voters, so I suspect once they see me and get to know me, I'll pick up a lot of support."

"What about Ron Wells' claim that you have no political or governmental experience and that the district's clout in Austin would be severely diminished by your election?"

Kristina's eyes narrowed. She hadn't been expecting such a tough interview. Her stomach was in knots, and she was struggling to maintain her composure. She took a deep breath. "Well, Veronica, for the last two weeks, I've been talking to many of the people of the 67th District, and they tell me Ron Wells has sold out to the special interest lobbyists and they don't think he really represents them anymore. I would say it's better to have a rookie Representative who works for the people of this district rather than an entrenched politician who only looks out for himself or the special interest groups he's sold out to for his own personal gain."

Veronica looked at Kristina, wide-eyed. "Whoa! Okay. You're a feisty one, I see."

Kristina laughed. "Well, I've never been accused of being soft on scum."

Veronica laughed. "Alright. We'll be right back after a commercial break."

In the waiting room, Stan watched the reaction of the guests waiting to go on. Kristina had them laughing, and soon everyone was huddled around the TV. When the show went to commercial, they all started talking excitedly.

"Who is that? She's funny," one lady said.

"Now that's the kind of Representative we need in Austin," another noted.

A minute later, the interview continued, and the room quieted. Everyone watched now with great anticipation.

"Alright, Kristina, seriously now… You admit you don't have any experience in government, right?"

"Sure, but did you know in the last ten years that

forty-two percent of all state representatives who were elected to office had no previous governmental experience and 100 percent had no legislative experience when they were elected to the state legislature for the first time."

"Really? Well, I see you've done your homework. Are you always on top of things this way?"

"Oh, yes. I'm a quick study, and although at this moment I obviously have a lot to learn, it won't take me long to get up to speed on the legislative process."

"Alright. Well, that's all the time we have. It was great meeting you, Kristina."

"Likewise. Thank you for having me on your show."

"You're welcome, best of luck to you on election day. If I lived in your district, you'd have my vote."

"Thank you. That means a lot to me."

Veronica turned to the camera and said, "Well, I think you will agree Ron Wells may have his hands full fending off Kristina Tenison's challenge for his seat in the 67th District. That's all for today. Until tomorrow, this is Veronica Brooks. Good day."

Stan stood up, elated after the interview. The producer leaned out over the receptionist's counter and gave Stan a thumbs up. Stan smiled. A minute later, Kristina and Veronica came through the door laughing and talking.

Veronica looked at Stan. "Where did you find this girl?" she asked playfully.

Stan shrugged. "I don't know. She just showed up one day at Republican headquarters, and life's never been the same."

Kristina latched on to Stan's arm, blushing.

"Well, I think you've got a keeper. I want the first interview after you're elected," Veronica said.

Stan nodded. "Absolutely. We'll send you an invitation to our victory party."

"Oh, Stan, I didn't have a chance to ask how you're doing since the kidnapping?"

"Oh. I'm fine."

"I can't imagine what you went through. If you feel up to it, I'd like to have you on the show."

Stan thought about it a moment, wondering if that would be wise. Then he realized it would be a great opportunity to plead his case for Rob's innocence. It might even spur the police to reopen the investigation.

"Sure," Stan replied. "That would be great."

"Good. I've got an opening next Thursday. Will that work for you?"

"Yeah, I think so."

"Good. See you on Thursday then."

On the way home, Stan and Kristina stopped for a late lunch at Steak & Ale. Kristina was feeling relieved that the interview was over and glad it had turned out well. Stan was happy for Kristina and excited about the opportunity to tell the public what really happened the day of the Shepard murders. After they'd ordered, Kristina's mood changed.

"What about the Dallas Morning News poll?"

"You handled it perfectly, just like we talked about."

"I know, but ten points? That's going to be nearly impossible to overcome."

Stan shook his head. "Don't be negative now. I'm sure you closed the gap a bunch today. You were great."

"Yeah, but who's going to see this interview? A few housewives and unemployed husbands?"

"Don't underestimate the daytime TV audience. The women who saw you today will talk about it to their husbands, and everyone in the media saw it. I wouldn't be surprised if some other networks want in on the action."

"Hmm. I can see you're not going to let me feel sorry for myself."

Stan laughed. "No, that's not allowed."

After lunch, Stan dropped off Kristina at her place and went home. Rebekah had watched the interview and was excited to see him.

"Kristina did wonderful. I didn't know she was so funny."

"Yeah. I knew she'd be a great candidate."

"She's my kind of woman. She's not going to take shit from anyone."

Stan laughed.

"Oh, Lynn Jenkins is looking for you. He came by earlier. I hold him you'd be home about now. He said he'd come by later."

"What does he want?"

"Something about Cindy's necklace and the woman who pawned it."

"Hmm."

Twenty minutes later, Office Jenkins rang the doorbell. He was out of uniform and had a six-pack of Coors in a bag under his arm. Stan answered the door and let him in.

"I brought us some liquid refreshment," he said, handing Stan the bag.

Stan peered inside. "Oh, good man."

They went into the den, and Stan pulled off a beer for each of them as they sat down.

"So, Rebekah said you found out something about Cindy's necklace."

"Yes. You mentioned Molly Rogers fit the description of the woman who fenced the necklace, right?"

"Uh huh."

"Well, I went to the Rogers' place and got a picture of her as she was getting in her car."

"Really?"

"Yes. I wanted to show the owner of the pawn shop her picture to see if she was the one who'd pawned the necklace."

"So, was she?"

"He wasn't sure, but he did recognize her. He says she'd been in the shop several times over the past few months selling different items."

"So, did you find a record of any of those transactions?"

"Yes, but the names don't match. Apparently, she's been using an assumed name."

"Did you run a criminal check on Molly Rogers?"

"Yes. No felonies, just a couple of hot check charges. Small stuff."

"What about her husband?"

"Squeaky clean."

"Hmm," Stan said. "Say, I forgot to ask you. How many unidentified fingerprints did they find at the Shepard house on the night of murders?"

"I don't know how many, but there were a few."

"You think you can get them to send those prints to the FBI so they can cross-check them with the suspects in custody?"

"I don't know. The investigation is closed."

"I know. See what you can do. If there was a match, it would tie them to the murders."

"I'll bring it up, but don't hold your breath."

"I won't, thanks."

Stan didn't really think the killers would be stupid enough to leave any prints at the Shepard house, but he'd be remiss not to have it checked out. Criminals often made mistakes, so Stan figured there was a slight chance they may have left a print.

The next day was trash day, so Stan decided to go see if the Rogers' had put out their trash yet. He knew a lot could be learned about someone by going through their trash, and the courts had ruled it was not technically illegal. When a person put out their trash, there was a presumption that the property within it had been abandoned, so Stan drove up next to the trash bag, opened the door, and yanked it into his car without stopping. When he got home, he put the bag in his garage for later processing, as he had a lot of homework to do for class the next morning.

The next morning before Stan left for school, Agent Rutledge called to tell him the US Attorney had made a decision on Pablo Gomez' immunity request.

"He's agreed to the deal," Agent Rutledge advised, "but can't grant immunity on the Shepard case since he lacks jurisdiction."

"Will Gomez still talk?"

"Not unless the DA agrees to give him immunity on any state murder charges."

"Oh, great. So, we're back to ground zero."

"He's still going to go down for your kidnapping."

"I know," Stan replied dejectedly, "but that doesn't get Rob off the hook."

"Our canine team also found several more bodies up at the dump."

"Really? Have you identified them?"

"Not yet. That will take some time. They are all Hispanic males in their twenties and thirties. None of them had any identification, and some of them are, well… decomposed a bit."

"Well, thanks for calling."

"So, what are you going to do now?" Agent

Rutledge asked.

"Keep digging," Stan replied.

"You know, you can quit now if you want. You've been a big help and we appreciate all you've done, but we don't expect you to risk your life again."

Stan sighed. "Thank you, but I can't quit until I've cleared Rob's name—particularly now that I know for sure he didn't do it."

"Okay, but keep me informed so we can provide effective backup."

"I will. Don't worry."

"Oh, by the way. Mrs. Thornton wanted me to ask you to come visit her when you get a chance."

"Really? Did she say why?"

"No, but she seemed pretty anxious to talk to you. You ought to try to fit it in your schedule if you can. She might have some more useful information for us."

"Where is she?"

"She's in the Collin County Jail temporarily. She'll be there another week or so until the US Attorney decides whether to charge her or not."

"Alright. I don't really have the time, but I'll go after class this afternoon if I can."

"Thanks. Call me after you talk to her."

On the way to SMU, Stan wondered what his next move would be to prove Rob innocent. It was so frustrating to know he was innocent but not be able to prove it. He just hoped his appearance the following week on The Veronica Brooks Show would turn public opinion in his favor and force the police to reopen the case. He wished he had Kristina's natural charisma, but he knew he didn't, so he'd just have to be doubly prepared. If he wasn't successful, he may never be able to clear Rob's name and put the real killers behind bars.

Chapter 15

The Collin County Jail was a pretty dismal place, and Stan felt very uncomfortable as he waited to see Melissa Thornton. Dozens of people lingered around, many of them unsavory looking characters that Stan thought ought to be in a jail cell rather than in the waiting room. The scene brought back horrific memories of his time in the brig at Quantico, Virginia after he was arrested for the murder of his drill sergeant. His neck and shoulders began to tense up and he felt a headache coming on.

While he waited he wondered how they were treating Melissa. He felt sorry for her having to endure this ordeal while here husband was off somewhere hiding from the FBI. Finally, the deputy escorted him to a visitors room where Melissa was seated at a small table with a screen between them to prevent any physical contact. Stan walked over and sat down.

"How you holding up?" Stan asked.

"It's miserable in here. I can't wait to get out."

"What does your lawyer say about that?"

"He thinks if I cooperate with the prosecutor, they'll make me a deal."

"Good. I know you didn't have any control over Brad. It wasn't your fault."

"I don't know. I wonder what he'd have done had I put my foot down."

Stan shrugged. "Probably ignored you."

Melissa laughed. "Probably."

"So, what did you want to talk about?" Stan asked.

"I'm worried about Brad. He hasn't contacted me in over a week. I think something may have happened to him."

"When was he supposed to be back?"

"In just a few days. He should be home by now."

"Do you think he's intentionally staying away to avoid being arrested?"

"No, I don't think so. He never mentioned running to me. I think he thought he could beat this thing."

"How can I help?"

"I don't know, but you're the only one who seems to care about anybody. I know Brad shouldn't have gotten involved with Rubio, but he doesn't deserve to die over it."

"No, he doesn't, but I have no idea where to look for him."

"You told me your professor had hired a private investigator. Put them on the case. I'll pay for it."

"I really don't have time for another project. I've got school, Kristina's campaign, and work—not to mention a family that would like to see me once in a while. . . . Why don't I have one of them come see you, and you can hire them directly?"

"No. They need someone to direct them and keep a close eye on what they are doing. If I hire them, I'll just be throwing money away."

"I really don't have the time," Stan repeated.

"I understand, but if you find Brad, he can help clear Rob's name."

Stan thought about that a moment. That was the first reason she'd given that tempted him a bit. He sighed. "I can't promise anything, but I'll talk to him and see if he thinks they can help."

"That's all I ask. Go see Don Karnes at the bank. He'll give you a $5,000 retainer. Use it as you think is best to find Brad."

"You know if I find him the FBI will arrest him, don't you?"

"Yes, but better behind bars than dead."

Stan nodded and got up. A jailer immediately entered the room and took Melissa away. Stan watched her leave and then hurried out of the jail, praying he wouldn't ever have to go back to that grim, depressing place. On the way home, he stopped by the bank and asked for Don Karnes. The receptionist said he could go on back. Stan walked back to Karnes' office and knocked on the door. Don invited him in, and Stan took a seat.

"How are you holding up after the kidnapping? Don asked.

Stan shrugged. "It seems like it happened a long time ago, although I know it's been less than a week."

"No permanent injury?"

"I don't think so. I knew the FBI was following us, so I was fairly sure they'd intervene before things got out of hand."

"Good. . . . So, what can I do for you?"

"Melissa Thornton wants me to hire a PI firm to find Don. I have reluctantly agreed to see what I can do. She said you would give me $5,000 to get started."

"Right. Well, that's about all I can give you. Her trust fund is getting rather depleted with lawyer bills and the regular monthly expenses. Normally, Brad would have paid the regular expenses, but the feds have frozen all his bank accounts pending completion of their investigation."

"Well, if you don't have the money—"

"No, no. Finding Brad has to be a top priority. We need him back here to sort this mess out."

"You don't have any idea where he might be, do you?"

Don shrugged. "Well, he usually goes to Maui when he wants to get away and think things out, but I doubt that was his destination this time. That's the first place the FBI would look for him."

"You think he's hiding from the FBI?"

"That or Carlos Morales has taken him somewhere to lay low for a while."

"Do you have any idea where they would take him?"

"Probably Mexico. He likes San Antonio del Mar a lot."

"Yeah, but I doubt he could have gotten out of the country with an FBI investigation going on."

"Well, don't forget you're dealing with the Burilo Cartel. They own the border. If they want to get him into Mexico, they won't have any trouble doing it."

"Okay. I'll send the investigators down there to look for him. Maybe they'll get lucky."

"The trick will be getting him to come home. He may want to, but I'm pretty sure Morales wouldn't allow it."

"Well, we'll cross that bridge when we come to it," Stan said.

Don gave Stan a check and wished him well. When he got home, he told Rebekah about his latest assignment, and she was livid.

"Why did you agree to help her? Her husband was responsible for your kidnapping! She almost got you killed!"

"We don't know that. More likely it was Morales. I don't think Brad Thornton is calling the shots anymore."

"You promised me this would be over soon, and now you're jumping right back into the fire. What's wrong with you?"

"I'm sorry. I'm going to let the private investigators handle it. All I'm doing is hiring them and giving them a little direction."

"You're still going to be involved, and Morales and his thugs are going to find out what you're doing. You want them to come after you again—after us?"

Stan took a deep breath. "All I have to do is have a couple of conversations, it's no big deal. The cartel won't even know I'm involved. Anyway, it's already done. I'm sorry. I can't back out now."

Rebekah shook her head angrily and stomped out of the room. Stan ran his hands through his hair anxiously. He understood Rebekah's concern, but he really wanted to find Brad. He agreed with Karnes that Brad was the key to sorting this whole mess out. In his mind, he had no choice but to go forward with Melissa's assignment.

Since Rebekah wasn't talking to him, he went upstairs to see what the kids were doing. They were all glad to see him and soon talked him into playing a game of Go Fish. An hour later, Rebekah came up and told the kids it was time for bed. She continued to ignore Stan, so he went out to the garage to look through the Rogers' trash. He gagged when he inhaled the pungent odor of rotten garbage as he opened the big black bag. After he'd sorted out the discarded paperwork, he closed up the bag and went to his workbench and laid them out.

There was an assortment of junk mail and then he came across an American Express bill. It was ninety days past due. Putting that aside, he looked in the next envelope—a demand letter for eighty-six dollars due to the Columbia Records Club. Quickly, he sorted through the envelopes until he came across one from a law firm named Page & Smith. He searched for the letter that had been in the envelope but couldn't find it. He'd heard of the law firm before but couldn't remember anything about them.

Remembering he had a chapter of his oil and gas textbook to read, he went back into the house. After checking on the kids, he went to his desk and retrieved the textbook. Stan found oil and gas interesting but couldn't see himself practicing in that area of the law. He knew living in Texas, however, that it would likely come in handy sooner or later. When he finally made it to bed, Rebekah was asleep, so he slipped in next to her and soon fell into a deep slumber.

The next morning, Stan woke up at first light. He was excited about hiring a private investigation firm to look for Brad. He'd never even met a private investigator before, so he was a little nervous. After he'd put on a pot of coffee, he went outside to get the local newspaper. He brought it in, but before he opened it, he poured himself a cup of coffee. When he finally opened the newspaper, his eyes widened as he read the headline, 'Representative Ron Wells Calls Opponent 'Irresponsible Nobody':

> State representative Ron Wells today lashed out at his new opponent, Republican Kristina Tenison, who he characterized as an "irresponsible nobody who he will crush on election day." He claimed she was trying to attract attention by spreading "outlandish lies" about him, but "it won't work." Wells denied accusations that he has sold out to

> special interest groups and is more interested in pleasing them than his own constituents. He pointed out he was responsible for pushing through more bills in the last session than any other state representative...

The story went on to explain how Kristina had been the third opponent facing Wells since Rob Shepard won the primary election. Then it detailed Commissioner's Barnes' switch to the Republican Party and appointment to fill Shepard's spot after his untimely death. Finally, it related that most experts believed that Kristina Tenison had little chance of upsetting the incumbent, Ron Wells.

Stan's heart sank. He knew Kristina would be devastated by the article. He looked at his watch. She wouldn't call before seven o'clock, he figured, but it wouldn't be too long after that he'd be hearing from her. At 7:12 the phone rang and Stan picked it up quickly, hoping Rebekah wouldn't be awakened.

"Hello," Stan said.

"Stan, did you see the Star Courier?"

"Yes. It's no big deal."

"No big deal? The pig called me a nobody!"

"Come on. You've got to have a thick skin to be a politician. You didn't expect Wells to ignore your accusations, did you? He had to say something after your scathing attack."

She sighed. "I guess you're right."

"Don't worry about it. You're getting some good press. People need to hear your name as often as possible so they'll remember you on election day."

"The experts don't think I can win. Maybe they're right. I'm just wasting my time."

"No, you're not. You can win this thing. Trust me. The dirt I've got on Wells is going to even the playing field. The only way you can lose is to give up now."

"Okay. I'm going to take a hot shower. Maybe that will make me feel better. I have a Kiwanis luncheon today and an appearance at the Small Business Section meeting of the Chamber of Commerce tonight."

"Good. That should keep your mind off of Wells. Just be yourself and you'll be fine."

"Alright. Sorry to bother you so early."

"It's alright. I've got to get to school. I've got a big day."

"Really? What's up?"

Stan told her about Melissa and the search for Brad Thornton.

"Well, let me know how that turns out."

"I'll call you tonight," Stan replied and then hung up the phone just as Rebekah walked in with a sour look on her face.

"Who was that calling so early?"

"Kristina. There was an article in the newspaper this morning that upset her."

"Well, she ought to have a little consideration. What does she expect you to do about it anyway?"

"I don't know. She just needed a little reassurance."

"Well, tell her to go find it somewhere else and leave you alone."

"Okay," Stan said, forcing a smile. "I think you need a cup of coffee."

Rebekah sighed. "I'm just sick of everyone expecting you to solve their problems. You've got your own problems to worry about, like graduating from law school and selling enough insurance so we don't starve."

"Well, the election will be over in less than a

month, so things should quiet down after that."

"Right. I'm not holding my breath," Rebekah spat.

Stan finished his coffee, gave Rebekah a peck on the cheek, and left to go to school. He hoped she'd be in a better mood when he returned that night, but he knew that was a long shot, as her anger usually took a few days to subside. When he got to SMU, he went straight to Professor Hertel's office, hoping to talk to him before class. He knocked on the door, and the professor said to come in.

"Stan! I wasn't expecting you to be in today."

"Oh, I'm okay. I can't afford to be missing class. It's hard enough keeping up when I'm here every day."

Professor Hertel nodded. "So, you were lucky the FBI was watching Mrs. Thornton, huh? If they hadn't been you may have been killed."

"Yes, that was fortunate. Speaking of Mrs. Thornton, she'd like your PI to locate Brad for her. He seems to have disappeared."

"Well, that's not really my problem."

"True, but since they're already investigating the Burilo cartel, she thought they could find him quicker than a new firm. She's willing to fund the investigation, and Brad's favorable testimony is going to be needed to get the Commissioner off the hook."

Professor Hertel thought about what Stan said and then shrugged. "Well, if she's funding it, I don't have a problem with it."

"Good. What's the name of the firm?"

"Burger and Wolford Investigations. Greg Wolford is in charge of the case. I think I have one of his cards around here."

Professor Hertel searched his desk and then produced a card with Greg Wolford's contact information.

"Don Karnes, his banker, thinks he's in San Antonio del Mar. Apparently, that's one of his favorite hideaways."

"It's a fine resort with lots of beautiful senoritas. I've been there a time or two."

"Great. I'll call Mr. Wolford and get him started."

After class, Stan met up with Paula, and they went across the street to Dairy Queen for lunch. Stan thought Paula looked particularly sexy in her tight jeans. He was admiring her from behind as they walked across the street when Paula looked back. She frowned and then smiled wryly.

"You want some of this?" she asked playfully.

"Sorry," Stan said meekly.

Stan knew she liked men admiring her but still felt a little embarrassed. He followed her inside, and they gave their orders and then found a table.

"I guess you're not too traumatized if you've got sex on your mind."

Stan shrugged.

"I was so worried when I heard on the news you'd been kidnapped. You must have been terrified."

"Yeah, I was really scared."

"I bet. How did Mrs. Thornton take it?"

"Pretty well, actually. She's a pretty tough woman. She wants me to hire Burger and Wolford to try to find Brad. His banker thinks he's in San Antonio del Mar."

"Really? Did you talk to Harry about that?"

Stan laughed. "Oh, so it's Harry now? Not Snake?"

She shrugged. "Ah. Snake didn't go over too well."

"Hmm. Yeah, he said it would be okay when I reminded him he needed Brad's favorable testimony to get Commissioner Barnes off."

"Stan, you're a genius," Paula said.

"Huh?" Stan replied warily.

"I need a vacation. San Antonio del Mar should be beautiful this time of the year."

Stan rolled his eyes. "Yeah, I think Harry had the same idea. His eyes kind of glazed over when I mentioned it."

She laughed. "That's because I know how to take care of my men. You should let me take care of you sometime."

Stan thought about that a moment. "I would, but then I'd be under your spell and would lose my free will."

"So. . . it would be worth it," Paula teased.

"Only in the short run. Eventually Rebekah would find out and kill us both."

The cashier yelled, "Twenty-one!"

Stan looked at his ticket and went to get their food. After lunch Stan went to the library where they had telephone booths and called Greg Wolford's office to try to get an appointment. His receptionist said he had some time late that afternoon, so Stan made the appointment. While he was waiting, he checked the Martendale Hubbell Legal Directory to check on the law firm of Page & Smith. When he found the listing, he discovered the firm represented mortgage lenders. Suddenly, he was pretty sure he knew what had happened the night of the Shepard murders. All he had to do was check the Collin County deed records to be sure.

After his federal taxation class, Stan went to Greg Wolford's office. It was located on the second floor of a strip center on Greenville Avenue. Professor Hertel had warned Stan that the firm operated out of a dump, but not to be alarmed by that. Apparently, Greg Wolford liked to keep a low profile but was actually a bored multi-millionaire who did PI work for the sheer fun and excitement of it. Stan took a seat in front of Greg's beat-up steel desk.

"So, Snake said you want us to find Brad Thornton."

"Right. Actually, Mrs. Thornton is the one retaining your services. She would have come herself—"

"But she's in jail. Yeah, I read about that."

"His banker thinks he may be in San Antonio del Mar."

"Good. I've got some contacts down there. I'll put them on the lookout for him, and if he surfaces, I'll send someone down right away to keep an eye on him for you."

"That would be great. We need him as a witness, so try not to spook him. Also, Carlos Morales and Tony Rubio probably won't take kindly to us rescuing him and bringing him back to Texas."

"No, they won't. That's why we're only going to locate him. You'll have to figure out how to get him back to Texas."

"Well, if you find him, the FBI will help me get him back, I'm sure."

"You and the FBI are tight? Why is that?" Wolford asked.

"What makes you think that?"

"Well, it's pretty unusual they would give you the time of day. They usually keep their investigations close to the vest."

Stan swallowed hard. He couldn't let on that he was a confidential informant for the FBI. They had warned him that if that information came out he'd immediately become a target. But then again he was already a target, it seemed. "They haven't told me much, actually. I'm just passing on anything I find out that might impact their case against Brad Thornton. It's my civic duty, right?"

"How does our client feel about that?"

"I told her the FBI would probably arrest him if we were able to find him and bring him back. She knows I'm cooperating with them."

Wolford nodded. "Okay. We charge $200 a day until we spot him, then it's $500 a day once I send a man down there, plus expenses."

"Okay. I'll give you $2,000 to start, okay?"

"Fine. That will last you a few days."

Stan counted out twenty $100 bills and handed them to Wolford. He took them and stuck them in his pocket. Stan filled out a client services contract and then left. On the way home, he wondered what the odds were that he'd actually find Thornton. He hoped he wasn't wasting Melissa Thornton's money. Then he worried about what he'd do if they found Thornton and the FBI couldn't help him get Thornton back to Dallas. If Professor Hertel and Paula went down there, they might be able to persuade him to come back, if he was on his own, but not if the Morales' or Rubio's men were babysitting him.

Chapter 16

Paula insisted she go with Stan to his interview on NBC Channel 5 with Veronica Brooks to provide moral support. Stan didn't mind her going along as long as Rebekah didn't find out. Stan hadn't told her about Paula, even though they were just friends. He knew Rebekah didn't like his propensity for befriending pretty women and would be angry if she found out about it. She barely tolerated his relationship with Kristina and constantly complained about it, even though she hung around with Kristina herself sometimes. On the way to the studio Paula advised Stan that Professor Hertel had invited her to go to San Antonio del Mar for the weekend to help him do research on the Burilo cartel.

"Right. I'm sure you're going to get a lot of research done at a beautiful resort."

"Well, Harry says if it's a business trip, he can write it off on his taxes. He's going to have a meeting with Wolford's contact down there just to make it an official business trip."

"Oh, I see. Well, if you see Brad Thornton down there, be sure and call me."

"I will. Don't worry."

"This is going to be a tricky interview," Stan said.

"Yeah, I bet. I'm glad it's you and not me."

Stan had wrestled for several days on what exactly he wanted to reveal in the interview. A lot would depend on Veronica's questions and what interested her, but he also knew he could steer the interview in other directions during his response if he wanted to. Since his main objective was to clear Rob's name, he decided on two major courses of conversation. First, he wanted to tell the world about Rob Shepard in such a way that they'd know he wasn't capable of murdering his family. Secondly, he wanted to flush out the witness who he was sure had seen the killers responsible for murdering the Shepard family. If he was successful, the police would have no choice but to reopen the Shepard family murder investigation and get it right this time. He knew this was a dangerous move, so he asked Lynn Jenkins to arrange for some off-duty police officers to watch his house for the next twenty-four hours.

Stan didn't have much time for watching TV, so he hadn't seen any of Channel 5's extensive promotion of the interview. When he and Paula walked into the station, they were a bit surprised to see the reception room packed with people. In an unusual move for The Veronica Brooks Show, the producers had set up a small audience area like the ones in late-night talk shows. Stan was already nervous, and the live audience did not help. He looked out over a sea of strange faces, the knots in his stomach tightening, and he wondered why he had agreed to the interview.

While a technician fitted Stan's microphone on his jacket pocket, Veronica smiled at him. Stan forced a return smile and then heard the director say, "On the air in ten seconds." Stan took a deep breath and smiled at the camera.

"Good afternoon. Thanks for tuning into The Veronica Brooks Show."

The crowd yelled and screamed enthusiastically while the show's theme music was played. After a minute Veronica raised one hand. "Okay, okay. Thank you. Today we have with us Stan Turner, who, as you may know, was recently kidnapped and taken to a remote location apparently to be murdered by members of the Burilo drug cartel. Fortunately, Stan and Melissa Thornton, wife of millionaire Brad Thornton, were rescued by the FBI just seconds before the execution was to take place. I know it sounds like an episode of Harry O, but it's real-life drama here in north Texas. Do you feel lucky to be alive, Stan?"

Stan nodded. "Oh, yes. Had it not been for the FBI's surveillance of the Thornton home, Melissa and I would be dead right now."

"Now, for those listeners who haven't been following your exploits, explain to us why the Burilo drug cartel is after you. We know you're a Republican County Chairman, a law student, and the campaign manager for the feisty Kristina Tenison, candidate for state representative in District 67, but I doubt any of those activities would upset the Burilo drug cartel."

"No. What apparently has them upset is my efforts to clear the name of my good friend, the late Rob Shepard," Stan explained.

"I think everyone is familiar with the Shepard murder-suicide."

"Right, but I don't believe Rob murdered anyone, and I've been conducting my own investigation to prove that he didn't."

"Do you think the Burilo drug cartel had Rob Shepard murdered?"

"Well, if you remember, the murders took place just days after the FBI launched their investigation of Brad Thornton for allegedly laundering money for the Burilo drug cartel. It's my belief that Rob Shepard had knowledge or evidence that could have connected the cartel to Brad Thornton, and the only way to make sure the evidence never made it to a court of law was to kill him. Obviously, the person responsible didn't want the authorities to know they were responsible for the murder, so they staged a murder-suicide."

"Yes, but the police and coroner at the time indicated that Rob Shepard was severely depressed over the investigation, his expected indictment, and the prospect of having to drop out of the race for state representative. That certainly would be reason enough for anyone to take their life."

"Maybe, but I was with Rob just hours before the murders. We were attending a reception honoring President Ford. Rob and I got to personally meet the President and shake his hand. Rob was in a good mood and didn't seem the least bit depressed."

"Yes, but some people are good at hiding their depression from their friends."

"Perhaps, but I was Rob's best friend. He confided in me. He didn't believe he was going to be indicted. He knew nothing of any money laundering and, at worst, was guilty of being naïve."

"So, the murder-suicide decision shocked you?"

"Yes, because even if Rob was as depressed as the police and medical examiner say, he would never kill his wife and children. He loved them and would be incapable of hurting them in any way. I am absolutely certain about that."

"Okay, so obviously your investigation was making some headway if the cartel decided to have you killed."

"Yes, in the course of my investigation, I was fortunate to get my hands on some very incriminating evidence against a man named Carlos Morales. He's heavily into the Silver Springs Ventures and reportedly the front man for the cartel. Of course, I turned that evidence immediately over to the FBI. I believe that act is what precipitated my abduction."

The crowd stirred from the revelation. Stan looked out at them and wondered what they were thinking. He hoped his message was getting across to them.

"How does Melissa Thornton fit into the scheme of things?" Veronica asked. "Why was she kidnapped?"

"Like Rob Shepard, she probably has knowledge that could tie her husband to Carlos Morales or others in the cartel. Someone thought it would be clever to get us together and then get rid of two birds with one stone."

"Where are you on the investigation now? Any progress?"

"Yes, I'm glad you asked. I have identified a witness who I believe saw the killers leave the Shepard house that night. Unfortunately, this person has not come forward for personal reasons."

"Wow! Can you tell us who it is?"

"Not now. If I did, the witness would be dead by morning. No…what I'm hoping the witness will do is go to the police immediately and tell them what was seen. If the witness does that, the FBI can arrange protection, but if the witness stays silent any longer, then I will be compelled to go to the police and tell them what I know. After I've given the police this information, I'll call you and reveal the witness's identity."

"An exclusive?"

"Yes. Since you've given me the opportunity to get my message out to the public, I'm giving you an exclusive on the identity of the witness."

"Fantastic! What do you think this witness saw?"

"I don't want to give out any details because that might help the cartel figure out the identity of the witness."

"I see. So why not go to the police or the FBI with the identity of the witness rather than air it on live TV?"

"Because neither the police nor the district attorney's office are likely to do anything right away after I give them the information. If the witness shows up and confesses, they'll be forced to reopen the investigation, and Rob Shepard's name will be cleared."

Many in the audience began to clap. Stan smiled at them.

"So, Stan, I hope you have a bodyguard with you tonight. It seems like the cartel would have good reason to get rid of you before you go to the police in the morning."

Stan smiled. "Don't worry about that. My house is being protected by off-duty police officers tonight, and I've already arranged for the evidence I have to be delivered to the police, the FBI, and to you by courier or overnight mail by 10:00 a.m. tomorrow. If I don't make it through the night, will you be sure the information is reported to the public?"

"Yes, absolutely, but I hope that's not necessary."

"Me too."

The audience laughed.

"Alright, ladies and gentlemen, tune in tomorrow and find out who this mystery witness turns out to be and whether Stan Turner's bold actions here today bear fruit. Thank you, Stan, for being my guest today. It was definitely the most exciting and dramatic interview I've ever conducted."

As Stan stood up, the crowd applauded and cheered. Stan nodded and then left the studio, quite relieved the ordeal was over. When he reached the reception area, he was mobbed by the crowd. Everyone wanted to shake his hand or pat him on the back. Paula watched with tears in her eyes as he made his way to her.

A woman grabbed his arm. "You're a good man, Stan Turner," she said. "Rob Shepard was lucky to have you as a friend."

Stan smiled at the woman and took a step forward.

An elderly man shook Stan's hand. "Good luck to you, boy! I'll be praying for your witness to do the right thing."

"Thank you," Stan replied.

Another woman grabbed Stan's arm. "You be careful, Stan," she said. "Don't go home. Go to a motel."

Stan laughed. "I don't think my wife would appreciate that."

"She would if it saved your life."

Finally, Stan reached Paula, and they made a quick exit. Stan looked around the parking lot warily, as there were many people standing around. He didn't think any of Morales' men could have made it to the studio that fast unless they'd already been following him. Stan felt better once they were on the road, but he kept looking in his rearview mirror to see if anyone was following him. At first, he thought he'd made a clean escape, but then he saw a blue Mercedes a few cars behind him.

He watched the Mercedes. When he changed lanes, the Mercedes changed lanes too. Just to be sure he was being followed, he turned right at the next signal and went completely around the block, ending up where they had started. The Mercedes followed his every move.

"We've got someone tailing us," he said.

"Yeah. I wondered what in the hell you were doing." Paula turned around and looked at the cars behind them. "Which car?" she asked.

"The blue Mercedes."

She squinted, trying to read the license plate. "MXV 249," she said.

"Write it down. I'll never remember it."

She opened her purse, pulled out a piece of paper, and wrote down the license number. "Okay, got it. What should we do?"

"Nothing. I don't think they'll try anything as long as we stay on busy streets."

"I hope you're right," she said apprehensively.

"It won't do them any good to kill me. I've already sent the information to the police."

"So who is this witness? Molly Rogers?"

"Right."

"How do you know she witnessed the killers leaving the house?"

"I've done some research and discovered that she and her husband were in deep financial trouble. In fact, their home was posted for foreclosure and set to be sold on the first Tuesday of November. When Molly went upstairs just moments after the last shot was fired, she must have seen or heard the killers crawling out the window and dropping onto the roof. I bet she even went over to the window and watched them leave."

"Oh, I see. She comes back to inspect the bodies and sees Cindy's necklace. She figures Cindy won't have any use for it anymore, so she steals it. The next day, she takes it to the pawn shop and gets just enough money to catch up her mortgage payment and avoid foreclosure."

"Right, but she can't tell the police the truth because she doesn't want the killers to know she saw them or the police to do much digging for fear they'll find out she's stolen the necklace."

"But what if you're wrong?"

"I'm not. I know that's what happened. If you'd have seen Molly Roger's face the night I showed up at her house, you'd be as confident as I am."

"Well, I hope you're right. I hate for anything bad to happen to Molly."

Paula's misgivings bothered Stan. He prayed he hadn't made a mistake about Molly and endangered her life. Suddenly Stan realized they were coming up to the on ramp of I30. He went up the ramp and pushed hard on the gas pedal. The car lurched forward and accelerated to seventy. The Mercedes stayed right on Stan's tail as they wove through traffic, trying to keep some distance. Paula looked back nervously.

"They're catching up to us. I think they may try to ram us."

"Well, we can't outrun them," Stan said. "I saw this in a movie once."

Paula looked at him incredulously. "You saw what in a movie?"

Just as the Mercedes was about to rear-end them, Stan swung the car two lanes to the left and slammed on the brakes. The Mercedes flew past them like a lightning bolt. Several cars in the left-hand lane had to take evasive action to avoid hitting them. Then Stan did a U-turn over the grass median and headed back down I-30 in the opposite direction.

Paula looked back and saw the Mercedes trying the same maneuver but farther up the road where the median was impassible and had gotten bogged down.

"Nice work!" Paula said. "I didn't know you were an Indy driver."

"We were lucky. We could have gotten rear-ended or mired in the mud trying to cross the median. But if they had rammed us from behind I might have lost control of the car and we could have ended up dead."

"No. You handled the situation perfectly. I'll drive with you in a car chase anytime."

Stan laughed tentatively as his racing heart began to slow. On the way back home, he worried about his family. He knew Jenkins was there, but that didn't completely allay his fears. After he left Paula off at SMU, he drove home praying everyone was okay. Jenkins' police car was parked in front of his house, along with Agent Rutlege's blue Malibu. When Stan walked in the door, Reggie ran to him.

"Dad! You're okay," he said, wrapping his arms around Stan.

"Yeah, I'm fine," Stan said, picking him up and holding him. Mark and Peter looked on curiously.

"Is someone trying to hurt you?" Reggie asked.

"No," Stan lied. "Why don't you and your brothers go upstairs and play? I need to talk to Agent Rutledge and Officer Jenkins."

Stan put Reggie down, and they all ran upstairs. Rebekah glared at Stan, shook her head, and went into the kitchen.

"So, I guess you saw the broadcast."

"Are you nuts?" Jenkins scolded. "That was a very dangerous thing to do."

"I know, but how else will I flush out the witness?"

"You should have brought the evidence to me," Agent Rutledge said. "We would have interrogated the suspect and discovered the truth."

"But it's not your case," Stan protested.

"It's our case now if what you say is true. If the Shepard family was executed by the Burilo cartel, that puts it under our jurisdiction since they were tampering with our witnesses."

Stan shrugged. "Well, I did send you the info. You

should have it at 10:00 a.m. tomorrow."

"Who's the suspect? I want to get some protection out to him. I've got two agents in the neighborhood, but it would be nice to be able to focus on one residence."

"Molly Rogers."

Stan explained about her financial problems and theft of Cindy Shepard's necklace. He told them that the pawn shop owner had identified her photograph as a regular at his place of business.

"Well, I hope she comes in and confesses. That would make life easier for us all. I've talked to Detective Moore, and he's going to advise us immediately if she comes in."

"You might want to pick up her husband when he goes to work at eight. I don't think he realizes what she did. He might be helpful in getting her to come clean."

"Okay. We'll do that."

"So, any trouble on the way home?" Agent Rutledge asked.

Stan raised his eyebrows. "Well, now that you mention it, we did have a bit of a problem."

Stan described the car chase and gave Agent Rutledge the license plate number of the Mercedes.

She just shook her head. "I hope I don't end up visiting you in the morgue," she said.

Stan smiled cautiously. "You and me both."

Agent Rutledge left, and Stan thanked Jenkins for lining up the off-duty police officers to watch the house. He gave him some of the cash from Melissa's retainer to pay the officers, and then Jenkins left. Stan sighed as he looked toward the kitchen door where Rebekah's wrath awaited him. After summoning his courage, he stepped through the kitchen door.

Chapter 17

The next morning, Stan woke up at seven, but when he tried to go back to sleep, he kept thinking of Molly Rogers. Would she come forward or continue to hide? Since he had three more hours before he'd find out, he got up, made coffee, and got the newspaper. When he opened it, there was an article about his TV interview and his challenge to the witness to come forward. He read it quickly and then began flipping through the rest of the newspaper. In the Metro section was another poll showing that whereas Kristina had gained ground on Ron Wells in the race, he still led by seven percentage points. Knowing that Kristina was an early riser, he gave her a call.

"Good morning."

"Hi," she said sleepily.

"I didn't wake you, did I?"

"No, I was up. Did you see the latest poll?"

"Yeah. You're making progress."

"Not enough. We're running out of time."

"Don't worry. Things can change in a hurry."

"You've certainly proved that. Do you have a death wish or something?"

"No. I just ran out of patience. I'm getting burned out over this investigation. Rebekah's about to divorce me. I had to do something drastic to get it over with."

"Well, I hope it works out."

"I'm optimistic."

"So, I'm getting tired of being behind in this race.

When are you going to drop your bomb on Wells?"

"Soon. But the timing's not right yet."

"Care to enlighten me as to what dirt you have on him?"

"No. You'd just worry about how it would play out. It's a distraction you don't need right now."

Kristina sighed. "Alright then. I've got to get going. I've got a breakfast meeting with the Executive Committee of the Junior League."

"Great. They should be all over your campaign, being a women's organization."

"I'll soon find out."

"Okay. I'll call you over the weekend to see how it turned out."

"Thanks. Hope your witness shows up."

"Me too. See you."

As Stan hung up the phone, Rebekah walked in and grabbed a cup of coffee. "Who was that?" she asked.

"Kristina. Just checking in to see how she was doing."

"She's ten points behind in the polls. She's going to lose."

"Seven points as of this morning, and she's going to win."

Rebekah rolled her eyes. A wave of anger washed over Stan, but he managed to stifle it. He turned to the sports page to see how UCLA was doing in the football standings. He noticed his alma mater was 7-2-1 and had a good shot at going to the Liberty Bowl. A few minutes later, Reggie and Mark walked in, and Rebekah poured them both a bowl of cereal.

"Go get your daughter," Rebekah said. "I heard her playing in her crib."

Stan got up and went across the house to Marcia's room. She was standing up in her crib when he entered the room. He swept her up out of the crib and set her on the changing table. She laughed and smiled at him.

"Okay, little girl. You hungry?"

Hearing Stan, Peter ran into the room. "What are you doing, Daddy?" he asked.

"Getting your sister ready for breakfast. Are you hungry?"

"Yep," he said and ran out of the room.

Stan picked Marcia up and carried her to the kitchen. After depositing her in her highchair, he sat down to finish reading the paper.

"When do you have to leave?" Rebekah asked.

"I'm going to hang around until Agent Rutledge calls. It could be anytime now. I don't have class until eleven."

"Are you sure Molly Rogers even watched your interview yesterday?" Rebekah asked.

"I hope so. I had someone call her and tell her to be sure and watch it. Even if she didn't, it was on all the news channels at six and ten last night, and there was a blurb about it in this morning's paper."

"I hope she saw it."

After breakfast, Stan tried to study but found it difficult as the anticipation was killing him. Finally, at ten fifteen, he got the call from Agent Rutledge.

"She showed up at police headquarters about fifteen minutes ago," Agent Rutledge said. "I'm on my way to pick her up."

Stan breathed a sigh of relief, told the good news to Rebekah, and then left for SMU. When he got there, he went to Professor Hertel's office and discovered that Paula and Professor Hertel had indeed gone off to San Antonio del Mar. Hertel's secretary gave Stan a note with their hotel name and room number written on it.

After class, Stan called Greg Wolford for an update.

"One of our men spotted Brad Thornton a few minutes ago," Wolford advised. "He's not being held hostage or anything, but there are three of Morales' goons there keeping an eye on him."

"Excellent. Professor Hertel's down there with Paula Waters as we speak."

"I know. My man's going to meet with them tonight to confirm the sighting."

"Alright. I'm going to go meet with Melissa Thornton and then Agent Rutledge to advise them of the situation and discuss strategy. I'll call you late this afternoon for an update."

"Very good. Talk to you later," Wolford said.

It took Stan over an hour to get to the jail in McKinney and get in to see Melissa Thornton. She was very glad to see him.

"You must have found Brad," she said.

"Yes. He's at a resort in San Antonio del Mar with three of Morales' men."

"Hmm. They're keeping him in Mexico so he won't be arrested and can't cooperate with the FBI."

"It looks that way," Stan agreed.

"You've got to go down there and rescue him."

"Not me," Stan protested. "I just agreed to help you find him."

"We've got to get Brad back here. They're not going to babysit him forever. Eventually, they'll just kill him to be sure he doesn't talk."

"Maybe the FBI can have him extradited?"

"You think so? I'm so worried about him."

"Possibly," Stan replied. "I'm going over there in a little while to discuss another matter. I'll ask them about it."

"Good. I don't want to lose him. Whatever you do,

you've got to act quickly."

"Like I said, I'm going over there right now."

"Thanks, Stan. You're a good friend."

After driving all the way to McKinney, Stan wasn't thrilled about having to go all the way back to FBI headquarters in Dallas, but time was critical, so he had no choice. It was nearly four o'clock when he stepped into the lobby and checked in with security. They made him wait until Agent Rutledge came down to pick him up.

"Stan! You finally made it. Where have you been?"

"I had a class I couldn't skip and then I had to go up to McKinney to tell Melissa Thornton that they found her husband in San Antonio del Mar."

"Who found him?"

"The PI firm we hired—Burger & Wolford."

"They're sure he's there?"

"Yeah. He's being babysat by a three of Morales' men. She wants you guys to extradite him back to the US. Can you do that?"

"No. He hasn't been charged yet, and even if he was, extradition takes time."

"But wouldn't he be in protective custody pending the extradition?" Stan asked.

"In the US, that might mean something, but in Mexico, a prison is a very dangerous place to be stuck."

"Hmm. She's afraid they're going to kill him if he's not rescued soon."

"She's probably right."

"So, what can we do?"

"I don't know. Probably nothing, unless—"

"Unless what?" Stan asked.

"Unless, you wanted to organize a rescue?"

"Me? How in the hell would I do that?"

"You couldn't do it by land, but since the resort is on the ocean there wouldn't be too much risk."

"Really?"

Agent Rutledge told him her plan, and Stan listened with great interest. She told him the investigation of Brad Thornton and his money laundering operation was about finished, and with or without Melissa's cooperation, they were about ready to go to the grand jury to ask for several indictments. Since Brad Thornton was their primary target, his absence was a huge problem. If they tried to extradite Thornton, he'd likely be killed by the cartel before he made it back to the US. If, however, someone rescued him and brought him back voluntarily, they could arrest him immediately, put him in protective custody, and go forward with their cases.

"We can put you in contact with some ex-Navy seals who can help you with the rescue."

"Why don't you just hire them to do it. I have no military training."

"We can't legally do that, but you could. Besides, Brad doesn't know them. He may not be anxious to leave with a stranger. He knows you and is much more likely to cooperate if he sees a familiar face. But, it will be dangerous, so I wouldn't blame you for declining the suggestion."

"It's just that Rebekah will have a stroke and I've got so much going on right now."

"It would be a way you could help save Brad Thornton's life and at the same time help the FBI finally put the Burilo Cartel out of business."

Stan sighed. "Okay. I don't give a rats ass about Brad Thornton, but I'll do it for Melissa. I like her. She's a nice lady."

"Good. I'll make the arrangements."

Stan nodded. “What did Molly Rogers have to say?”

“She admitted to taking the necklace and seeing two men leave the Shepard house that night, so Rob Shepard is off the hook. The medical examiner is going to revise his determination as to the cause of Rob’s death from suicide to murder.”

“Oh, thank God. What a relief.”

“We had Mrs. Rogers take a look at the two men who tried to kill you and Mrs. Thornton, but she couldn’t identify them. She says she only saw them from the back as they were climbing out the upstairs window.”

“Oh, that’s too bad. It would have been nice to have been able to wrap that case up and be done with it. Were you able to compare the extra prints they found at the Shepard house with your two prisoners?”

“Yes. They weren’t a match.”

“Damn. That’s a shame.”

“I know, but we still might find some evidence to link them to the murders.”

“I hope so. If they did it, we can’t let them get away with it.”

When Stan got home, Rebekah was elated with the news that Rob had been cleared of the murders of his family. Stan suggested they go tell Tom and Marge Shepard in person, but since they couldn’t find a babysitter, they settled for a telephone call. Stan made the call, and Rebekah picked up their second line.

“Tom, this is Stan Turner, and Rebekah’s on the line as well.”

“Oh, hi, Stan, Rebekah. How are you?”

“Wonderful. You should put Marge on the line. I’ve got good news.”

“Okay… just a moment,” Tom said.

“Hi, Marge said.”

"Hi. I've got good news."

"What?" Marge asked.

"I just left the FBI, and I wanted to be the first to tell you that Rob has been cleared of all murder charges. The witness came in this morning and acknowledged she saw two men leaving the house just after the murders. She also admitted to stealing Cindy's necklace."

"Oh, my God! I can't believe it," Marge said. "Thank you, Stan. This is wonderful news."

"Yes, I'm so relieved," Tom said "I knew Rob couldn't have done something so terrible."

"No. We knew it too," Rebekah said.

"So, do they know who was responsible for murdering our children and grandchildren?" Tom asked.

"It may have been the same two guys who tried to kill Melissa and me, but they don't have any proof of that yet."

"Well, just clearing Rob's name is enough for now. We really owe you big time, Stan. I know you put yourself and your family at great risk to clear Rob's name. If there is ever anything we can do for you, please let us know."

"Yes, Stan," Marge said. "Please let us do something for you."

"No, that's not necessary," Stan said. "I did it as much for Rebekah and me as I did it for you. Cindy and Rob were friends, and we couldn't let their lives end in a lie."

"God bless you, Stan," Marge said tearfully.

Stan and Rebekah hung up the phone, feeling pretty good for the moment. Stan used the happy moment to tell Rebekah about his plan to rescue Brad Thornton.

"You're going to do what!" she screamed.

Chapter 18

Stan went upstairs to pack a few things for his weekend trip to San Antonio del Mar. Rebekah was furious about the trip, so Stan didn't want to hang around the house any longer than he had to. Once he'd gathered his things, he kissed the kids goodbye and left. From the airport, he called Paula to enlist their help in the rescue. After listening to what a great time they were having, he explained to her his rescue plans and what he needed her and Professor Hertel to do.

"This sounds like fun," Paula said. "I'll go get Harry, and we'll get started right away."

"Good. You can't let them know who you are, or they'll immediately be suspicious."

"Oh, don't worry. I just hope Brad Thornton picks up on the con and doesn't give it away.

"Me too."

"I'll make sure we're alone when I explain what's happening."

"Good. Tell Professor Hertel I'm sorry for messing up his holiday."

"Oh, don't worry. He'll love this charade."

"Good. Eight o'clock tomorrow night, Pacific standard time. Don't be late."

"Got it. You be careful."

"I will. Bye."

After Stan hung up the telephone, he called another number. A bored sounding man answered the telephone. "Horizon Charters."

Hi. This is Stan Turner. I was referred to you by Ruth Rutledge."

"Oh, right. We've got most of the details worked out for your tour of Baja."

"Good. What am I going to have to do?"

"Ah. We'll talk about it when you get here."

"Okay, I'm about to board my plane."

"You have our address?"

"Yes."

"Alright then. See you tomorrow. Ask for Brett."

"Thanks, Brett."

Stan hung up the phone and took a deep breath. He could feel adrenaline flowing into his blood just from the anticipation of the rescue. He wondered how the extraction would work and what he'd have to do. There were a lot of things that could go wrong, and if they slipped up, someone could be killed. He played Paula and Snake's part of the plan over and over in his head and couldn't see how Paula or Professor Hertel could get hurt unless Morales' men realized who they were. That seemed unlikely, and Paula and Professor Hertel were well aware of that risk and knew they'd have to have a quick escape plan ready after the ruse had played out.

More worrisome possibilities were that the cartel would have a boat handy to pursue them once they realized Brad Thornton was gone, that Brad Thornton didn't want to be rescued, or that Paula and Harry's cover might be blown. Stan felt sick after thinking of all these possibilities and wondered if he should abort the mission. He could still call Paula and Professor Hertel and call the whole thing off. He was contemplating this possibility when his plane was called.

He boarded Flight 422 from Dallas to San Diego at 6:00 p.m. Due to the two time zones they'd be crossing, they'd arrive in San Diego at 7;20 p.m. Stan hadn't reserved a motel room, as he wanted to stay close to the private airport where he'd be meeting his team. After they took off, a stewardess delivered a light dinner and a cold drink. He ate appreciatively since he'd skipped lunch. After dinner, Stan fell asleep and began to dream.

In his dream, he was rowing a raft toward the shore when he saw the tail fin of a shark circling him. He saw himself rowing faster and faster, trying to outrun the sharks, with no success. Finally his pace became so frantic he didn't see an approaching wave. Suddenly, the raft was flipped over, sending him naked into the warm water. He felt a fin graze his leg, and he screamed in terror.

The stewardess shook him. "Sir? Are you alright? Sir!"

Stan opened his eyes and looked up at the stewardess, much relieved. He sighed, "Yes, sorry. Just a dream."

"Can I get you a glass of water or something?" she asked, seemingly concerned.

"No. I'm fine," Stan said. A little embarrassed he looked around and noticed people staring at him. "Sorry," he whispered.

Intense dreams weren't unusual for Stan. He had a vivid imagination and often had intricate dreams that he later made into short stories for his kids. They loved to hear his bizarre tales of strange creatures and great adventures. Rebekah, of course, said she'd always known he was crazy. Stan wondered what his kids would think of this real-life adventure he was about to embark upon.

They arrived in San Diego right on schedule. It was fifty miles to Brown Field, the small airport where Stan was meeting the extraction team, so he rented a car and bought a map of Southern California. When he arrived at the airport, he located the hangar for Horizon Charters and then went back to a Best Western motel he'd passed about four miles earlier. Once he was settled, he called Rebekah to tell her he had arrived safely. She was cool to him, but he could tell she was glad he had called. After he had talked to Reggie, Mark, and Peter, he hung up the phone and went to bed.

He slept soundly but had more dreams about the raft. In one of them, he was nearly at the plane when a speedboat came bearing down upon him, guns blazing. Just as he was about to climb aboard the plane, it started up and took off without him. In yet another version, they made it to the plane and Brad Thornton climbed aboard, but then the speedboat showed up and he was shot in the back. Needless to say, Stan was somewhat nervous when morning rolled around, but he kept telling himself they were only dreams and soon forgot them.

There was a small diner near the motel, so Stan walked over to it, bought a newspaper from the stand out front, and went inside to have breakfast. The waitress brought him a cup of coffee and took his order. When she'd left. he started to read the newspaper. Buried deep in the San Diego Union, he found an article about the Shepard murders and how the police had reopened the investigation and the medical examiner had revised his report to eliminate any reference to a suicide. Stan was a little surprised, but he was pleased the story had made it all the way to San Diego.

At eleven thirty, Stan packed up his things and checked out of the motel. He drove to the airport and parked near Horizon Charters. The front door was wide open, so Stan walked in and looked around. He approached a stout man in overalls inspecting a plane.

"Hi. Is Brett around?" Stan asked.

The man looked up and gave Stan a once-over. Then he pointed and said, "In the office over there."

Stan looked in that direction and saw a door with a sign on it that read PRIVATE. He walked over to it and knocked on the door.

A man with an athletic build and a sober demeanor opened the door. "What do you want?"

"Brett. I'm Stan Turner."

"Oh. Welcome, Mr. Turner. Come in."

Stan stepped inside and looked around the cluttered office. The place stunk of oil and burnt coffee.

"I have your plane all ready. Why don't we go take a look at it?"

"Sounds good," Stan replied.

Brett walked over to a golf cart, got in, and then drove it up to Stan. "Hop in."

Stan sat next to Brett and they were off. They drove all the way around the terminal to where a small Piper Cub J-3 was parked.

Stan looked at the plane and frowned. "This can't land in the ocean," he noted.

"No. We'll fly this one up to Lake Cuyamaca, where the extraction team is waiting with a Cessna A185F."

"Oh," Stan said. "I see."

"That's why I got you here early. I've got to brief you on the details of the extraction and then get you up to the lake to join the extraction team."

"Right," Stan said nervously.

"Let's go to the office and get started," he said as they took off back to the front of the hangar.

Brett drove them up to a chart room with a long walnut table occupying one end. A map of Baja California was spread out on the table. Brett picked up a ruler and drew lines showing their expected flight path.

"We leave from Lake Cuyamaca and fly west out over the Pacific Ocean about four miles. Then we turn south and fly toward San Antonio del Mar. We have to stay at least three miles from the coastline in order to be in international waters. When we are directly west of San Antonio del Mar, we'll fly low toward the coastline and set down about a mile from shore. You and Paul will have to row the raft to shore, pick up your package, and row back. It will be dark, so it's not likely that you'll be seen."

"If it's dark, will we be able to find the plane coming back?"

"I'll turn on a small running light. If anyone sees it from the shore, they'll just think it's a fishing boat."

"Is there much current? Will we have trouble landing at the right spot?"

"The Rosarita Beach Hotel will be all lit up. You shouldn't have any trouble finding it."

"Okay," Stan said nervously. "Let's go."

Brett nodded, folded up the map, and handed it to Stan. "Alright. I'll fly you up to Lake Cuyamaca. Your team will meet us there."

Ten minutes later, Stan climbed into the plane, buckled his seatbelt, and put on his headset. Brett did his pre-flight check, and they began taxiing down the runway. Soon they were airborne. While they were flying, Stan played over the plans in his mind. He was worried about the mile row into shore. He'd done plenty of rowing when he was young and knew it was more difficult than it looked. He remembered his father getting caught in a strong current on a river in northern California and nearly being washed out to sea. He imagined a sea current could be just as powerful.

Then, he worried about visibility. Having lived near the sea as a child, Stan knew fog could be a problem. If a fog bank drifted between them and the sea plane, he knew they'd lose sight of the plane and may never find it. He felt a sharp pain in his stomach and wondered how he'd been so stupid to volunteer for such a rescue. It had seemed like a great adventure when it first came up, but now it seem like pure foolishness.

When they got to Lake Cuyamaca, they landed at a small airport and taxied to the south end where a Jeep was waiting for them. They deplaned, and Brett introduced Stan to the pilot, Phil, and his boatman, Paul."

"Nice to meet you, Stan, Phil said. "We need to get moving if we're going to make the rendezvous on time."

"Alright," Stan said as he climbed into the Jeep.

Stan waved goodbye to Brett, who wished him good luck. Phil drove fast across the runway to a connecting dirt road. It was a bumpy ride, and Stan had to hold on tight to keep from being thrown from the vehicle. Soon the lake appeared in the distance, and then they were descending down toward the shoreline. The Cessna sea plane was floating in a cove and appeared loaded and ready to go. Stan saw the small inflatable raft tied to the pontoons, and a chill darted up his spine.

When the Jeep abruptly stopped and Stan noticed the identification numbers on the plane tail, he remembered he needed to call Agent Rutledge and give her the ID number so the Border Patrol would leave them alone.

"Is there a telephone around here?"

Ruben pointed to a bait shop a few hundred yards away. "Inside the shop there's a pay phone."

"Thanks," Stan said. "I'll be right back."

The FBI telephone receptionist indicated Agent Rutledge was in a meeting. When Stan told her who it was, Agent Adams came on the line.

"So, how does your team look?" Agent Adams asked.

"They seem capable. I just hope I don't screw up the mission," Stan replied.

"Don't worry. They're not expecting you to do much."

"Right? All I have to do is help row the raft less than a mile. I think I can handle that."

"I'm sure you can."

"Here's the ID number—N275RF you wanted. We're in a red and white Cessna A185F."

"Alright. I'll pass on the info to Agent Rutledge. Good luck."

Stan hung up the phone and ran back to the plane. Paul helped him aboard, made sure he was buckled in, and then took his seat and fastened his seatbelt. Phil started the engine. The plane took off quickly toward the center of the lake, gained speed, and then lifted out of the water. As Stan looked down at the beautiful landscape, he wondered if he'd ever see it again.

The plane gained altitude, rising high above the mountains. Soon they were flying over an urban area just south of San Diego. They continued until they reached the shoreline and plunged due west over the Pacific Ocean. When they reached international waters, the sun was setting, and the sea beneath was dark. Suddenly the plane banked left, and Stan could only see a few dim lights on the Baja peninsula to his left and nothing but utter blackness beneath them.

As the minutes wore on, Stan felt more and more nervous about the mission. A sinking feeling came over him as he realized that very soon, they'd be dropped off in the middle of the ocean completely on their own. There would be no one to rescue them if anything went wrong, and if they were discovered they'd likely be killed. He thought about aborting the mission right then but couldn't force himself to do it.

Suddenly, the plane began to descend. Stan looked at his boatman in horror, but fortunately in the darkness, Paul couldn't see Stan's pale face. The plane dipped, then leveled off, and dropped into the choppy waters. Stan took a deep breath, summoned his courage, and unbuckled his seatbelt. Paul opened the cockpit door and began unfastening the raft. A strong wind whipped across Stan's face as he struggled to get out the door. Once outside, he dropped down onto the pontoon next to Paul. Bobbing up and down in the darkness, Paul had difficulty inflating the raft but eventually got it ready for boarding. After he placed the oars into the locks on each side, he handed Stan a life jacket. Stan put it on and dropped into the raft.

As Paul shoved them off, Stan looked toward the shore and saw the Rosarita Beach Hotel in the distance. It was supposed to be only a mile away, but it looked much farther. He looked at his watch and saw that time was passing quickly. Soon they were rowing as fast as they could toward the shore.

It had been ten years since Stan had rowed a boat and even longer since he'd been out on the ocean. He'd forgotten how high the swells grew and what they did to his stomach. He didn't have time to stop to puke, so he stifled his nausea and kept on rowing. Halfway to shore, his arms began to ache. He realized how out of shape he'd become in the eighteen months since he'd been discharged from the Marine Corps. Now he wondered if he'd have the strength to row all the way to ashore. He stopped a moment to rest and take a deep breath but Paul gave him a dirty look, so he started rowing again. In the silence, he heard the sound of a ship's engine. He looked to his right and saw a large fishing boat coming straight at them.

Chapter 19

Paula slipped on a short black cocktail dress and looked at herself in the mirror. Harry looked at her admiringly from the doorway but with a bit of concern showing on his face. She smiled at him as she dug into her purse looking for her lipstick and eyeliner. She carefully applied them, and when she was satisfied with her appearance, turned to him expectantly.

"Wow! You look great," Harry said. "Be careful with those thugs. They don't have much respect for women."

"Don't worry. I'll be Brad Thornton's date, so they should leave me alone."

"Don't let him go to the bathroom. One of them might try to lure you away."

"If he has to go, I'll go too. That way I won't be standing around alone."

"I'll be watching you, but if I have to intervene, it will blow our cover."

"Don't worry. I know how to handle men."

Harry nodded knowingly. A few minutes later, Paula left the room and walked to the hotel lobby. She looked at the bar but decided first to check out access to the beach. She walked out onto the terrace overlooking the beach and was dazzled by the incredible sunset. The hot sun looked like it was just about to dip into the Pacific Ocean. She halfway expected to hear an incredible sizzle as the molten sun sank into the sea, but there was only silence.

When the sun disappeared and night claimed the sky, Paula went into the bar looking for her date. Brad Thornton was already there, nursing a drink. Paula walked up briskly and sat beside him. Morales' thugs were at the bar, too, but giving Thornton plenty of space. Earlier in the day, Paula had made a point to run into him and strike up a conversation. They'd talked for some time and agreed to meet later for dinner.

"Oh, hi," Brad said as Paula walked up.

"Hello. Sorry I'm late. I was watching that gorgeous sunset out on the terrace."

"Oh, really? I guess I missed it."

"Well, I'm sure it will be just as nice tomorrow night. Perhaps we can watch it together."

Thornton's eyes lit up. "Yeah, absolutely. Can I get you a drink?"

"Gin and tonic, please," Paula said.

Thornton snapped his fingers, and the bartender looked at him. "Gin and tonic for the lady," he advised. The bartender nodded and continued what he was doing.

"So, how long will you be staying in San Antonio del Mar?" Paula asked.

"Oh, I don't know. I've got some business down here I've got to straighten out before I go back. How about you?"

"Oh, me? I'm just here for the weekend—needed a break from studying."

"Law, isn't it?" Thornton said.

"Right. My final year, thank God."

"Well, that's a good profession. You can do about anything with a law degree."

The bartender leaned over and set a drink down next to Paula. She picked it up and held the glass out to Thornton. He picked up a glass and said, "Cheers."

"Cheers," Paula said, taking a drink.

One of Morales' men looked over at Paula disapprovingly. She met his gaze and smiled at him. He turned away.

"Are you hungry?" Thornton asked.

"Not yet. Why don't we take a stroll on the beach?" Paula suggested.

Thornton frowned. "The beach?"

"Yeah. Let's kick off our shoes and take a stroll along the water. It's beautiful out, and we'll be all alone."

Thornton shrugged. "Well, okay. I'm not really dressed for the beach."

"Oh, don't worry. We'll just take off our shoes, and you can roll up your pants. Plus, it's dark out there. We can—"

"Oh, right," Thornton said. "That's a great idea."

They finished their drinks and slipped out the back door to the terrace. Paula suggested Thornton take off his shoes and leave them there so he could find them later. He nodded and pulled them off awkwardly. Then Paula took his arm and they walked down the steps to the beach.

Halfway to the water, Paula glanced back and saw one of Morales' men come out the back door onto the terrace. He watched them a moment and then decided to follow them.

"Brad," Paula said.

"Yeah?"

"Listen carefully and don't say anything. Morales' goons are watching us."

Brad's eyes narrowed as he looked at her in surprise. "I know you're not down here because you want to be. Your wife sent us down to rescue you."

"Rescue me? Why?"

"Because your life's in danger. Morales is going to

kill you."

"Who told you that?"

"Think about it. Your money laundering days are over. You are of no use to the Burilo cartel anymore. Your being alive is a major risk to them. It's only a matter of time before they kill you." Paula glanced at the man watching them twenty yards down the beach. "Kiss me."

"Huh?"

"Kiss me, or your friend watching us will get suspicious."

Brad gave the man an annoyed look and then grabbed Paula's neck and pulled her to him. They kissed passionately for a long minute. The man turned around and walked slowly back toward the hotel.

Paula broke away. "Stan Turner is out there with an extraction team just beyond the breakers. They're in a raft to take you out to a seaplane. It's your only chance. If you stay here, you're a dead man."

Brad looked nervously out to sea. "He's out there right now?" he asked skeptically. "Why would he want to help me?"

"Your wife begged him to rescue you. They've already tried to kill him, so he's got to help the FBI take down the Cartel to save his own skin. The prosecutors need your testimony to take down Carlos Morales. They'll be lenient with you and Melissa if you cooperate."

"Okay, what do I have to do?"

"Kiss me again."

Brad looked back toward the hotel. The man was still watching them. They kissed once more, longer and harder.

"Take off your clothes. You can't swim in your clothes."

"What?"

"Take them off now. We're running out of time. Give me the key to your room. You won't be needing it."

They kissed again and started removing their clothing, one piece at a time. The man watching them smiled and started walking up the stairway to the hotel. He stopped on the terrace and looked back again. They were waist deep in the water, falling all over each other.

"Okay, Brad. Just swim past the waves, and Stan should be there."

"Are you sure?" he said fearfully.

"Yes. Go."

"Alright. Thanks, Paula. Are you going to be okay?"

"Yes, I'll be fine. Just get going."

Brad started swimming out to sea. Paula watched him until he disappeared into the darkness. Suddenly, she felt hands wrap around her waist and squeeze her breasts.

"Hey, watch that!" she said as Harry pulled her to him.

"Where were you? I didn't see you."

"I've been watching your little performance. You should be on Broadway."

"Oh, yeah. Actually, I wasn't acting. Brad's quite a hunk. I kind of enjoyed kissing him."

"Well, I'm not worried. He's got a date with a federal judge. He'll be in Club Fed for a long time."

"Come on. We better make our escape while we got the chance."

Harry and Paula noisily left the water, stopping from time to time to kiss and fondle each other like lovers do. When they reached the shore, they ran back through the cover of the sand dunes to their room. Hastily, they got dressed and made their escape in the rental car they'd procured at San Diego's Lindbergh

Field.

When Morales' man saw them running away, he went into the bar and told his comrades what had happened. They talked it over for a while and decided to go check the room to be sure Thornton was still there.

In the room, Paula had left a tape running she'd made of Harry and her having sex. Harry didn't make much noise when they made love, so Paula didn't think Morales men would realize it wasn't Thornton in the room. When they got to the door to Thornton's room, they heard Paula moaning and her frequent gasps of sexual bliss. They listened for a moment and then went back to the bar with smiles on their faces.

Harry and Paula drove all night until they reached Tijuana and crossed the border. They didn't want to be in Mexico when Carlos Morales discovered Brad Thornton had disappeared right under their noses. They breathed a sigh of relief when they reached the Airport Holiday Inn where they had reservations for the night. After they checked in and got settled in their room, Harry poured them a drink and sat next to Paula on the bed.

"I wonder if Stan was out there with the boat?" Paula asked.

"I'm sure he must have been. I didn't hear Thornton screaming or anything."

"I doubt you could have heard him over the pounding surf."

"Oh, God. What if they find Thornton dead on the beach tomorrow?"

"Oh, I'm sure he's fine," Harry assured her.

"Oh, God. I hope you're right."

Harry put his free hand around Paula and squeezed her. She looked at him and sighed. "What if something happened to Stan?" Paula suddenly blurted out. “What if they both die?”

Harry shook his head and then got up and poured them another drink. “I can see the only way you’re going to sleep tonight is if I get you drunk.”

Paula laughed and took the glass. “You’re right about that,” she agreed. “Just keep ‘em coming.”

Chapter 20

Stan looked on in horror as the fishing boat headed straight at them. They began rowing furiously but the ship hit them in the stern and Stan heard a loud thud as Paul's head hit the hull of the ship. The raft flipped over and Stan was thrown into the ocean. Stan had on his life vest, so he didn't sink very far before he came bobbing out of the cold water. Much to his distress, however, the raft had drifted fifty yards away and was being quickly washed toward the shore. He looked frantically for Paul but couldn't see him in the darkness. Finally, he gave up and focused on his own survival.

Stan knew he'd never be able to catch up with the raft in his life vest. It would cut his speed in half. In his youth as a Boy Scout, he had to swim a mile in order to earn a merit badge. He wondered now, ten years later, if he could still do it. The raft was drifting farther away, so he finally ditched the life vest and shoes and began swimming as fast as he could toward it.

When he was about halfway to the raft, he felt his energy faltering and wondered if he was going to make it. He stopped a second, flipped over on his back, and floated awhile until he caught his breath. Seeing the raft continuing to drift, he started swimming again until he finally grabbed the side of it and pulled himself aboard. He was relieved to be out of the water but soon began to shiver as the wind blew through his wet clothes.

He searched again for Paul, but couldn't find him. He figured his life jacket would keep his head afloat even if he were unconscious, but he could only see twenty-five feet or so ahead, so searching for him would have been a futile effort.

As his mind cleared from the trauma of the collision, he looked toward the shore at the Rosarita Beach Hotel, which looked much closer now. He realized if he began rowing, it would probably warm him up, so he got in the proper position, fumbled with the oars, and began rowing once more. Soon, he sensed he was near the rendezvous spot and began calling, "Brad! Where are you? . . . Brad, do you hear me? . . . Brad!"

A wave caught the raft and pushed it toward the shore. Stan looked around but could see very little in the darkness. Then he heard a splash behind him.

"Over here!" a voice yelled.

Stan pulled out a flashlight, but when he turned it on, nothing happened. "Brad! Where are you?"

"Over here!" Brad said.

Stan began to row the raft in the direction of the voice. There was another splash, and Stan saw a hand waving at him.

"Okay. I'm coming. Hang on."

Stan rowed over to where Brad was treading water and stretched out his hand. Brad grabbed the side of the raft and pulled himself up next to it.

"Thank God. Where have you been?" Brad gasped. "Are you alone? I thought you had a team."

"I did, but we got run over by a fishing boat coming into to get you. You're lucky I was able to catch the raft before it got away."

"Yeah. I was about to swim back to the shore."

"Sorry," Stan replied. "We need to look for Paul on the way back. He was wearing a lift jacket so hopefully he hasn't drowned."

"Sure."

Stan helped Brad aboard and they began rowing back in the general direction of the plane.

"I can't believe you came down here to rescue me. This is crazy."

"I know. Your wife is very persuasive."

"So, the feds are waiting for me when I get back?" Brad asked.

"I'm afraid so, but there may be a way out for you," Stan said.

"How's that?"

"The feds want Carlos Morales and the Burilo cartel. If you help them bring them down, they may cut you a pretty nice deal."

"Yeah? That's what Paula said. Is she FBI?"

"No. She's a friend of mine from SMU. She's been helping me clear Rob's name."

"How's that going?"

"Mission accomplished. The medical examiner has changed his findings and cleared Rob's name."

"Good. Rob was a good kid. He didn't know anything about what was going on."

Stan looked into the darkness, checking for any sign of Paul.

"I can't see behind me, so keep a lookout for a blinking light. That will be our ride."

"Okay," Brad said, looking off into the darkness.

Stan rowed for a long time and began to tire when Brad finally said. "There it is!"

Stan turned and saw the dim blinking light in the distance. "Thank God!" he said, altering his course slightly in order to reach the plane. Rowing frantically, they finally reached the plane, and Brad tied a line to the pontoon. As they were climbing aboard, the door to the cockpit opened, and Phil stuck out his head.

"You made it. Where's Paul."

Stan explained what had happened.

"Shit! Get aboard. I'll get us airborne and we can search for him."

When Brad was safely aboard, Stan set the raft adrift and climbed into the cockpit. "Okay, we're set."

Phil nodded and started the engine. Turning the plane to face the wind, he pushed the throttle forward, and the plane started to pick up speed until it was airborne. Phil circled around and came in low so they could see the surface of the water.

They searched for a half hour without seeing anything but choppy water.

"Damn it. I'm getting low on fuel. We can't search much longer."

Stan's stomach twisted another notch as a wave of guilt washed over him. He didn't know if he could live with himself if Paul died because he hadn't been able to find him. He wondered if he should have just forgotten about Brad and kept searching for Paul.

"I'll call search and rescue," Phil finally said. "If we don't head back now they'll be searching for all of us."

"Oh, Jesus!" Stan said. "The fishing boat came out of nowhere."

"Maybe they felt the collision and stopped to see what they hit," Brad conjectured.

"That's a possibility Phil said. They may have rescued him. He might be aboard the fishing boat."

Stan felt a little better, but not much. "I hope Paula and Professor Hertel are okay."

"They seemed to know what they were doing," Brad said. "Boy, does that girl know how to kiss."

In the distance, Stan could see the lights of Tijuana. He couldn't wait to be back in the United

States. Finally, the Cessna banked to the right, and he knew they'd soon be back to Lake Cuyamaca. When they reached the lake, a string of lights illuminated the Cessna's landing lane. Ruben brought the plane in and set it down in the water with hardly a ripple.

As the plane taxied over to the dock, Stan saw Agent Rutledge and a tall, dark-haired man in a suit waiting for them. Stan gave them a thumbs up. When the plane stopped, Stan stepped out of the plane first and looked back as Brad Thornton carefully stepped out. The dark-haired man rushed up to Thornton and flashed a badge.

"Robert Thornton, I'm Special Agent Vincent Ross of the FBI. You are under arrest." Ross put one hand on Thornton's shoulder and adroitly spun him around and cuffed him.

Stan frowned. "Is that necessary?" he complained.

Before Agent Ross could respond, there was a flash of light, the sound of a gunshot, followed by a dull thud. Stan looked out into the darkness in the direction of the flash of light and then back at Thornton. Blood began to spread in a rough, dark circle over Thornton's left breast. Agent Rutledge slammed into Stan, knocking him to the ground, and Agent Ross tackled Thornton. There was a second flash, the sound of a gunshot, and a splash in the water behind them. Stan looked up into the darkness, realizing someone had just tried to kill them.

"Stay down!" Agent Rutledge screamed, pulling out her gun and taking cover behind a thick post.

Stan crawled over to Thornton and cradled his head in his hands. "Brad! Can you hear me?" Stan yelled, pulling off his t-shirt and pressing it against the gushing wound. Brad's eyes glazed over and then closed. Stan felt his pulse; it was very weak. "We need a doctor!" he yelled.

“There’s a doctor in town,” Ruben advised. “I’ll go call him.”

Phil ran across the dock, down the dirt road to the bait shop, and went inside. Agent Ross took off in the direction of the shooter while Agent Rutledge stood guard over Thornton and Stan.

“Did you tell anyone we were picking you up here?” Agent Rutledge asked angrily.

“No,” Stan replied irritably. “I didn’t know about this place until yesterday when they flew me up here.”

“What about Horizon Charters? Did you tell anyone you were chartering from them?”

“Only Melissa since she was paying for the operation.”

Agent Rutledge shook her head irritably. “How about Paula or the professor?”

“They were in Mexico. I’m sure they didn’t tell anyone.”

“They may have told someone over the telephone.”

“No. They knew secrecy was important.”

Stan looked up as he heard the sound of a car coming quickly down the dirt road. A beat-up Chevy Malibu skidded to a stop near the dock. An elderly man got out and rushed over, carrying a medical bag.

“What happened?” he asked.

“He’s been shot,” Agent Rutledge replied. “He’s lost a lot of blood.

The doctor felt his pulse, looked at the wound, and sighed. “There’s a medivac helicopter on the way, but I don’t think it will get here in time. He’s barely hanging on.”

Stan stood up and walked a few steps away. He noticed Agent Ross returning from the hill where the sniper had taken his shot.

"He got away. I found two shell casings and some tire tracks, but that's about it."

"I can't believe this," Stan said tears welling in his eyes. "Paul's probably dead and now Brad may die."

Agent Ross shrugged. "The cartel must have discovered him missing."

"But how could they set up a hit so fast? It's only been a few hours," Stan said angrily.

"I don't know. Maybe they have a mole at Horizon Charters and put two and two together. An organization like the Burilo cartel probably has members sitting around waiting for sensitive assignments like this one."

The doctor felt Thornton's pulse again and then began pushing hard on his chest. In the distance, the sound of a helicopter floated over the trees. A moment later, it appeared overhead and set down on the road between the dock and the bait shop. Two medics came out, rushed over, and began taking vitals. A third medic brought out a rolling stretcher and rushed it over to where they were working on Thornton. A few seconds later, they loaded him aboard and rushed to the helicopter.

"Where are you taking him?" Agent Rutledge asked.

"Sharp Memorial," the medic replied.

Agent Rutledge nodded as the helicopter took off and disappeared into the darkness.

"Come on, Stan," Agent Rutledge said, seeing Stan wrapping his arms around himself to keep warm, "I think I've got an extra shirt in the car."

Stan followed her to their car and watched her as she rummaged through the trunk. After a few seconds, she pulled out and FBI T-shirt and handed it to him.

"Thanks," Stan said. "I can't believe we went through all this for nothing."

“Maybe Thornton will make it.”

“The doctor doesn’t’ think he will.”

“Let’s just wait and see. We should get you to your hotel. I bet you could use a hot shower and a good night’s sleep.”

“Aren’t you going to the hospital?” Stan asked.

“Yes, right after I drop you off at your hotel.”

“I’ll come with you.”

“No. You need your rest after the ordeal you’ve been through, and you have a flight bright and early tomorrow morning.”

“Okay. I should call my wife, too, and tell her I’m still alive.”

Agent Rutledge laughed. “I pity your wife having to put up with your escapades.”

“What about your husband? He must love waiting up for you at night, wondering if you’ll come home in one piece.”

“I’m not married. I wouldn’t put a man through that.”

“Good for you. Unfortunately, I didn’t plan the way my life has turned out. It just kind of fell into place.”

Agent Rutledge smiled ruefully and handed Stan her cell phone. “Call her now. No need to make her suffer any longer than necessary.”

“Oh, thanks,” Stan said, taking the phone and stepping a few yards away for privacy. He dialed the number and waited. “Hello. It’s me.”

“Oh, thank God! I was so worried.”

“Piece a cake,” he lied.

“Yeah, I bet.”

“Unfortunately, a sniper just shot Brad and my boatman is missing. They’re taking Brad by helicopter to your old hospital.”

"Sharp?"

"I think that's what I heard them say, Sharp Memorial."

"Maybe I'll call my friend Cecilia and see how he's doing."

"Yeah, do that, and I'll call you from my motel in about an hour."

"Alright. I'm so glad you're okay."

"Me too. I'll talk to you later."

Agent Rutledge watched Stan curiously as he talked to Rebekah. She had never known someone so dauntless. She envied his wonderful family and wondered if he knew how lucky he was to have them. She feared he didn't and one day would lose them.

Stan hit the end button, walked over to Agent Rutledge, and handed her the phone back. "Thanks," he said.

"You're welcome. Let's get you to your hotel."

Stan yawned. "Good idea."

It was almost an hour drive back to the hotel, and Stan dozed off several times on the way. When they left him off at the motel, instead of going to his room, he went across the street to the diner to eat some dinner since he hadn't eaten anything since breakfast. The nightly special was Philadelphia cheese steak, so he ordered that and iced tea. While he was eating, all he could think about was Brad Thornton and his missing boatman. He just couldn't understand how the killer could have known he was going to be landing on Lake Cuyamaca. He finally figured it just had to be bad luck. When the men babysitting Thornton realized what had happened, they guessed he'd been taken out by seaplane, and Lake Cuyamaca was the likely place to land.

After dinner, Stan went to his room, called the front desk for a wake-up call, and then called Rebekah to see if she had an update on Thornton's condition. "So, what did you find out from Celia?" he asked.

"He died, Stan. He was dead when he arrived at the hospital."

"Damn it! I suppose I should call Melissa."

"Let the FBI do it."

"No. I was supposed to call and give her a report on the mission anyway, so she's waiting by the telephone."

"You want me to call her?" Rebekah asked.

"No. I need to explain some things to her."

"Alright. I'll see you in the morning. I love you."

"I love you, too. Bye," Stan said and hung up the telephone.

Stan found his wallet and located Melissa's home telephone number. She had been released on her own recognizance due to the deal she'd made with the US Attorney.

"Stan, how did it go?"

"The mission went well. We got Brad out of Mexico, but—"

"But what?"

Stan sighed. "There was someone waiting for us when we landed the plane."

Stan explained to her what had happened and how horrible he felt that Brad had been murdered. She was sobbing when he finished, struggling to keep her composure.

"I'm sorry. It's just that I was expecting good news. I was sure you'd get him out safely."

"I don't know how the cartel found out where we were taking him. They must have had an assassin in the San Diego area that they called the moment they discovered Brad was gone."

"They do have many contacts in that area. A lot

of their drug trafficking takes place along the border between Mexico and California."

"I guess we made the mistake of thinking he'd be safe once we got him back into the United States. I'm so sorry. I thought with the FBI there, everything would be okay."

"No. It was my fault. I know this isn't your line of business. I was foolish to force it on you. I'm just glad you didn't get hurt. You were an angel for going through with my stupid plan."

"Well, no one can blame you for trying. We almost got him home safely. Had you done nothing, he'd have died anyway. We all did what we could for Brad."

"I'll let you go. I know you must be very tired."

"Exhausted, actually," Stan admitted.

"Thank you, Stan. You're a good man."

"Well, you were a good wife. Not many women would have had the resourcefulness and determination to organize a rescue party to save a husband held by thugs in a foreign country."

"Oh, I don't know. The FBI made all the arrangements. I just spent every last dime I had funding it. Anyway, have a good night's sleep."

Stan hung up the telephone, turned out the light, and then went to bed. He slept soundly, his exhaustion trumping all the myriad of emotions he'd experienced over the last twenty-four hours. When he awoke at first light, it all seemed like it had been a dream until he realized he was in a motel room, then the reality of it came crashing down upon him. He wondered if Paula and Professor Hertel were okay. He looked at the clock and tried to think. They should be at their hotel by now if everything had gone as planned. He called the hotel and asked for Paula Waters' room.

"We have no one at the hotel under that name,"

a man advised.

"Oh? Hmm. Try Harry Hertel."

"Harry...Harry...oh, yes. I'll connect you."

"Hello," Paula said.

"Oh, thank God!" Stan exclaimed. "You're okay."

"Yes, and since you're calling, you must be too."

"Not entirely. Did you hear about Brad?"

"No. What happened?"

Stan explained what had happened after they'd landed the sea plane.

"Oh, no. Damn it! I can't believe the FBI let that happen."

"We can't blame it on them. We all underestimated the Burilo cartel. In retrospect, we should have thought more about what dangers there would be after we rescued him. We should never have landed at the same place we took off. That just made it too easy for them."

"Oh, it was my fault too. I encouraged you too much without thinking of the possible consequences of what we were undertaking. I was just so got caught up in the excitement of it all, and I didn't think it through."

"Well, we'll know better for our next covert operation."

"Huh? You know something I don't know?" Paula questioned.

"No. . . . Just kidding."

"Good. We should probably just concentrate on graduating from law school."

"Probably," Stan agreed.

"Well, I'll see you Monday in class."

"Alright. See you then."

Stan hung up the phone, called Rebekah and the kids, and then left for the airport. His flight was uneventful, and early in the afternoon, he arrived at

Dallas Love Field. He'd left his car there, so he drove straight home. As he drove, he started to think about how Thornton's death would affect Carlos Morales and the investors in Silver Springs Ventures. He hoped Carlos Morales wouldn't be off the hook now with Thornton out of the way because Stan considered him responsible for the murder of the Shepard family, as well as Brad Thornton. But he wondered about Commissioner Barnes and the other names he'd seen on the investor list. Would the FBI still indict them? Thinking back to his conversation with Rob, he could understand how they'd gotten hooked into the scheme. He almost felt sorry for them, because he knew if criminal indictments came out on them, their lives would quickly crumble.

Chapter 21

It was one week before the November elections, and Stan had just picked up Kristina to take her to a candidate forum sponsored by the Richardson Chamber of Commerce. It wasn't a full fledged debate, but after each candidate had spoken, they did have an opportunity to ask their opponents a few questions. Kristina was nervous about this aspect of the event and asked Stan about it.

"So, what do you think Wells will ask me?" Kristina asked.

"I don't know. Do you have any skeletons in your closet?"

"No. I don't think so."

"Then your tender age and lack of experience would be my guess."

"Well, I hope you're right. I've answered that question a hundred times already."

"What are you going to ask him?" Stan inquired.

"Oh, I've got three good ones."

"Really? What are they?"

"I did some research and discovered he always manages to show up for a vote one of his lobbyist friends is behind but only half the time on other legislation."

"That is a good one. What else?"

"Did you know he took eleven trips out of the country at taxpayer expense?"

"Really? That's a bit odd for a state representative, but I'm sure he'll come up with a good reason for each trip."

"Good. I want to hear him try to explain it. The voters need to know this kind of stuff."

"And your final question?"

"I'm not quite sure yet. I've got a couple possibilities."

"Forget them. I've got one for you."

"Really? What is it?"

"Ask him what he's going to do if the government indicts everyone on the Silver Springs Ventures investor list."

Kristina frowned, and then her eyes lit up. "You dog! His name is on the list. That's your dirt on him?"

"Yes. What do you think?"

"Oh, my God! What do I think? I may win this election."

"That's what I've been telling you. Now he'll probably try to ignore the question or say something irrelevant."

"Okay. Should I have a follow-up question?" Kristina asked.

"No. Don't say anything else. The reporters will ask you why you asked the question later. You can respond by simply saying you have been told by informed sources that Representative Wells will be extremely tied up, so to speak, if everyone on the list is indicted.

Kristina laughed. "You're wicked."

"No, I just think the public has a right to know his name is on the list. What it means he'll have to explain to them. Maybe he is just an innocent victim, who knows, but the voters can consider that possibility on election day."

When they arrived at Plano Senior High where the event was being held, a good sized crowd had already gathered. This was one of only a few opportunities for the voters to see all the candidates together and ask questions, so it always drew well. Stan went with Kristina to where the candidates had gathered, wished her good luck, and went into the main auditorium. Spotting Don Karnes, Stan went over to him.

"This should be interesting," Stan observed.

"Hey, Stan. How you feeling? Have you recovered from your trip to Mexico?"

Stan sighed. "I think so. How's Melissa holding up?"

"Oh, she's a tough woman. She'll move on."

"Yeah. I guess that's about all you can do."

"What did the FBI say to her after Brad's murder?"

"Oh, they still expect her to testify against the other investors."

"So, they're still going through with the indictments?"

"Uh huh. Apparently."

"Did they find that mercenary that got hit by the fishing boat?"

"Yeah. Two days later he showed up in a Mexican hospital. I guess he was knocked unconscious but his life jacket kept him from drowning. When he woke up he was able to swim to shore. Someone found him on the beach and took him to the hospital."

"Wow. That will be something to tell the grand kids about. . . Do the feds have any leads on Morales?"

"I don't know. I've been focusing on politics. I haven't' talked the FBI lately."

"So, is there any hope for Kristina?"

Stan nodded. "Yes, after this forum is over, things are going to heat up in the state representative race."

"Oh, really? Kristina's still five points down in the last poll that was out."

"Right. Like I said, things are going to change. I'm going to need you to talk to your friends at the paper and make sure they don't let Ron Wells weasel out of what's coming down on him today."

"What do you know that I don't?"

"You'll find out soon enough. I don't want to spoil the surprise."

Don just stared at Stan as he moved on to someone else he'd spotted in the audience—his law school buddy Lamar Jones.

"Hey, you made it," Stan said.

"Yeah, well, you said this event would enhance my political education, so how could I miss it?"

"You're a smart man. Today you're going to see how to supercharge a hopeless campaign."

"Okay. You're definitely going to need that since I see your lady is way behind in the polls."

"Come on. Let's go find a seat. The show's about to begin."

Stan and Lamar found a spot and sat down. The moderator, Martin Vince, opened the meeting and thanked everyone for attending. There were eleven different races with state representative being near the end. Stan and Lamar listened impatiently for over an hour before the moderator finally announced that the next speakers would be Kristina Tenison and Ron Wells. After he'd introduced them, they both gave brief statements about themselves and then took questions from the audience. When the last question had been answered, the moderator asked each candidate to ask their questions.

"Representative Wells, what is your first question for your challenger?"

"Thank you, Martin. Well, Ms. Tenison, do you plan to recklessly attack the leadership of the state legislature for the obvious influence lobbyists have on them as you claim they have on me? I'm not the only legislator who spends time with lobbyists."

Martin turned to Kristina.

"Yes, if you take out the word recklessly, then that's exactly what I plan to do. Anyone who is taking orders from anyone other than their constituents is fair game."

Martin raised his eyebrows. "Okay, Kristina. It's your turn."

"Representative Wells, since we're talking about lobbyist, I did some research and discovered you always manage to show up for a vote that's important to one of your lobbyist friends, but on the basic legislative agenda, you miss nearly half the votes that come up. How can you say you're a good representative of the people here in the 67th District when you don't even bother to vote half the time?"

Martin stifled a laugh. "Representative Wells, how do you respond to that?"

Martin scowled at Kristina. "Well, here again, Ms. Tenison's lack of experience is showing. Anybody who knows anything about the legislative process knows that most of the votes that take place are procedural or votes on amendments to bills. A legislator is so busy he can't be bothered with many of these insignificant votes. If my vote will make a difference in anything that comes to the floor of the House, my staff notifies me, and I show up immediately."

"Alright, Mr. Wells. Do you have a second question for Ms. Tenison?"

"Yes, I do. Since she just got in the campaign, I would like to know who she supported in the primary—Ford or Reagan?"

"Ms. Tenison?" Martin said.

"I like them both, actually, and since, at the time of the primary, I was working for the County Chairman, I made it a point not to support either one. Today, of course, I stand firmly behind the President."

Stan smiled at the answer. She'd answered the question without revealing her true political position, thereby not alienating any of the Ford or Reagan supporters.

"Alright, Ms. Tenison. do you have another question for the incumbent?"

"Yes. How do you justify taking eleven trips out of the country at taxpayer expense when your job doesn't involve anything going on outside the state of Texas?"

Mr. Martin bowed slightly. "How do you respond to that one, Mr. Wells?"

"That's simple, and if Ms. Tenison were not so inexperienced, she'd know that the state of Texas does much business abroad and our relationship with foreign governments and foreign corporations is very important."

"What business were you attending to when you took your two sons on a two-week safari to Africa and spent six days gambling in Monte Carlo?"

The audience laughed.

"I'm sorry, Ms. Tenison. Under the rules, you can't ask follow-up questions."

"I'm sure Mr. Wells is grateful for that rule," Kristina retorted.

The audience laughed again. Wells turned red but kept his mouth shut. Lamar looked at Stan and smiled.

"Alright, Representative Wells, do you have a final question for the challenger?"

"Well, I must set the record straight. I paid for the safari as well as the R&R in Monte Carlo. Since we were traveling in those areas anyway, we decided to take a few extra days, and it didn't cost the taxpayers a dime."

"Okay, Ms. Tenison. What is your response to that?"

"Well, I'd beg to differ about it not costing the taxpayers a dime. I believe on these junkets Representative Wells travels with a secretary and two other staff members. I'm sure the record will show he paid for the safari and gambling, but who was paying the hotel bills for this staff?—and I doubt they were staying at Motel Six."

The audience laughed again, and Wells shifted in his seat.

"Ms. Tenison," Martin said, "your final question, please."

"I was curious as to what he's going to do if the government indicts everyone on the Silver Springs Ventures investor list."

Martin frowned and then looked at Wells expectantly. Wells' mouth opened and then closed. He looked around, seemingly confused. Finally, he said, "I have no idea what you're talking about."

Martin looked back at Kristina for clarification, but she just smiled at him. "Okay, ladies and gentlemen, that's it for the state representative race. Thank you, Representative Wells and Ms. Tenison. That was very interesting."

Wells and Kristina left the stage. Stan motioned to Lamar that they should leave. When they caught up with Kristina, she was talking to two journalists.

"All I know is I've been informed that Representative Wells will be quite distracted when the indictments come down. I was hoping he would clarify why those indictments would have any impact on him,"

Kristina said.

"Are you saying he's going to be indicted?" one of the reporters asked.

"No. I'm not saying anything. I'm as much in the dark as you. You should check with your sources and find out how the indictments will affect him. I don't know for sure. I'm just telling you what a very reliable source has told me."

"Can you identify the source?" the second reporter asked.

Kristina looked at Stan and smiled. "Oh, no. Of course not. If I revealed my sources, they'd quit giving me juicy information."

"But—"

"That's all. I've got to get home. Thank you."

Kristina walked off, and Stan and Lamar joined her, motioning for the journalist to back off. When they were alone, Stan congratulated her.

"That was perfect."

"You think?" Kristina asked.

"You were awesome, Ms. Tenison," Lamar agreed.

"Oh, Kristina. Have you met Lamar Jones? He's a friend from law school. He wants to be a politician, so I suggested he come today to get a lesson in political maneuvering."

"Oh, nice to meet you, Lamar. Well, Stan's the pro. I'm just doing what he tells me."

"I don't know," Lamar said admiringly. "You seemed to be a tiger up there. It didn't sound scripted."

"Well, the last question was."

"I have no idea what the last question was all about," Lamar confessed. "I guess I'll understand as the week plays out. What I loved were your questions and how you managed to get him on the defensive. It was a knockout in my book."

"Yes, it was," Stan said. "Unfortunately, there are not enough voters here to do much good. That is why we had to resort to pointing out that our dear state representative is on the verge of being indicted for money laundering."

"Oh, really?"

"I'm not sure he'll be indicted, but his name was definitely on the list, and the people have a right to know about it before election day."

"I agree," Lamar said. "The voters definitely have a right to know all the facts. So, how about I buy you both a drink?"

"Oh, that sounds great," Stan replied, "but I've got to get back to the family. I promised them I'd take them to dinner and a movie. Have you seen Rocky yet?"

"No. I heard it was good though," Lamar said.

"Yeah, me too. You guys go ahead."

Kristina looked at Lamar and smiled. "This is a dry area, but I've got a membership at Friday's. We can go there."

"Fine. I'll buy you dinner too."

"Oh, that sounds good," Kristina said excitedly.

Stan shook Lamar's hand, gave Kristina a hug, and then headed for the exit. On the way, he was accosted by the two journalists who'd interviewed Kristina.

"Mr. Turner, I was wondering if you know what Ms. Tenison was getting at in her last question to Representative Wells."

"Did you ask Wells?" Stan asked.

"He left immediately after the program and wouldn't answer any questions."

"Well, I'd keep pressing him for a response, or you could go to the US Attorney's office. They're handling the investigation into Silver Spring Ventures' involvement in the Burilo drug cartel. I was told a number of indictments would be coming down soon. They should be able to give you more specific information."

"So, you're saying Ron Wells is going to be indicted."

"I didn't say that at all. Grand jury deliberations are private. I have no knowledge as to who they indicted, if anybody."

"Alright. Thanks a lot, Mr. Turner," the reporter said sarcastically.

When Stan got home, Rebekah and the kids were all ready to go out to dinner, so when he pulled into the driveway, the door opened and they all came running out. Stan got out and helped them get seated, then Rebekah handed Marcia to him, and he put her in the car seat. On the way to Cici's Pizza Stan filled Rebekah in on Kristina's confrontation with Ron Wells and her interview with the reporters afterward.

"So, you think that will be enough to win?"

"I don't know. It depends on how the media spins it. It would help if the grand jury indicted him, but the government works very slowly."

"So, Kristina went out with Lamar, huh?"

"Yeah. They seemed to hit if off very well. Lamar would be a good catch for Kristina."

"Lamar wants to be a politician. He may not be willing to support Kristina."

"That's true. He could just be intrigued by her charisma—trying to figure out why people react positively to her."

"I could tell him that," Rebekah said. "She's honest and straightforward, a real genuine human being with strong moral fiber, and she's very passionate. It doesn't hurt that she's funny too."

"Wow! I didn't know you were such a fan."

"I like her a lot. I'd like her even more if she didn't have such an obvious crush on you."

"Huh?" Stan said, feigning ignorance.

"You know she does. Tell me you don't flirt with her."

"I wouldn't call it flirting, per se. We just kid around."

"Uh huh. Well, I'm sure she thinks you're flirting. You need to be more businesslike. You're her campaign manager and that's it."

"She knows that."

"I bet a lot of people think she's your girlfriend the way you two act."

"No. That's not true."

Fortunately for Stan, they arrived at Cici's Pizza, and the place was so hectic, there was no way to continue the conversation. The ride to the movie theater was so short the matter didn't come up again, and by the time Rocky was over, the topic of Kristina was forgotten—or at least Stan hoped that was the case.

When they got home, Rebekah took the kids upstairs to get them ready for bed, and Stan turned on the TV. The lead story on the ten o'clock news was Ron Wells' connection to the Burilo drug cartel.

"We're taking you live to Veronica Brooks, who is at the home of State Representative Ron Wells," the newscaster said.

"Veronica Brooks here at the home of State Representative Ron Wells, where we're waiting for a statement confirming or denying that he was a partner in the Silver Springs Ventures currently under investigation by the FBI and the United States Attorney's office.

"The possibility that the state representative was involved in this questionable venture first surfaced in a candidates' night sponsored by the Richardson Chamber of Commerce. Since then, the media has been frantically searching for answers.

"In a related matter, I've been advised that a story will appear tomorrow in the Austin American Statesman analyzing another allegation from Kristina Tenison concerning Wells' frequent travel out of the country at public expense. The story reported will confirm what she said today and expose even more abuses.

"Okay. . . . I'm told Ron Wells will be out in a minute to make a brief statement." In the background, the front door opened and Ron Wells stepped out.

"Ladies and gentlemen," he said, "questions have come out today about my investment in the Silver Springs Ventures. It is true that I am a partner in that investment, however, I do not manage my finances and can say with a clear conscience that I wasn't even aware of the investment until Commissioner Barnes resigned from the race. His resignation prompted my staff to review my investment portfolio for anything questionable. When I was advised of the investment, I immediately told my staff to divest me of it, however, due to the FBI investigation, it couldn't be done at that time. That's all there is to it and all I have to say about it at this time."

"Will you be withdrawing your bid for re-election?" a reporter asked.

"No—absolutely not. Like I said, I knew nothing about the investment, so it shouldn't be a factor in the race. Thank you."

Wells turned and went back into the house amidst a barrage of questions from reporters.

"So, there you have it," Veronica said. "Representative Ron Wells has confirmed he is an investor in the notorious Silver Springs Ventures currently under investigation by the FBI. If you will recall just a few days after the FBI launched its investigation into the venture one of its investors, Rob Shepard, and his family were murdered. Since then, the founder of the venture, Brad Thornton, has also been murdered. Finally, the abduction and attempted murder of Stan Turner and Melissa Thornton are also connected to this suspected money laundering operation. This is Veronica Brooks for NBC Channel 5 News."

Stan turned off the TV, a little concerned. Everything had gone as planned, but Wells' profession of innocence bothered him. Would the voters buy into his claim he knew nothing about the investment? The more he thought about it, the more worried he became.

Chapter 22

That night a dream about Brad Thornton's murder woke Stan up with a start. It frustrated him that Carlos Morales seemed to be untouchable, off in Mexico where the feds had no jurisdiction. He thought about it as he drifted in and out of sleep until he had an epiphany. Suddenly, he realized how he could find Carlos Morales and turn him over to the FBI. The thought of bringing down Morales made Stan so excited he didn't sleep a wink the rest of the night. He couldn't wait for daybreak to come so he could set his plan in motion.

What he realized was that the Silver Springs Ventures was but one of many of the Burilo Cartel's money laundering operations. This meant that Carlos Morales was sure to be visiting the United States on a regular basis to monitor the cartel's various operations. If that were true, all he'd have to do is identify one or more of the other operations and then wait for Morales to appear. He thought that would be a good project for his criminal law class.

The next morning, Stan went to see Greg Wolford to gather information for his quest. He didn't have any money left to hire Wolford to do more work, but he figured he owed him what information he'd already gathered. Wolford seemed surprised to see him.

"Why are you still interested in the Burilo cartel?

I thought your investigation was over."

"I don't like people committing murder with impunity. He had Rob and his family killed, then Brad. Who's going to be next? Carlos Morales needs to be stopped."

"Why don't you let the FBI do it?"

"I'm not stopping them from doing anything. I just have an idea of how I might help them."

"Do they know about this?"

"No. They probably don't want to know. They'd have to tell me not to do it even though secretly they'd love any help they can get. You see, I don't have to follow their strict rules. I can do things that they couldn't dream of doing for fear of tainting the evidence or entrapment. "

"Hmm. I doubt Morales will be doing much traveling in the US with the FBI looking for him. I'm sure they have alerted the Border Patrol to be on the lookout for him."

"Oh, he doesn't cross through any legal ports of entry. I'm sure he crosses in the night at one of the cartel's entry points they use to bring in their drugs, illegal immigrants, and cash that needs laundering."

"Perhaps, but aren't you worried that if Morales finds out you're looking for him, he'll kill you and your family?"

"He's not going to find out I'm looking for him. Don't mention to anyone that I came by today, okay? This is going to be a low-key, off-the-radar investigation. I only told you about it because I know I can trust you and I need whatever intel you have on the cartel."

"Alright. What do you want to know?"

"First of all. I need a photo of Morales so that I'll recognize him if I find him."

"No problem. I've got that."

"I also need any information you have on the cartel's business organizations. I've got a lot of information already, but I'm sure you've got more."

"You can look through the file and make copies of what you need."

"Good. Finally, I need to know where Morales has stayed in the US in the past. People are creatures of habit, so I might accidently find him in one of his old stomping grounds."

"One of our men followed him for a while. I'll give you those notes."

"Good. Thanks, Greg."

"You sure you don't want us to help you out on this? I could assign a man to help you."

"No. I don't have any money to hire you, and like I said, I'm trying to keep this low profile so the cartel won't know I'm even looking for them."

"I understand, but this is dangerous work you're doing, low profile or not. Why don't you let me talk to Melissa Thornton? I'm sure she'd spring for our fee. After all, you're searching for her husband's killer."

"No, thanks. Maybe I'll take you up on that later if I'm not making any progress. Melissa's liable to tell someone I'm working on the case, and then I'll end up dead."

"That's probably true. Okay. Good luck."

After Stan had gathered the information he needed from Wolford, he went to class. Paula was already seated in the classroom, so Stan sat down beside her. Her eyes lit up when she saw him. She gave him a hard look.

"Hi. You look tired."

"I am a little tired. I didn't sleep well. I was trying to figure out how we can find Morales and turn him over to the FBI."

Paula laughed. "You never give up, do you?"

Stan smiled. "No. I guess not. I don't take failure well."

"Me neither. So, what do you have in mind?"

"You know your research on the Burilo cartel?"

"Yeah."

"Well, as brilliant as it was, we've got to do much more. What you've uncovered is only the tip of the iceberg. If we can identify other money laundering operations, I'm sure we'll be able to find Carlos Morales while he's in the US. Then we can tip off the FBI so they can arrest him."

"You think he'd dare set foot in the United States with the FBI looking for him?"

"I don't think he has much respect for our law enforcement agencies. He thinks he can outsmart them, and so far he has."

"He's certainly outsmarted us," Paula noted.

"Yes, he has, and that's why we can't give up. We've got to bring him down."

"Alright, I'm in. What's next?"

"Are you free late this afternoon?"

"Yes. I usually study in the afternoons."

"Good. I'll meet you in one of the private study rooms in the library. We can spread out all our intel and figure out a research strategy."

"Okay. Maybe I'll round up some of kids from class to help out."

"No, let's keep this to ourselves. If we get too many people involved our covert operation may be compromised. I know I can trust you, but I really don't know the others that well."

"Right."

"I had to tell Greg Wolford we were working on the case since I needed what was in his files, but I didn't tell him our plans exactly, so it's gonna be just you and me, okay?"

"Fine. I won't tell a soul."

"Good. I knew I could count on you."

After he left Paula, Stan had lunch with Lamar Jones. He wanted to find out how his dinner with Kristina had gone. Stan took him to the Highland Park Cafeteria, not too far from campus. They both loaded their plates like they didn't expect to have time for dinner.

"So, how was your dinner with Kristina?"

"It was fun. She was so keyed up over your little bombshell she could hardly sit still. I think now she's starting to believe she can win."

"Good. I think she will. Wells has already admitted he made the investment. I doubt the voters will believe he knew nothing about it."

"Yes, it may be true, but the public won't buy it. He's still responsible for what his agents do."

"That's right. You've got to be careful who you hire. I wonder if the Burilo cartel has someone on his staff."

Lamar's eyes widened. "You think so?"

"Well, if he claims not to know about it, it makes sense. They either have a man on the staff or bribed someone already there to make the investment. Then when a critical vote comes up, they let Wells know how they want him to vote, and if he refuses, they threaten to go public with his illegal investment."

"Holy crap!" Lamar exclaimed. "I had no idea they'd go to such lengths."

"Yeah, well, it's just a theory, but a definite possibility. There's a lot of corruption in politics, but it's often so subtle it's overlooked."

"Are you going to tell the FBI about your theory?"

Lamar asked.

"No. I'm done with my investigation," Stan lied. "I've cleared Rob's name, and that's enough, don't you think?"

"Of course," Lamar agreed.

"So, are you and Kristina going to go out again?"

Lamar smiled. "Maybe. She's pretty busy now, but after the election his over I plan to ask her out. She invited me to the victory party."

"Oh, good. I'll see you Tuesday night then."

"Wouldn't miss it for the world," Lamar replied.

At three o'clock, Stan had spread out all his information in one of the study rooms in the library. Paula showed up shortly thereafter, and they began sorting through the stacks of reports.

"Okay. This isn't going to be easy," Stan noted. "What we have to do is identify another one of the cartel's money laundering organizations. It will probably be very similar to the Silver Springs structure. If we do that, we can figure out where Carlos Morales is likely to show up."

"Where do we start?" Paula asked.

"We're looking for business names. You go through your research and make a list of any business names you come across. I'll go through Wolford's report."

"What do we do with the list?"

"Well, since this is a money laundering business, the dirty cash has to end up in legitimate businesses. That means these businesseses will be legally organized corporations, partnerships, or business trusts. These legitimate business must file tax returns and file periodic reports with the Secretary of State, Comptroller, and SEC. A lot of these reports are public records, so we can access them. Some of these reports require disclosure of ownership, which could lead us to other cartel businesses. If we find a cartel business name, we may be able to identify its owners and affiliated entities by searching these records."

"Don't you think the cartel will be careful not to leave a trail?"

"Probably, but when you're dealing with something as complicated as this, it's easy to make mistakes. Ordinary people are often careless, and criminals even more so."

"It sounds like a long shot."

"It may be, but I say we give it a try."

"Okay," Paula said. "So, I'm supposed to make a list?"

"Right. For each company, list the name, address, incorporator, officers, registered agent and address, shareholders, partners, assumed names, and affiliated entities. I'll do the same. Tomorrow we'll go to Austin and research all of the new entity filings for the last year."

"How do we do that?"

"We look at each new entity formed during the year, looking for any common names, addresses, shareholders, incorporators, etc. If we find a match, there is a good chance it's a cartel business."

"I see. So once we identify a cartel business, we go check it out and hope to find Morales there."

"Right."

"Okay, but you're going to owe me dinner after all this hard work."

"No problem," Stan said as he started working on his list. Several hours later, they finished, having identified sixteen separate entities, fifty-seven individual names, eleven lawyers who acted as incorporators, and seventy-seven separate addresses. When they were done reviewing the list, Stan took Paula to Dickey's Barbecue for dinner and then went home. Rebekah wasn't thrilled to hear Stan was going to Austin the next day.

"I thought you were done with this investigation?" Rebekah moaned.

"Well, I've got this idea of how we might find Carlos Morales. I really think it might work. If it does, we can let the FBI know where he is."

Rebekah shook her head. "Go ahead. Do whatever you want. You're not going to listen to me anyway."

"Don't you want Rob and Cindy's murderers to be caught?"

"Yes, but I don't want the father of my children killed."

"I'm going to be very careful. Don't worry. I'm not going to be in any danger."

"That's what you always say, and then you narrowly escape death."

The next day, Stan picked up Paula early, and they drove to Austin. Going through the records was tedious work, as they had to compare each new filing with their lists, and there were thousands of new entities that had been filed during the year. In the first few hours, they'd gone through over 200 filings and hadn't come up with a match. Then, Stan noticed something.

"Look! This company, Blue Bayou Condominiums, Ltd., has the same mailing address as Calidad Interests, Ltd."

"Oh, my God!" Paula said. "Do you think we've found another cartel property?"

"Maybe. Let's check it out. The general partner is Avalanche Marketing, Inc."

"Cute name," Paula remarked.

"It has a Longview address, and the incorporator

is Simon Lansing."

"What's the business address?"

"It's another Longview address," Stan replied.

"So, now what?"

"Well, I'll keep looking for more matches, and you go check out Blue Bayou and Avalanche Marketing with the Comptroller's office. They'll have current officer and director information. While you're at it, call Longview information and see if they have a listing for the condos."

"Alright," Paula said, getting up to leave. "I'll be back when I'm done."

"Okay. I'll be here."

Stan continued comparing new filings with his list and almost immediately came up with another hit. The incorporator of a new company called Summit Leasing, Inc., was also the incorporator of a known cartel business, Matamoros Logistics, Inc. Stan was starting to get excited. Morales had been careful to create new entities to do his money laundering but careless in setting them up. He knew he'd find even more before the day was done.

When Paula came back from the Comptroller's office, Stan had a new list of entities for her to check out, so she immediately left, as time was running out. When the state offices finally closed at five, Stan and Paula had identified eleven new cartel businesses. Unfortunately, there was no time to celebrate, as they had to get back to Dallas. Paula was concerned she was falling behind in classes, and Stan knew he'd been neglecting Rebekah and his family and wanted to spend the evening with them.

Rebekah was glad to see Stan and seemed to be in good spirits when he walked in the door. This greatly relieved him, as he'd been worried all the way back from Austin about her being angry with him. The source of

Rebekah's good spirits turned out to be a conversation she'd had with Reggie's teacher. The teacher had gone out of her way to tell Rebekah what a wonderful student he was, a joy to teach.

"Way to go!" Stan said to Reggie. "Good man!"

Reggie shrugged. "I didn't do anything really."

"Look at that! He's modest too," Stan teased. "A chip off the old block."

Rebekah feigned choking on her food. "Ah, I don't think so. He takes after his mother obviously."

Stan raised his eyebrows. "Uh huh."

Rebekah slugged Stan playfully, and he grabbed her and wrestled her to the couch, laughing. Reggie shook his head at his crazy parents and left the room. Mark watched, eyes wide. Soon they were kissing passionately. Mark frowned and ran up the stairs.

"Get off me!" Rebekah ordered, sitting up. "Look. You've scared away the kids."

"Good. Now we can get down to business."

"In your dreams."

"Come on!" Stan pleaded. "You've got me stirred up. You can't quit now."

Rebekah looked at Stan and laughed. "Too bad."

At that, Stan swept her off her feet, carried her into the bedroom, and shut the door with his foot. He'd have to do something special for Reggie's teacher, he thought, as he flung Rebekah on the bed and started undressing her. She looked up at him blissfully with her big brown eyes and then pulled him down upon her.

Chapter 23

The next day, Stan skipped another day of classes and drove two hours to Tyler, Texas where Summit Leasing supposedly did business. He didn't know exactly what he was going to do there, but he wanted to check it out to see if it really existed or if it was just a sham. When he arrived at the address, he was amazed to see a thriving business with a retail outlet out front and a huge warehouse in the back. He started to go in the retail outlet to check it out when he saw a Peakload Personnel truck drive up and let off some temporary workers. Stan was familiar with Peakload, as he'd had to resort to day labor when he first came back after being discharged from the Marines Corps. He noted the address on the side of the truck and then consulted his map to see how to get there.

When he got to Peakload, he went inside and filled out an application for a job. Then he went up to the dispatcher and handed it to him.

"You got any work today?"

"Got some work at a battery acid factory, a lumber yard, and Summit Leasing needs warehousemen and clerks."

Stan smiled. "I can do either. I type eighty words a minute, and I've done inventory at a hardware store back in California."

"Alright then. You can take the next van to Summit. They only pay minimum wage."

Stan nodded and took a seat to wait. A few

minutes later, he was summoned to a departing van. When they got to Summit Leasing, he was let off near the loading dock. A red-faced man in a flannel shirt asked for his paperwork, so Stan handed it to him.

"You type eighty words a minute?" the man questioned.

"On a good day," Stan said confidently. "One of the few things I did right in high school—took typing."

"Yeah, I wish I'd have done that. I wouldn't be stuck out here in the warehouse. Go ahead in and report to Blanche in Receivables."

"Okay," Stan replied and went off in the direction the man pointed.

After wandering around a while and memorizing the layout of the offices, Stan walked through a door marked ACCOUNTING and looked around. A sign hung from the ceiling off to the left that read ACCOUNTS RECEIVABLE. Stan noticed a blonde-headed lady with a clipboard barking orders to a woman who didn't look too happy. He figured that was Blanche and walked over to her.

"Hi. I'm here from Peakload."

"A man! They sent a man?"

Stan looked around self-consciously. "Yeah. Is that okay?"

"I've never seen a man who could type eighty words a minute," she explained.

"Well, prepare to be dazzled," Stan said flirtatiously.

She smiled "Hmm. Okay, take that cubicle, and I better be impressed."

Stan took a seat in front of the typewriter and soon had piles of work dropped in the bin next to him. He looked through the stack and saw he was to complete several leases. While he was typing in the blanks with the names of the lessees, he scanned the terms and conditions and noted each company name on the back of an envelope. When he was done with the leases, he started working on invoices and was astounded at the high lease payments being charged each customer. Later, when he was asked to work on an accounts receivable aging report, he was shocked to see there were hardly any past-due accounts.

When it came time for lunch, Blanche offered to take him to the lunch room. He accepted with alacrity, and they went off like they were best friends. At lunch, Stan did what he did best—listen.

"I'm sorry they only pay minimum wage here. I know you're probably worth ten dollars an hour."

"Yeah, well, I'm just a little short this month, so I thought I'd work a few days to help make ends meet."

"I know what you mean. The owners of this place are so tight. They should be paying me twice what I'm getting, and we don't even have group insurance."

"Huh? That's surprising with business booming the way it is. You'd think they'd treat their employees better."

She nodded and rolled her eyes.

"I don't think I've seen such a low rate of delinquent accounts," Stan observed. "The economy isn't exactly booming right now."

"Yeah, well they sell primarily to affiliated companies, so paying family is a first priority."

"Who owns the company? Do you know?"

"Yeah. Some hotshot from Mexico."

"Have you ever met him?"

"No," she chuckled. "He doesn't' even know I exist. He comes around once a week to collect his profits and confer with the manager and then takes off."

"What's his name?"

"Hell, I don't know—Carlos something. Nobody ever talks about him. At staff meetings, it's all about efficient operations and keeping the employees in line."

"Hmm. Glad I'm not working here full time."

"Yeah, if I could find something better, I'd quit."

"So, when does Carlos come around?"

"Thursdays, usually. He comes in about ten and leaves in the early afternoon."

"So he's here now?" Stan asked.

"I don't know. I haven't seen him yet, but he may be in with the manager."

"How fast do you type, Blanche?" Stan teased.

Blanche smiled wryly. "Typing isn't required for my job."

On the way back to the A/R Department Stan went by the manager's office. There was a drinking fountain nearby, so Stan lingered there a while. After a few minutes, a short, dark-haired man walked out, followed by Carlos Morales. They gave Stan a hard look as they walked by and then disappeared around the corner. Stan went to the office door, but it was locked, so he turned around and followed the manager and Carlos. They were standing outside talking, so Stan took up a position nearby where he could hear their conversation but was out of their sight.

"If any police or federal agents come by, don't talk to them. Call me immediately."

"Of course. Are you going to Longview now?"

"No, not until tomorrow. I've got a luncheon appointment with the Mayor, and then we're going to play a round of golf. You know, in America it pays to have friends in high places."

The manager nodded in agreement, and then Carlos strolled out to his car. The manager waved and then turned and walked quickly back inside. Stan pretended to just be walking by and smiled.

"Who are you?" the manager demanded.

Stan stopped and gave him a bewildered look. "Uh, just a temp in Accounting."

Blanche suddenly appeared and walked up to them. "There you are. Did you get lost?"

"Oh, yeah. I'm sorry. This place is a maze."

The manager's eyes narrowed.

"Come on," Blanche said. "I'll guide you back."

"Thanks," Stan replied gratefully.

After they were away from the manager, Blanche asked, "What are you doing here?"

Stan gave her a blank look. "What do you mean? I'm trying to pick up a few bucks."

"Bullshit. You're way overqualified for this job, and I doubt you need the pittance this job pays. What is it you are really after?"

"Nothing."

"Don't worry. I'm not going to blow your cover," Blanche said. "I'm just curious."

Stan cleared his throat and looked around. "Well, in a few days you'll probably know why I was here. In the meantime, you should look for a new job."

A knowing smile came over Blanche's face. "Okay. So I was right."

Stan shrugged and went back to his cubicle. When the shift was over, Stan caught the first Peakload van back, collected his day's wage, and then searched for a payphone. When he found one at a gas station, he called Agent Rutledge, collect.

"Hi, Stan. Haven't heard from you in a while. What are you doing in Tyler?"

"Just a little temp work at Summit Leasing."

"Summit Leasing?"

"Right. It's quite a place. It's operated by a guy

named Carlos Morales. You know him?"

"Don't be a wise-ass. How do you know Carlos Morales operates it?"

"Well, I just saw him there and I've been told he comes every Thursday to check on things."

"Where are you now?"

"At a payphone. I just left there."

"I see. So, where is Morales right now?"

"Having lunch with the mayor, and then they're going to the country club for a bit of golf."

"Okay, but we have one problem."

Stan's heart sank. "What's that?"

"We don't have enough on Morales or Rubio to convict them yet. We can arrest him but the U.S. Attorney is not ready to prosecute him."

"Damn it! I thought with Melissa and the three Mexicans in custody that would be enough to take down the cartel."

"No. Melissa will testify that Brad knew Rubio in college, but its all hearsay. It's not enough to tie him to the Silver Springs Ventures. We need Brad Thornton, but, as you know, he's dead."

"So, you're just going to let him skate?"

"Well, has your cover been blown?"

"Ah. Well my supervisor knows I'm up to something but she's friendly. She hates Morales."

"Then since you've gone out on a limb already, can you stay on the job a few days and gather evidence. With the right evidence and you and your supervisor's testimony that would probably be enough to convince the U.S. Attorney to go forward with the indictments."

Stan took a deep breath. "I don't know. The manager is already a little suspicious of me and I'd hate to get Blanche killed."

"Well, you found Morales and identified another

money laundering operation. That's not too shabby. I don't blame you for quitting while you're ahead. It's the sensible thing to do. I'll call our Tyler office and get a tail put on Morales. Maybe he'll lead us to Rubio and we can keep an eye on both of them. At least we know where he is now, that's something."

Stan shook his head. "No. Don't do that. I'll do it. We can't let him get away with this."

"You sure?"

"Yeah. Rebekah may divorce me, but at least there will be one less drug cartel in operation."

"Good. I'll get a team put together and we can all meet tonight and plan the operation."

"Okay. I'll be at the Best Western Motel. Call me."

"I will. And thank you, Stan. We've been trying to bring the Burilo Cartel down for years. With your help maybe we can finally do it."

Stan hung up the phone and immediately began to worry. How was he was going to break the news to Rebekah. She was going to be livid if he didn't come home tonight? How was he going to handle Blanche? Was she trustworthy enough to tell her what was coming down? Nothing came to him immediately except a splitting headache, so he decided to take a shower. Sometimes a steady stream of hot water relaxed him and cleared his mind.

After thirty minutes in the shower he felt a lot better and mustered up enough courage to call Rebekah. He decided to go with the truth rather than try to concoct a lie. Rebekah would be mad but she'd be even more upset if she thought he was lying to her. He dialed the number.

"Stan, where are you?"

"Still in Tyler."

"You said you'd be back for dinner."

"Something came up. I spotted Carlos Morales and the feds want me to help gather a little more evidence before they arrest him."

"No! You promised me you wouldn't put yourself in danger."

"I know and I won't be in danger. Morales has no idea who I am. I stared him right in the face and he didn't recognize me. He was probably in Mexico when I was in all the papers and on the TV news."

"Yes, but one of his men may have been in town. If one of them spots you they'll drag you off again and kill you."

"The FBI will be all over the place. They will protect me."

"You've got an election in a few days. Don't you have last minute things that have to be done?"

"Sure, but someone else can do them. This is more important."

"Of course. Whatever you're doing is always more important than us!"

The phone went dead. Stan slammed down the receiver and began pacing back and forth. He thought about calling Agent Rutlege and backing out of the operation, but couldn't bring himself to do it. He picked up the telephone and dialed Kristina's number.

"Hello."

"Kristina. This is Stan."

"Oh. Hi Stan. How are you?"

"Fine. I just wanted to let you know I'm going to be out of pocket for a day or two so If you can't find me don't be alarmed."

"But it's so close to the election."

"I know. But I've done everything I can to make sure you are elected. It's really up to you and the voters now."

Kristina sighed. "Right. So, what are you up to now?"

"I can't say but if I'm successful it could be a positive for your campaign."

"You're not doing something dangerous again, are you?"

Stan didn't respond.

"Stan, what am I going to do with you? Let the cops and the FBI deal with the cartel. They're trained for it."

"I'm just helping them out. I'll be fine."

"So, your working with them. They'll have your back?"

"Yes. Don't worry. I'll be fine."

"Right," she said tears welling in her eyes.

"I don't know how Rebekah does it. I'm a nervous wreck and I'm not even married to you. Remind me not to marry a soldier, a cop or a suicidal attorney."

Stan laughed. "Thanks a lot."

"Well, be safe. Don't worry about me."

"I won't. I know you're going to win. You've got charisma. . . . You're irresistible."

"Huh. Except to you?"

Stan didn't respond.

"Goodnight, Stan."

"Bye."

Stan hung up the phone wishing Kristina were there with him. He wanted to hold her tight and feel her body against his, to stroke her hair and feel her lips on his. She was irresistible. How had he managed to keep his distance? When he was with her it was like trying to stand up in a hurricane. He so much wanted to let go and be consumed by her. But somehow he stayed upright and kept his distance, not by conscious reason but driven by something deep down within himself that he couldn't begin to fathom.

Chapter 24

Stan was hungry so he drove down the street to Denny's and ordered chicken friend steak. He knew it would probably be a long night, so he ate heartily. As he was leaving he bought a copy of the Dallas Morning News. He was anxious to see if there was any new polling on the State Representative's race or stories about Representative Ron Wells.

When he got to his motel room he went through the paper cover to cover but didn't see anything. He wondered if the press had swallowed Well's claim that he had no knowledge that he was an investor in Silver Springs Ventures. The phone rang and he picked it up.

"Stan. We're here and setting up downstairs in the conference room."

"You're here at the Best Western?"

"Yes, we don't have a lot of preparation time, so we decided to come to you."

"Great. I'll come down."

"Good. See you in a minute."

Stan put down the newspaper and went into the bathroom to take a look at himself. On careful inspection he noticed he had dark shadows under his eyes from lack of sleep. He suddenly felt exhausted. How long could he keep up his insane schedule? As soon as the election was over it would be different he told himself. After splashing water on his face he grabbed a towel, dried himself and then went downstairs. He saw a pot of coffee as he stepped in the room so he went directly over to it and poured himself a cup. He didn't really like coffee that much but needed the caffeine to stay awake.

"Hi. Stan," Agent Rutledge said from behind him.

He turned and smiled. "Hey."

"Did you get a good nights' sleep?"

Stan shrugged. "Not really."

Rutledge laughed. "Have a seat."

Stan took a seat at the conference table and the others joined him.

"So, tell us. How did you track Morales down?" Agent Rutledge asked.

Stan looked around the table and counted Rutledge, Adams and six others. He explained how he and Paula had poured through all the records and then cross referenced them with new business entities that were set up through the Secretary of State's office.

"Impressive," Agent Rutledge said.

"Well, luckily I was taking Business Entities at SMU, and I picked my professor's brain. I don't think he's ever had a student ask so many questions. Usually they have to pry questions out of students."

"That's great—very resourceful. You've got to bring Paula around to meet me sometime."

"I will. I also figured out how they used Summit Leasing to launder their money."

"You did?" Agent Adams asked.

"Yeah. Judging from their overpriced leasing contracts, they buy an asset for say $1,000 and then lease it for $150 a month for five years. That way, they are able to launder $9,000 for every $1,000 of investment. Since all of their new companies lease all of their assets, the amount of money they launder is staggering, but if you look at the books, it all looks legit. The only thing out of whack is the owner capital account, but as that grows, it just makes the business appear stronger. Of course, the IRS would have a field day auditing them.

"So, how do you know so much about accounting?" Agent Adams asked.

"Oh. I minored in business and finance at UCLA. I figured a lawyer would have to understand business, and accounting and bookkeeping were major facets of every business."

"That's certainly true," Agent Adams said. "Now the problem we have right now is like you say, everything on paper looks legit. The cartel has the best accountants money can buy, so to nail them for money laundering is not going to be easy."

"Right," Stan acknowledged. "So, what do you need me to do."

"We need to prove the books are fraudulent, that assets don't exist or income and expenses are bogus."

"Well, I would hazard a guess that some of the leased equipment doesn't exist. There are so many companies involved it would be easy to fabricate purchase orders and bills of sale."

"Right. So, we need all of Summit's leases and leased asset records."

"That's too many documents to copy or steal from the office. Plus I doubt I could get access to the copier or the files to do it."

"Right. All you need to do is get us enough evidence to convince a judge to give us a search warrant."

"What kind of evidence?"

"Proof that a crime is being committed. Even if you found one lease that you could prove was bogus, that would be enough for the warrant."

Stan handed Agent Adams two envelopes. "Well,

yesterday they had me working on new leases. These are the ones I did yesterday. All the pertinent info on each I wrote down on those two envelopes. The lessees, terms, equipment being leased, etc. You can start with those and go to those affiliated businesses and see if the equipment is there. If it's not, then you'd have probably cause."

"Unfortunately, if we start walking into Morales's business operations it will throw up a red flag and Morales may run."

"We could send somebody in posing as a county tax auditor," Agent Rutledge said. They could say they were auditing the company's personal property tax return. If they weren't paying taxes on the leased equipment or it wasn't there, we'd have what we needed."

Agent Adams looked at a female at the table. "Okay, Margo. Take Stan's list and do that first thing tomorrow."

"Yes, sir," Margo replied.

Agent Adams got up and retrieved a set of plans of Summit's building and spread it out on the table. Stan recognized the layout of the building.

"Stan, can you tell us what's in all of these rooms?"

Stan nodded. "Most of it." He stood up and started pointing. "That's the warehouse. This is the office. The accounts receivable office is on this side of the room and payables on the other. A couple of supervisor are at the front of the room." He pointed to a string of offices in the back. "Here we have the offices of the operations officer, production manager and a conference room, janitor's closet."

Agent Adams pointed to a large closet connected to the operations officer's room. "What's this."

"I tried to get in that office while the operations officer was talking to Morales but it was locked. Unfortunately, they didn't have a class on lock picking at UCLA."

They all laughed.

"They reason I ask," Adams said, "is that this room is coded for special construction. In other words, it's not to be constructed like the rest of the offices. The walls are shown to be thicker and reinforced. Unfortunately, this drawing doesn't give us the exact specifications for the room, but it obviously has a special purpose."

"You mean like a vault?" Stan said.

"Precisely. They may keep sensitive documents there, cash, drugs, who the hell knows?"

"So you want me to see what's inside that closet."

"That would be ideal, but we don't want to you to get hurt either. See if you can at least get into the office. Maybe the door will be open and you can take a peak inside."

"Maybe Blanche has reason to go into that office. If so, she might be able to take a look or she can send me there."

"Right. Just try to find out what's in there. And give us all the info on the new leases you process. In the meantime we'll be working other angles."

"Okay."

"We'll have a couple of agents apply at Peakload and go in as temps tomorrow to provide you backup. If anything goes awry they'll only be seconds away. We'll wire you up so you can feed us info during the day."

Stan sighed. "Okay. Is that it?"

"Yes. Get a good nights' sleep and we'll see you here tomorrow at six."

Stan thanked them and retired to his room. He

called Rebekah again to say good night but she didn't pick up the phone. He then called Paula to update her on what was happening.

"You're staying another day?"

"Yeah. They need more evidence to nail Morales."

"Do you want me to come help?"

"No. You can't miss anymore school and I'm not sure what you could do anyway. There will be a couple agents hiring on at Peakload, so I'll have backup."

"Hmm. You always have all the fun," Paula teased.

"Yeah. Well, I seemed to remember you having fun down at San Antonio Del Mar."

"Right. That was awesome. Next time write me into your script, okay?"

"Alright. Sorry."

"Keep me posted and keep safe."

"I will. Thanks for all your help."

"Bye."

Stan called Rebekah again but she didn't pick up. He watched the ten o'clock news and then went to bed. The next thing he knew the phone was ringing. He picked it up. "This is your wake-up call," a cheerful voice said.

"Thanks," he moaned and turned over.

Reluctantly he got dressed and went downstairs. The team was already hard at work. He went to the coffee pot and poured himself a cup and grabbed a donut. Agent Rutledge looked up and waived him over.

"Hey, Stan. Sleep good?"

He shrugged. "As well as to be expected."

"I guest your first task will be to talk to Blanche and get her onboard."

"Right."

Agent Rutledge handed Stan an envelope. "We

did some research on Blanche and she's in desperate financial straights. Here is $2,000. Give this to her and tell her if we are successful at getting the evidence we need on Morales they'll be another two grand for her."

"Okay," Stan replied, surprised by the gesture.

"I think she would have done it for nothing, but the cash can't hurt."

"No. . . . Okay, Agent Adams will wire you up and then you will be good to go."

"Alright. I have to go to Peakload and get assigned to Summit for the day."

"Right. Do what you have to do."

After the wire was installed Stan drove his car to Peakload. Two agents followed him and they all walked into the office together. There was a long line so they waited impatiently while everyone in front of them were processed. When Stan finally got to the front of the line he gave the clerk his info sheet.

"Okay, we have the battery acid plant, Gordon's Nursery and Community Hospital available."

Stan felt weak. "What? No Summit Leasing? That's where I want to go."

"Well, we haven't got any requests for them today."

"Are you sure?" Stan said desperately.

The clerk rolled her eyes. "Yes, I'm sure. Do you see their name on the list."

Stan sighed. "No, but I was told to come back there today."

"Well, there's no request."

"Can you call over there? Ask for Blanche."

The clerk just gave Stan a long stare. Finally she said, "Okay. I'll give Blanche a call."

The clerk dialed the number and waited. She asked for Blanche and waited again. There was a short exchange and then the clerk handed Stan the phone. “She wants to talk to you.”

Stan took the phone. “Blanche.”

“What’s going on Stan. I thought you were through here?”

“Something came up. I need another day. I’ll make it worth your while.”

“You know how hard it is to find a decent job?”

“Yes. Like I said. I’ll make it worth your while. Just give me another day. Please, and you need to request two other laborers.”

She laughed. “You don’t want much, do you? How am I supposed to explain this to my boss?”

“You’ll think of something. You’re a smart girl.”

She sighed. “Okay, put the clerk back on the phone.”

Stan handed the phone to the clerk and she put the phone up to her ear. She nodded and then wrote Summit Leasing on her list. “Right. I’ll send them right over.”

The clerk looked up at Stan. “Okay, she said she did need you. Go ahead on over there.”

“Great,” Stan said, relief washing over him.

“They need two general laborers’ too.”

The two agents standing behind Stan raised their hands. The clerk waived them forward and gave them their credentials. They all left in separate cars.

When Stan got there he went straight to Blanche’s desk. She looked up at him skeptically. “So, you couldn’t stay away, huh?”

“No. I enjoyed working with you so much I had to come back.”

“Right. I was expecting the place to be closed down today.”

“Yeah. Me too, but we’re not quite ready. Can I do

what I was doing yesterday?"

Blanche looked over at a desk where a young girl was working. "Gail. Go help Jill with payables."

The girl nodded and left the desk.

"It's all yours."

"Lets talk at break," Stan suggested.

"Yes. Definitely."

Stan resumed where he had left off the day before and managed to document twelve more leases before it was time for the ten o'clock break. When the buzzer sounded Stan followed Blanche to the break room. They both got a Coke and a bag of potato chips and then took a walk in the equipment yard behind the building.

"So, you're back," Blanche said.

"Yes. I need your help?. . . We need your help."

"Who's we?"

"Me and the FBI. We need your help in gathering evidence so we can get a warrant to search this place. We're close to having enough already but we need more."

"So, how can I help?"

"You know the room or large closed attached to the Manager's office?"

"The storage room?"

"Is that what it's called?"

"Yes."

"Have you ever been in there?"

"No."

"Have you ever looked inside it?"

"No. I rarely go into the Manager's office. He usually comes out here to talk to us."

"Well, we suspect there may be incriminating evidence in there. One of us needs to get a look inside."

"It's locked and it's not a cheap lock. You have to have two separate keys."

"How do you know that?"

"I was in there one time when it was opened. Carlos had one key and the Manager had the other."

"But you didn't see what was inside."

"No. I couldn't see inside from where I was standing."

"Damn it. I need to see what's in there."

"It's opened every night at five when the Brinks truck comes to pick up the days' receipts from the retail store."

"So it is a vault?"

"They don't call it a vault, but it may be. I don't know."

"Okay, will you help us?"

She sighed. "I don't know. Carlos Morales isn't the kind of guy a girl wants to cross."

"No. You're right. But I don't think he'll ever pick up that you've helped us."

Blanche didn't say anything.

"Ah. If you help I've two grand for you and if we get what we need there will be another two grand for you."

Blanche's eyes lit up. "Seriously?"

"Yes. This is very important. I'll give you two grand right now if you agree."

Blanche smiled. "Count me in then. I get to help nail the bastard and get paid for it to boot. How can a girl turn down such a good deal?"

Stan laughed and pulled the envelope from his pocket and handed it to Blanche.

"Okay. We better get back. Break time is about over."

She nodded and they walked back into the building and resumed their work. At lunch Stan made a point to eat with one of the undercover agents and told him his idea. Agent Rutledge was listening in down in the utility van down the street and gave them the go ahead. On the way back to his work station, Stan wandered through the facility looking for anything suspicious. As he walked by the loading van he saw a white van and two men unloading boxes. He watched where the two men bring the boxes in but was surprised when, instead of taking them into the warehouse they took them to the manager's office. He verbally stated the vans make, model and license number and destination of its cargo and then went back to his station.

At the three o'clock break Stan called Rebekah. She picked up.

"Are you done yet. Are you on your way home?" she asked.

"Almost. Hopefully it will all be over at five. I tried to call you last night but you didn't answer."

"I went to bed early."

"Hmm. You feeling alright?"

"I miss you and the kids don't understand why you're not home."

"I know. I'm sorry. In a few days this will all be over. The election will be over and life can get back to normal."

"Yeah, but normal for you is still exhausting."

Stan laughed. "We'll that's true."

"Be careful, okay. We need you."

"I will. See you soon."

Stan hung up feeling better that Rebekah was talking to him again. He looked at his watch and wondered if there was anything else he could do before the five o'clock fireworks began and all hell broke loose. He noticed one of the men who had been unloading the van go out in the yard and light up a cigarette. Stan didn't smoke, but he decided today he might have to take it up again. He followed the man outside and bummed a cigarette from him.

"Did you hire on with Peakload?" he asked.

The man shook his head. "No, man. I don't work for Summit."

"Oh. Just a delivery driver, huh?"

"Un huh."

"Have to travel a long way?"

"No. Just from Dallas."

"Hmm. I'm just working temporary. I really need a full time job. Does your company have any openings."

He laughed. "No, you don't want to work for my boss."

Stan laughed with him. "Why not?"

"Well, the pay is good, but there's no benefits and if you screw up the boss will put a bullet in your head."

"Excuse me!" Stan exclaimed.

The man tossed his cigarette to the ground and crushed it with his boot. "Forget it, man. You're better off where you are, trust me."

Stan lost his cigarette and then went inside. He grimaced over the foul taste in his mouth from smoking. Agent Rutledge came on through his ear piece.

"Nice work, Stan. You might have just got us what we needed. The judge will love the part about his boss putting a bullet in his head. But you need the guy's name and the company he works for."

"I know. I was trying to get that out of him, but I couldn't."

"Look in his truck. There may be something in the cab with that information."

Stan walked over to the van and looked around. He didn't see anyone so he looked into the open window. There was a clipboard and a packing slip attached to it. The company name was Cabrillo Couriers and the signature at the bottom read Luis Reyes. Stan turned to leave and Luis was staring him in the face.

"What you doing, man?" he demanded pushing Stan away.

Stan raised his hands. "Nothing? Just checking out your new van. Pretty nice. How does it ride? I was thinking about buying a conversion van for the family. They say on TV these new vans ride like a passenger car. Are they right?"

Luis shook his head. "No. They're lying. It rides like a regular truck, man. Now get away. If Jose sees you messing with his van he'll kick your ass."

"Oh, sorry," Stan said making a hasty retreat.

When Stan got back inside he whispered what he'd learned for Agent Rutledge's benefit. "Cabrillo Couriers, driven by Jose, last name unknown, and Luis Reyes, both Hispanic males in their mid-twenties."

"Got it. Thanks, Stan."

Stan entered the office and headed for his desk. Blanche looked at him nervously as he went by. She nodded toward a tall man with a shaved head by the door. Stan took a deep breath, glanced at the man, and then smiled back at her. He looked again and noticed the man's arms were covered with tattoos and he had a scowl on his face. Stan looked at his watch and saw that it was four o'clock. He still had an hour to kill until the storage room would be opened. He started going through leases again wondering why the man was there and trying no to look at him. Finally, he turned and left.

At 4:55 Blanche got up and went out into the hallway. A moment later Stan left and went directly to the manager's office. Precisely at 5:00 p.m. Blanche tripped the fire alarm. Stan immediately broke into the Manager's office and yelled. "There's a fire. Everybody out. There's a fire."

The manager rose from his desk as Stan rushed

by him toward the storage room. The two men in the room looked up in surprise. Stan took a quick mental inventory of the room. "Fire! Fire! Everyone evacuate!"

The manager came around his desk and tried to stop Stan but he eluded him and went back out into the hallway.

"Okay. I saw two pallets of cash, I couldn't tell the denomination and I saw guns, lots of guns."

"What kind of guns," Agent Rutledge asked. "Rifles, machine guns, all kinds of guns."

"Alright. We've got an agent with the Judge. He's sighing the search warrant as we speak.."

The two FBI agents working undercover stepped inside the managers' office, showed their badges and took the three men into custody without resistence. Then the main FBI SWAT team began swarming in from all directions. Stan left and went out the front door to his car.

"Am I done?" Stan asked.

"Yes. For now," Agent Rutledge replied. "Go over to the command center and let us remove your wire. Then you can go. We'll need to debrief you tomorrow."

"Okay. Did you arrest Morales?"

"No. But we will soon. He's in Texarkana right now. We've got a tail on him."

"Don't let him get away."

"We won't."

"Alright. I'm on my way over."

"Thanks Stan. You did a great job."

"No. Problem. Glad it worked out."

As soon as the wire had been removed Stan drove back to Dallas, praying the FBI would arrest Morales soon. If they didn't find him, all his efforts would not only have been in vain, but Morales and Rubio would be after his blood. Stan pushed the speed limit as he sped down I20 toward Dallas.

When he walked in the door, Rebekah looked up at him, a look of astonishment on her face. "Stan! They caught Morales!" she exclaimed. "It was just on the news! They arrested Carlos Morales. Can you believe it?"

Stan smiled, relief surging over him like cool rain on a hot day. He went to Rebekah and swung her around like he hadn't seen her in a hundred years. She laughed and hugged him tightly.

"I feel like celebrating," Stan said. "Let's take the kids to your mother's and then go out on the town."

She laughed. "Are you serious?"

"Dead serious," he replied, drawing her close to him and giving her a long kiss. "Now all I have to worry about is the election."

Stan wondered now that Morales was in custody if the rest of the indictments would come down before election day. Realistically he didn't think that would happen. Seeing the concern on his face, Rebekah came over to him.

"What's wrong?"

"Nothing. Just worried about the election on Tuesday."

"Well, the latest poll said Kristina is only two points down, so she might pull it off."

Stan looked at Rebekah and raised his eyebrows. "Wow. Did I note a bit of optimism from my wife?"

Rebekah laughed. "Then again, two points is a lot to make up in three days."

Stan shook his head. "Call your mother. We should call Lynn Jenkins too. He'll probably want to celebrate."

"What about the Shepards? They certainly should be happy their son's killer has been arrested."

"Good idea. The more the merrier."

An hour later, they had all gathered at Cheddars to celebrated Carlos Morales' arrest. Stan filled everyone in on most of what had happened, and they all listened with amazement. Rebekah shook her head disapprovingly, as much of what he told them she hadn't yet heard about. After dinner, as they were preparing to leave, Stan noticed Melissa Thornton in a corner booth with a tall, muscular, Hispanic man. When their eyes met, she turned away. About that time, Tom grabbed the check and insisted on paying it. Stan protested, to no avail, and when he looked back over into the corner, Melissa and her friend were gone.

A moment later, there was a commotion at the door as several reporters and their cameramen entered the restaurant. Stan watched them argue with the manager, and finally they sat down and waited. A few moments later, the manager came to their table and advised them there were some members of the media who wanted to interview Stan and the Shepards.

Stan looked at Tom. "You feel like talking?" Stan asked.

Tom shook his head. "Not really."

"Me either," Stan agreed, turning to the manager. "Is there a back way out of here?"

The manager nodded and pointed to a back door. They all said their goodbyes and made their way outside, careful to avoid the reporters standing around the front door. On the way home, Stan couldn't get the image of Melissa Thornton eating dinner with a strange man out of his head. He wondered why she had looked at him the way she had and why she had left as soon as he noticed her. Something wasn't quite right, but he couldn't put his finger on what it could be.

The next day Stan went to FBI headquarters in Dallas for the debriefing. He was meticulously questioned by several agents and then made to write a full account of what happened. After he'd signed the statement Agent Rutledge called him into her office.

"Well. I guess that does it. Thanks again."

"So, did Morales lawyer up the moment you arrested him?"

"No. He did some talking. He denied knowing anything about Brad Thornton's assassination."

"Really?"

"Un huh."

"Well, I guess a confession would have been a lot to ask."

"Right."

Stan left feeling relieved that he was done with his criminal investigations. He decided he didn't like criminal law all that much and would probably stick to civil law when he graduated from SMU. He couldn't imagine having to defend people like Carlos Morales or even white collar criminals like Brad Thornton. He wanted to work with clients he liked and respected. But what he wanted and what fate had in store from him was quite different.

Chapter 25

On Saturday, Rebekah had to work, so Stan was stuck with the kids all day. In the morning, he played games with them, and in the afternoon he tried to study while Marcia and Peter were napping and Mark and Reggie played in the back yard. By the time Rebekah got home at three, Stan had developed cabin fever and wanted to get out. He'd been thinking a lot about Carlos Morales' arrest and his profession of innocence in Brad Thornton's murder. During the day, he got the idea that perhaps he should go see Brad's ex-bodyguard, Todd Watson, to see if he could shed any light on the subject. Now that Brad was dead, he figured Watson might be more inclined to talk, particularly since Stan had tried to rescue his boss. He didn't have Todd's telephone number, but he did have his girlfriend's, so he called it. Tina answered on the second ring.

"Hi, Tina. This is Stan Turner."

There was no response for a moment, and then she finally replied, "Yeah, what do you want?"

"I'm looking for Todd. Do you know how I could reach him?"

"He's right here. Hold on."

A minute later, Todd came on the line. "What do

you want, Turner? I thought I told you I have nothing to say."

"Right, but a lot has changed since then with Brad's death and all. What are you doing now that you don't have a body to guard?"

"Working security at the mall until I can find something better."

"I see. Listen, since Brad is dead, I thought maybe you might talk to me now. There are a lot of unanswered questions you might be able to enlighten me on."

"I've already talked to the FBI."

"Good, but they have a different agenda. I'm still trying to figure out who killed Brad and tried to kill me. I'm sure you'd like to find out who killed your old boss."

"I thought the FBI was looking at Carlos Morales for that?"

"They are, but he denies having anything to do with it, so I need to try to keep looking for answers in case he's telling the truth. I promise not to take too much of your time."

"Alright. I guess it can't hurt. You want to meet over at the mall where you tried to seduce my girlfriend?"

Stan felt a rush of guilt at the memory of his encounter with Tina Small. "Seducing her wasn't really my intention. Sorry."

Watson laughed. "Just pulling your chain. Tina told me you turned down a romp in the hay with her. I gotta thank you for that."

"Right. Okay. I'll see you in about an hour then," Stan confirmed.

"We'll be there," Watson said and hung up.

Stan told Rebekah he had to go to Republican headquarters for a few hours not wanting her to know he was still investigating the case. On the way to Northpark, he did stop there to check on a phone bank that was in full operation. It was the traditional get-out-the-vote drive that began on Friday night before the election and lasted until the polls closed on Tuesday. He talked to a few of the workers and made sure everything was going smoothly and then continued on to Northpark. Todd and Tina were sitting on a bench outside the restaurant when Stan walked up.

"Hi, Todd, Tina. Thanks for meeting me."

"No problem. Just make it fast. We've got plans for the evening."

Stan took a seat next to Todd and took out a sheet full of notes he'd made for the interview. "Alright. I was curious why you didn't go to Mexico with Brad, being his bodyguard and all."

"Morales told him he didn't need me in Mexico. He'd have all the protection he needed."

"So, what were you supposed to do while he was gone?"

"I was supposed to keep an eye on Melissa—make sure she was okay—but as soon as Brad was gone, she told me my services were no longer required."

"She fired you?"

"Pretty much."

"Huh. But Brad led you to believe you'd still be his bodyguard when he got back?"

"Yes. When he came back, everything was supposed to go back to how it had been before."

"You'd get your job back?" Stan asked.

"Yes. That's what I understood."

"Did you suspect Brad was laundering money?"

"No, not until the FBI started their investigation, and then I realized that was a possibility. It certainly did explain a lot of things."

"Did he ever acknowledge to you that he was doing anything illegal, or do you think he was just an unwitting accomplice?"

"He knew Morales and Rubio were connected with some powerful people in Mexico, but I don't think he appreciated the full extent of what he was involved in. He was in desperate need of money and simply did what he was told, so the cash he needed would keep coming in."

"So, he wouldn't have hired someone to kill me and his wife?"

Todd laughed. "No way. He was a businessman and wouldn't have resorted to something like that. Carlos assured him there was no danger that the FBI would come up with anything. Apparently, he thought they'd covered their tracks pretty carefully."

"So why the trip to Mexico?"

"Brad was pretty shaken by the Shepard murders, as he knew everyone would assume he was responsible. He assumed Carlos was behind it, but Carlos wouldn't confirm or deny that it was his doing. He finally convinced himself that the medical examiner was right and it was a murder-suicide. Then you came along and started your investigation, tried to talk to me, and then went on TV. He was so spooked by all of your high-profile maneuvering that Carlos suggested he take a vacation to Mexico where he could relax and let Carlos deal with you and feds."

"So, you think Carlos had Melissa and I kidnapped?" Stan asked.

"I don't know if it was his call or Rubio's but one of them made the decision."

"What about Melissa? Was she threatening to go to the FBI?"

"No. I think Brad was worried about her loyalty

though. They were getting into arguments a lot there at the end."

"What do you mean?"

"Their financial problems were destroying their marriage. They argued all the time, and Melissa blamed everything on Brad's incompetence."

"I see. What about Ron Wells? He claims he didn't know he had invested in the Silver Springs Ventures—that the investment was made by a money manager and he knew nothing about it."

"That's bullshit. He called and talked to Brad personally on more than one occasion."

"Really? How do you know it was him?"

"I used to answer the phone for Brad when he was busy. Brad bragged about all the bigwigs he had lured into his venture as insurance. He figured they'd protect him if anyone ever came after him. He didn't figure on the FBI coming down on him though. They don't care who's involved. In fact, they get real excited if they can nail a politician or two."

Stan nodded in agreement. "What triggered the FBI investigation, do you think?"

"I don't know. I heard something about a tax audit, but I don't have the particulars."

"Alright. Thanks for talking to me. You've clarified a lot of things for me, and I appreciate it."

"Well, I hope you nail Brad's killer. Brad wasn't a bad guy really. His wife really pushed him into bed with Carlos. He'd have just filed bankruptcy and started over had she not threatened to divorce him."

"Well, a lot of people think it's all over if you file bankruptcy, but that's not true at all. A lot of millionaires go broke before they finally discover the road to great wealth."

Stan thanked Todd again, walked to his car, and

drove home. On the way, he tried to sort out in his head what he'd learned. He'd definitely gotten a different perspective on things that made him re-think some of his prior beliefs and conclusions. It was all very complicated, and by the time he got home, he'd developed a headache.

On Sunday, Rebekah had to work again, so Stan took the kids to the park in the morning and to McDonald's for lunch. Since it was Sunday, after Rebekah got home, they went to six-o'clock mass and then picked up Kentucky Fried Chicken for dinner. When they got home, there was an urgent message from Kristina. While the family was eating chicken, Stan called her back.

"Ron Wells has called a news conference for tomorrow at 9:00 a.m. In his notification to the media, he says he'll have proof that he had no knowledge of the Silver Springs investment."

"He's a lying piece of slime," Stan spat.

"What are we going to do?"

"Don't worry about the news conference. I'll take care of it. If anyone asks you about it, just say 'The Silver Springs Ventures investment is between him and the FBI. I have no comment'."

"Okay."

"We're all going out to breakfast after we vote on Tuesday, right?"

"Uh huh."

"Is Lamar coming with us?"

"Yes. He said he is."

"Good. We should go over to the phone bank after breakfast and thank all the workers."

"Sure."

"I thought you could make an appearance at the Community Center to thank all the workers who are getting ready for your victory celebration."

"Uh huh. Don't forget, I've got a media luncheon at noon."

"Right. We don't want to miss that."

"No."

"So, I guess it's up to the voters now," Stan said. "We've done all that can be done."

"Thanks, Stan. No matter how it turns out, you've been great."

"Me? You've been the one who has dazzled everyone. You're going to make a fine state representative."

"I hope I get that opportunity, but, like you say, it's up to the voters now."

"Exactly. There's nothing you can do now but wait. So go to bed early and get a good night's sleep. You've got a hectic forty-eight hours coming up."

"Okay. Good night, Stan."

Stan said good night, hung up, and then searched for Veronica Brooks' telephone number. When he'd found it, he called but got an answering machine. The message on the machine gave an emergency number, so Stan called it. A woman from an answering service picked up.

"Veronica Brooks, please," Stan said.

"She doesn't work on Sundays."

"I didn't figure she did, but this is her emergency number."

"Is this an emergency?"

"Well, it's a matter of great urgency, and I'm sure Veronica would want to talk to me. I've got a scoop for her that she'd be very heartbroken if she missed.

"Alright. I'll put you through."

"Hello," Veronica said.

"Veronica? Stan Turner.

"Oh, hi, Stan. How did you get this number?"

"From your answering service. I told them it was

urgent."

"Really? What's up?"

"Are you going to Ron Wells' news conference tomorrow morning?"

"I don't know. I just heard about it. Should I go?"

"Yes, you should go. I don't know what kind of evidence he's going to produce, but I just talked to Todd Watson, Brad Thornton's bodyguard, and he says Ron Wells called Brad on several occasions about the Silver Springs investment."

Veronica laughed. "Well, that's very interesting. I'd need to confirm it with Todd. Do you think that will be a problem?"

"No. Can you do a conference call on your phone? We can call him now."

"Sure. What's the number?"

Stan gave her the number and got Todd on the line. He confirmed to Veronica that he'd personally taken phone calls from Ron Wells and overheard them discussing the Silver Springs investment. Once Veronica had that confirmation, she promised she'd ask Wells about it at the news conference.

The following morning, Stan dropped by Kristina's house to watch the press conference with her and Lamar. They turned on the TV just as Ron Wells escorted a tall, distinguished looking man up in front of the cameras set up just outside his campaign headquarters. He introduced the man as Wallace Witherspoon, a money manager who'd handled Wells' investments. After he made the introduction, Wells then stepped back and disappeared behind several campaign workers. Witherspoon smiled at the crowd of reporters.

"Ladies and gentlemen, Mr. Wells asked me to explain how it was that Silver Springs Ventures ended up in his investment portfolio. As you know, I handle all of Mr. Wells' investments since he is so busy representing his district and has no time for such matters. Over the years, I have done pretty well for Mr. Wells, so he trusts me to buy and sell as I deem prudent.

"About a year ago, a man I'd known and respected for many years, Brad Thornton, came to me and pitched Silver Springs Ventures as a potentially lucrative investment opportunity. I listened to him, studied the proposal, and made a determination that it would be a good deal.

"Regrettably, I did not look too closely into the venture, as I trusted my old friend, and I can assure you Ron Wells knew nothing about the Silver Springs Ventures until recently when the FBI investigation was announced.

"As soon as Mr. Wells heard about the investment and the possibility of illegal activities being involved, he instructed me to divest him of it immediately. Unfortunately, that wasn't possible with the FBI investigation already underway."

"Mr. Witherspoon," a reporter said, "how much did you invest in Silver Springs Ventures?"

"I'm not going to go into the details of the investment since Mr. Wells knew nothing about it."

"Mr. Witherspoon," Veronica said. "Veronica Brooks from NBC 5. You said Mr. Wells didn't know anything about the investment, yet last night I interviewed an employee of Brad Thornton, and he claims Ron Wells called Brad Thornton on several occasions specifically to discuss Silver Springs Ventures. Do you deny that?"

Mr. Witherspoon looked around for Ron Wells, but he had slipped away. "Um, I don't have any knowledge of that, so I couldn't comment other than it was my understanding that there had been no contact between them. I'm sorry. That's all I have. Thank you."

Mr. Witherspoon turned to leave. "Mr. Witherspoon!" Veronica persisted. "Isn't it true that you purchased a $100,000 interest in the Silver Springs Ventures and were repaid over $250,000 after only one year?"

"Sorry. Like I said. I'm not going into the details of the investment. Thank you."

When the press conference was over, Stan looked over at Kristina and smiled. She sighed. "Well, that wasn't so bad," she said.

"I told you not to worry about it," Stan reminded her. "Wells should have just let it alone. Now he's opened up a can of worms. That little press conference might be enough to put you over the top."

"Yeah, but how many people will see it?"

"It will be on the news at six and ten. A lot of people will see it and have second thoughts about returning Ron Wells to Austin."

"I hope you're right."

"I agree," Lamar said. "The press conference was a mistake. I don't know how Veronica Brooks got Todd Watson to talk to her, but that was brilliant."

Kristina looked at Stan. He smiled. "Todd's a nice guy once you get to know him," Stan confessed.

Kristina shook her head. "I should have known," she said.

Lamar laughed.

"Okay, I've got to go. Lots to do before the election tomorrow. I'll see you two for breakfast."

Stan gave Kristina a hug and then left to go back to Republican headquarters where his staff was monitoring the final hours of campaigning and dozens of volunteers were manning the phone banks. Inside, he saw some of his staff members crowded around a TV set.

"What's going on?" he asked.

"The latest polls show Carter leading Ford 51 percent to 48 percent in Texas," Glenda Green said. "If that holds up, we're in deep trouble. All our candidates will be buried in the landslide."

Stan sighed. "That's the problem with politics. Events you have no control over often determine your fate."

"If Reagan had been our candidate, things would have been different," she argued.

When Stan was satisfied everything was running smoothly, he went to see Melissa Thornton. Her life insurance policy had come back from underwriting, and he needed to deliver it to her. She seemed a bit nervous when she showed him into the den.

"Have a seat," she said. "Thank you for taking the time to bring this to me. I know how busy you must be with the election tomorrow."

"Yes, fortunately I just have to supervise, so it was no problem slipping away for a few minutes."

He opened his briefcase, pushed the button that started taping the meeting, and pulled out the policy. "It came back standard rate with no problems."

"Good."

He handed it to her. "So, how have you been holding up after Brad's death?"

"Oh, it's been difficult, obviously, with all our assets tied up."

"I bet. Did you have any life insurance on Brad?"

"Yes, but it's being held up pending his murder investigation."

"Hmm. Are you off the hook now with the FBI?"

"Yes, I think so. I signed a deal to testify against Carlos Morales and Tony Rubio in exchange for immunity on any money laundering charges."

"Good. You've been through enough," Stan said. "Do you think you'll ever get any of your assets back?"

"Actually, as part of the deal, I will get back anything I can prove we owned prior to the establishment of Silver Springs Ventures. It won't be a lot, but it's something."

"What about your Maui property?"

"We owned that before Silver Springs, so it will be released, however, there's a mortgage and taxes owed which I doubt I'll be able to swing unless the insurance proceeds come through in time."

"Hmm. That's too bad. I heard the Maui property was quite exquisite."

"Yes. It's right on the beach. I love it there. I'd hate to lose it."

"Any word on what's happening with our kidnappers?" Stan asked.

"No. I haven't heard a word."

"Well, I guess Carlos Morales and Tony Rubio are higher priorities for them now."

"Yes. I'm sure they are."

"Well, I should go. Oh, I saw you the other day at Cheddars. Who was the man you were with?"

"Oh, just an old friend who came to the funeral. He stayed a couple of days to make sure I was okay."

"Oh, right," Stan said, standing. "Well, if you need anything, just let me know."

"Thanks, Stan, for all you have done. I'm in your debt."

They embraced, and Stan left, pondering the conversation. He wondered how much insurance Melissa had carried on her husband, and he guessed it was at least a million. The way things stood, he figured, the insurance company couldn't hold it for long since she'd been half a continent away from where the murder took place. If she got the insurance and was able to keep the Maui property, Stan estimated she'd have over two million in assets—not a bad recovery from being on the verge of bankruptcy.

Chapter 26

Stan awoke Tuesday morning at seven and began his usual exercise routine. It felt a little chilly, so he went to the thermostat and turned the heat up. As he was returning to the den, he glanced outside and saw it was snowing. He smiled. Stan loved the snow and knew it was a good omen for Republican success at the polls, since Democrats were more likely to skip voting if the weather was bad. He went upstairs and woke up the kids so they could see the white carpet that Mother Nature had laid during the night.

"Daddy, Daddy, can we go outside and make a snowman?" Reggie asked excitedly.

"After breakfast, maybe," Stan replied. "Dress warmly and put on two pairs of socks."

Stan went into Marcia's room and picked her up out of the crib. He took her to the window. "See the snow, little lady? Isn't it beautiful?"

Marcia looked out at the white landscape, seemingly mesmerized. Rebekah walked in and smiled at them. "What a day to snow, huh? The driving is going to be terrible."

"Actually, it may not be that bad. The snow doesn't seem to be sticking on the pavement. The temperature is thirty-one now, but I'm sure it will be above freezing by noon."

After feeding the kids breakfast, Stan took them outside so they could make a snowman and have a snowball fight. They weren't happy when he made them come in after only twenty minutes when their grandparents arrived to babysit.

"It's election day, so your grandmother and grandfather are going to babysit," Rebekah told them. "We'll be gone most of the day, so you be good for them."

"Can't we play outside?" Reggie pleaded.

"No. Not while I'm not here," Rebekah replied.

"But, Mom!" Reggie complained.

"You heard your mother," Stan interjected.

Reggie sighed and stormed off. Rebekah shook her head and smiled at her mother and father. She promised them she'd check in from time to time to be sure they were behaving. On the way to IHOP, they stopped at their polling place and voted. There were no lines, so it only took them ten minutes. When they got to IHOP, Kristina and Lamar were waiting for them.

"The turnout looks pretty light so far," Kristina observed.

"Yeah," Stan replied. "This snow is going to keep a lot of people indoors today—mostly Democrats, hopefully."

"I hope so."

"I really loved your interview on The Veronica Brooks Show," Rebekah said. "You didn't pull any punches."

"Yeah, I got a little excited. Some of her questions were pretty cruel."

"She's a natural," Stan observed. "I wish I had her charisma."

Kristina shook her head. "Your interview wasn't so bad."

"No, but people don't react to me like they do to you. They love you and hang on every word."

Kristina laughed. "Oh, come on."

“I’m serious,” Stan said.

The waitress advised them their table was ready, so they followed her to a table and sat down. She gave them menus and took their drink orders.

“I’m so nervous,” Kristina confessed.

“Well, that’s to be expected,” Lamar replied. “This is a major turning point in your life. Tomorrow, you may be a member of the Texas legislature.”

“Oh, God. This is all so unreal. Just a few weeks ago I was just a party volunteer.”

“Well, you had an unexpected opportunity open up, and you took advantage of it. A lot of people wouldn’t have had the courage to jump into a campaign so late in the game.”

They talked for a while before the waitress brought them their breakfast. They ate heartily and with great anticipation of the day’s events. After breakfast, Stan and Rebekah went to Republican Headquarters to check on the phone banks. It had stopped snowing and the roads were wet but not icy. Next they went to the community room at the First National Bank to check on the preparations for the victory party that evening. At noon Stan called the poll watching coordinator, who was in charge of the army of poll watchers observing each polling place.

“How’s the turnout looking?” Stan asked.

“It was very light this morning, but it’s been picking up as the weather has improved.”

“Any idea how we’re doing?”

“No, not really.”

“Alright. I’ll check on you again in a few hours.”

Stan hung up, worried that the turnout was picking up. He went over to where a group of campaign workers were huddled around a television. “What’s happening?” he asked.

"The last poll taken last night gave Jimmy Carter a slight lead. He's winning even bigger in Texas," a woman advised

"Great," Stan moaned. "I hate waiting. I wish the polls were closed and we could get on with the vote counting."

"If it's close, it could be a long night."

"I hope not."

Stan left the TV watchers and went back to where Rebekah was talking to Don Karnes.

"Hey, Don," Stan said.

"Hi, Stan. Your wife was just telling me how you sabotaged Ron Wells' news conference."

"Yeah, it was just good luck, actually. It just happened I'd talked to Todd Watson Sunday night, and he finally opened up to me. It was beautiful."

"So, why are you still questioning people? Haven't you accomplished everything you set out to do?" Don asked.

"Not quite. I want to find out who killed Brad Thornton and took a shot at me."

"Hmm. That could be dangerous."

"Yes," Rebekah agreed. "I've been trying to tell him that."

"I saw Melissa Thornton today," Stan said, changing the subject. "She's about to collect on a big insurance policy on Brad's life—at least a million, I'm sure."

"More like two-and-a-half million," Don advised.

"How do you know that?" Stan asked.

"My brother-in-law works for Provincial. I referred Brad to him when he was looking to get some coverage."

"Hmm. Do you know the friend who she's been hanging around with lately? Tall, strong, Hispanic man in his thirties."

"I know who you're talking about, but I don't know his name. I've seen him a few times at El Chico when I've gone there for lunch. Apparently, he's taken a fancy to a waitress there."

"Oh, really? That's interesting. I'll have to keep on eye out for him. I get the feeling he's more than just a friend."

"You think they are romantically involved?" Don asked.

"I don't know, but I'm going to find out."

At six, Stan and Rebekah met up with Kristina and Lamar again for dinner. This time they were joined by Kristina's friends, Glenda and Bill Green and John and Jill Smart. They found a table at Black-eyed Pea with a clear view of a TV. Lamar gave the bartender twenty bucks, and he changed the station to NBC Channel 5, where election coverage had already begun.

Stan bought the first round of margaritas and an assortment of appetizers for everyone to enjoy while they watched the election results come in from the East coast. Unfortunately, Jimmy Carter took an early lead, dampening the group's spirits. When they had finished their dinner about seven thirty, they moved the party to the First National Bank's community room, where a good crowd of friends, party workers, press, and supporters had gathered to watch the election results come in and hopefully celebrate Kristina's election. When Kristina walked in, there was a stirring round of applause.

Kristina smiled and waved meekly to the crowd. It was obvious she wasn't accustomed to being the center of attention and felt a bit awkward. Stan knew from experience, however, that when the moment came for her to perform, she'd come through better than anyone expected.

"Speech! Speech! Speech!" people began to shout. Kristina looked at Stan, and he pointed to a podium with a microphone. Kristina rolled her eyes and started moving slowly toward it, shaking hands as she progressed. When she reached the podium she adjusted the microphone and then smiled warmly.

"Hi, everybody. Thanks for coming out tonight. I'm overwhelmed by the numbers of you that are here. I know when we started this race, it looked pretty hopeless. A lot of people thought I was just put up as a token candidate to sacrifice to the almighty incumbent, Ron Wells."

There was laughter.

"Well, I will confess it appeared that way to me at first, and I was prepared to be the sacrificial lamb for the benefit of the Republican Party because I thought it an important milestone to have a woman on the ballot. But my campaign manager, our own Stan Turner, quickly set me straight. I remember his words quite vividly… 'Don't accept the nomination unless you intend to win'. I thought he was just joking at first. I mean, how does a Republican candidate defeat an incumbent legislator in a district that has been Democratic since the carpetbaggers were thrown out after the Civil War—not to mention the fact that no woman has ever been elected to state office in this district? But I soon realized Stan was serious, so I adjusted my thinking and told him fervently. 'Okay, I'm going to win'."

The crowd yelled and applauded enthusiastically. Kristina waited for them to settle down and then continued. "But saying you intend to win and winning aren't exactly the same thing."

There was more laughter.

"I knew I had an uphill battle, but for the first

time, I could see myself as your state representative."

"Yeah, baby!" someone yelled, causing everyone to laugh.

"As my confidence grew, I could see your confidence in me grow, and the media begin to take me more seriously. Of course, good fortune is always welcome. You've got to love it when your opponent gets mired in scandal and his true colors are revealed on the eve of the election."

Laughter and applause erupted from the crowd. Kristina stood tall, smiling broadly.

"But, seriously, despite my good fortune up until tonight, the reality of the situation was that Ron Wells would likely be swept back into the legislature on the coattails of Jimmy Carter."

"No!" someone screamed.

"I said likely, not definitely. I suspect it will be a close vote—the scandal playing in my favor and history and the obvious national tide favoring my opponent. But, whatever the outcome I will always cherish this moment looking out over all of your faces, family, friends and supporters, knowing you were so staunchly behind me in this most difficult race. God bless you, and may the best woman win!"

There was great laughter and applause as Kristina stepped away from the podium and began shaking hands and talking to her fans. After a few moments, Stan went to the podium.

"Ladies and gentlemen, thank you all for coming out tonight to celebrate Kristina Tenison's election to the state legislature."

There were loud cheers.

"For your convenience, there are several television sets all around the room tuned to different stations, so you'll have the very latest results available at all times. Also, we have live music and dancing in the southwest corner of the hall, as well as an open bar for those of you who are serious about partying."

There were cheers and applause.

"Enjoy yourselves. It could be a long night," Stan concluded.

As Stan left the podium, Don Karnes took his place. "Excuse me... we have our first results in tonight from Precinct 23. Ron Wells 623 and Kristina Tenison 701!"

Cheers erupted from the crowd. There was excited conversation, and the band began to play. Stan looked over at Kristina and Lamar and gave them a thumbs up. Then he went to the bar and got himself a drink. With a bourbon and seven in hand, he joined a group watching NBC 5. The lead story was Jimmy Carter's sweep of the east and much of the south. Stan saw that he was slightly ahead in Texas as well, 51 to 48 percent with 3 percent of the vote counted. The local results started to roll along the bottom of the screen. He gasped when he saw the results for 67th District: Ron Wells 1321, Kristina Tenison 1113 with 2 percent of the vote counted.

Stan sighed and then looked at his watch. It was after eight, and he knew nothing significant would be happening for at least an hour or two. He wondered if he'd have time to run over to El Chico to see if Melissa Thornton's friend was hanging out there waiting for his girlfriend to get off. Looking around, he decided nobody would miss him, so he slipped out. As he was leaving the building, the thought occurred to him that he might need some backup if he did run into Melissa's friend. He decided to call Lynn Jenkins.

"Hey, Lynn. What you up to?"

"Oh, just watching the election returns. Where

are you? I hear a lot of noise in the background."

"I'm at Kristina's victory party, but I've got a lead I need to check out."

"Really? I thought your investigation was over."

"Yeah, well there are still a few loose ends. One of them is a guy that's been hanging around Melissa Thornton. She says he's a friend, but I think she's lying about that. I need to find out who he is and how he fits into the puzzle."

"What did you have in mind?"

"He might be over at El Chico. If he is, I may need some backup. He may not like me snooping around and asking questions. If he's not there, I'll buy you a drink."

"Sounds like a plan. I'll meet you over there in a little while. I'm in the middle of something right now."

"No hurry. I'll try not to get into any trouble before you arrive."

Jenkins laughed tentatively. Stan hung up and then drove over to El Chico. It wasn't terribly busy since it was a Tuesday night and the tail end of the dinner hour, but there were a number of patrons in the bar. Stan surveyed the bar and the nearby booths but didn't see Melissa's friend. Disappointed, he took a seat at the bar, ordered a beer, and waited for Jenkins.

A few minutes later, he heard laughing over in the corner of the restaurant and saw the man he was looking for, flirting with a waitress. The waitress was pretty and much younger than the tough-looking man, but she seemed very taken by him and kept coming back to talk and deliver him more drinks. The man was drinking beer and chain smoking in between visits from the waitress. Stan figured he'd have to go to the bathroom sooner or later and, when he did, Stan could go over and steal one of his beer bottles.

Stan noticed the man was drinking a Corona, so he ordered a Corona for himself. When the man finally got up and staggered to the bathroom, Stan dropped a ten-dollar bill on the bar, took his empty Corona, walked by the man's table, and deftly switched it for one of his. Holding it with a napkin so as not to disturb any of the prints, he took it to his car and threw it in the back seat on the floor.

He was about to get in the car and go back to the victory party when he remembered Jenkins was coming by for a drink. He thought about it a minute and decided he had better wait. At that moment, the waitress came running out of the bar, pointing at Stan. Her boyfriend came out a second later and peered menacingly at him. Stan got in the car and locked the doors as the man came at him and pounded on the windows.

"What were you doing at my table? Who are you!" he screamed.

Stan recoiled in terror as the man started kicking and beating on the car. Finally, the man stopped and looked around. Stan watched in horror as he ran to his car, opened the trunk, and pulled out an iron crowbar. Stan tried to start the engine, but in his haste to leave, he flooded the engine. There was a crashing sound as the back window was shattered by one ferocious blow from the crowbar. Stan tried to start the car again. The starter whined and coughed, but the engine wouldn't kick over.

Then the driver's side window disintegrated, and Stan was pelted by broken glass. The man raised the crowbar again, this time to strike at Stan's head, but Stan desperately crawled to the passenger's seat, escaping the blow. Just as the man started to run around the car, Stan heard a siren and saw the reflection of red and blue flashing lights in the front window.

Jenkins rushed over and opened the door. "Stan! You okay?"

Stan took a deep breath and smiled. "Yeah, I'm fine now that you're here. He was trying to kill me!"

"I noticed. Unfortunately, he got away."

Jenkins helped Stan out of the car and then started picking glass out of his hair. "You weren't kidding about getting in trouble."

Stan shrugged. "I'd have gotten away clean had the waitress not seen me."

"Hmm. Maybe I should take you to the emergency room. You're bleeding."

"No, no. I'm fine. A couple Band-aids should fix me up."

Jenkins shrugged. "Okay. I've got a first aid kit in the squad car. I'll get you a few," Jenkins said and walked over to his car and popped the trunk. A moment later, he returned and affixed a half dozen adhesive bandages to Stan's wounds.

"You wouldn't happen to have an evidence bag, would you?" Stan asked.

"An evidence bag?"

"Yeah. I need to preserve the evidence I collected."

Jenkins frowned, went back to the trunk of his squad car, and produced a brown paper lunch sack. "Will this do?" he asked.

Stan gave him a disappointed look and then replied, "Sure, that'll work."

After Stan had secured the bottle of Corona and put it in the trunk of his car, he wondered if he should offer to buy Lynn a drink like he had promised. He didn't want to go back into the bar, so he suggested Lynn come back to the victory party.

"Okay. I'll come by for a little while. Maybe you

should drive your car home and park it in the garage. If it snows anymore, it's going to be a mess.

"That's a good idea. I'll switch cars while I'm there."

Stan drove home with Jenkins in tow, and they switched cars. When they got back to the victory party, Stan and Lynn went looking for Rebekah. When they found her, she gasped in shock. "What the hell happened to you?"

Stan shrugged. "Just a little misunderstanding," Stan said evenly.

"Huh! What happened? What's with all the cuts on your face?" Rebekah asked as she examined them.

"I found a big brute smashing in all of Stan's windows with a crowbar. I didn't realize he was inside."

"Oh, my God! You're going to need a plastic surgeon."

"No. Don't be ridiculous. I'll be fine," Stan said, backing off a few steps.

"What happened? Why was he smashing in your window?"

Stan thought about telling her the truth but then thought better of it. He wasn't in the mood for a lecture on minding his own business. The reaction of Melissa's friend disturbed him. Obviously, he wasn't just an ordinary citizen. Ordinary citizens don't try to kill you if you steal their empty beer bottle. This guy was hiding something.

"How's the election coming?" Stan asked, attempting to change the subject.

"Kristina's trailing slightly," Rebekah replied, "but it's still pretty close. Ford's getting clobbered."

"Hmm. That's too bad. He's a good man. He deserves another term."

"He's doing better in the west. He may still pull

it out yet."

Don Karnes went up to the podium. "We just got another precinct vote in. It's Precinct 83, and the vote is Ron Wells 947, Kristina Tenison 1048."

There were yells and whistles from the crowd, and then Don continued. "That makes the total vote with 47 percent of the vote counted, Ron Wells 84,221 and Kristina Tenison 81,304." There were a few moans and then silence.

Stan went over to Don Karnes, leaving Rebekah shaking her head. Jenkins joined them. "What precincts are still out?" Stan asked.

"Mostly the west side of the district, which should be more favorable to Kristina."

"That's what I was thinking. So, she still has a chance?"

Don nodded. "What happened to your face?" he asked curiously.

"Uh, well, Melissa's friend didn't like me snooping around, so he took a crowbar to my car."

"Holy shit!"

"Yeah. Luckily, Officer Jenkins here showed up before the hothead killed me. Don't tell Rebekah. I don't want her to worry."

"So, what's his problem?" Don asked.

"I suspect he's not just hanging around to comfort and support the widow Thornton," Stan said sardonically.

Jenkins laughed.

"He may be hanging around to get a cut of that 2.5 million dollars Melissa's about to receive."

Jenkins eyes widened. "Did you say 2.5 million dollars?"

Stan nodded. "That's what Don here tells me she's getting."

"Whoa! That's a lot of bread," Jenkins observed. "Why do you suppose he thinks he deserves a cut of it?" Jenkins asked.

"He either knows something Melissa wants kept secret, or it's a payoff for something he's done for her," Stan suggested.

"Maybe he's threatened to kill her if she doesn't pay or kidnapped someone she loves," Don added.

"Perhaps. Whatever it is, we can't let him get away with it. I'm going to see Agent Rutledge in the morning and tell her everything I know."

"I could track down the bastard and arrest him for assault and battery," Jenkins said.

"No, not yet. We need to find out what's motivating him first—see if others are involved. Then we should let the FBI deal with him.

The three men sat silent for a moment, contemplating the situation, and then a worker walked up briskly and handed Don a sheet of paper.

Don read the results out loud. "Oh, Precinct 97. Wells 874, Tenison 1277."

"Alright. That's much better."

Don nodded and ran off to announce it to the crowd. Stan looked at Jenkins. "We should go talk with the bartender and find out what he knows about Melissa's friend."

"Right, good idea," Jenkins agreed.

"El Chico closes at midnight. We'll be here long after that, I'm afraid. Maybe we can take a break and catch him as he's leaving."

Jenkins looked at his watch. "I've got to go run some errands right now. I'll come back here in time to run us over there and visit with him."

"Good. I'll see you later then," Stan said.

Jenkins left, and Stan looked around the room for

Kristina. He knew she would be worried sick and wanted to reassure her everything would be okay. He spotted her and Lamar talking to Veronica Brooks and some other reporters. He made his way through the crowd and came up next to her.

"Stan. There you are. Where have you been?" she said, frowning. "What happened to your face?"

"Someone decided to take their rage out on my car with me in it. Luckily, the cops came before I was seriously injured."

"What did you do to piss the guy off?" Veronica asked wryly.

Stan laughed. "Now, Veronica, what makes you think I did anything to provoke him?"

"Because you have a propensity for that kind of thing. You should be an investigative reporter. You'd be good at it."

Stan turned to Kristina, wanting to change the subject. "So, the latest numbers are looking good, huh?"

"Yeah, but that's just one precinct, and I have a lot of ground to make up."

"You'll do it," Stan reassured her. "Your best precincts have yet to report in."

"I hope you're right, but I've got a concession speech written just in case."

"Did you ever really think you had a chance of winning?" Sherry Lester, another reporter, asked. "I mean, had it not been for this last-minute scandal, you wouldn't have had a chance."

Stan bit his lip. Kristina straightened up. "Yes, I wouldn't have accepted the nomination if I hadn't thought I could win. I knew Wells had skeletons in his closet, and one of them was bound to pop out before election day."

Lester raised her eyebrows. "Well, that was very

astute of you. I certainly wouldn't have been so optimistic."

"Well, having a campaign manager like Stan Turner helps. He wouldn't let me dwell on anything negative."

"That's right," Stan agreed. "You are what you think, and you can do whatever you can imagine yourself doing—or something like that. I listen to a lot of motivational tapes while I'm driving around."

"It shows," Veronica said, smiling.

Don Karnes went up to the podium and asked for everyone's attention. "Ladies and gentlemen. We have the results of Precinct 121. Wells 779, Tenison 1278!" The room went wild with yells and screams of delight, then quieted when Don continued. "This brings the overall totals to Wells 97,232 and Tenison 96,477 with 51 percent of the vote counted."

"Hmm. Now it's getting interesting," Stan observed.

Kristina smiled tentatively. "Yes, less than 1,000 votes."

"Congratulations!" Veronica said.

"Yes, that's marvelous," Lester said begrudgingly.

"Well, I'm going to go check in on the poll watchers—make sure everything is okay. We don't want anything spoiling our victory should Kristina pull this out," Stan advised. "I'll see you later."

Stan left the group and went to a phone booth to call his poll watching coordinator. He told him there were no problems, so he went to the bar to get a drink. He got one for Rebekah, too, and then went searching for her. She was talking to Glenda Green and her husband. He came up next to her and handed her the drink.

"Oh, there you," Rebekah said. "I've just been telling Glenda about your adventures tonight."

"I don't know how you live with this guy," Glenda teased. "He's always getting in trouble."

Stan smiled. "Well, I get bored easy. What can I say?"

They talked for thirty minutes, and then Don Karnes returned to the podium. "Alright. A few more precincts have come in. The total vote as of two minutes ago was Wells 103,297, Tenison 103,199.

"Oh, my God!" Glenda exclaimed. "She's less than 100 votes behind."

"Yes, that's wonderful," Rebekah said. "I think she's going to make it."

Stan smiled at Rebekah. She was usually a pessimist, so to hear her say Kristina was going to win was like a cool breeze on a hot summer day. As he was relishing the moment, he saw Lynn Jenkins approaching. Looking at his watch, he said, "Uh, if you'll excuse me for a while, Jenkins and I have an errand to run."

Rebekah's eyes narrowed. "What are you up to now?" she asked disapprovingly.

"Just need to talk to someone. Officer Jenkins will be with me, so you don't have to worry."

Rebekah sighed and turned away. Stan and Jenkins left the community center and went to his squad car. Ten minutes later, they were in front of El Chico's deserted parking lot. It was eleven forty-seven when they stepped inside the nearly deserted restaurant. The bartender looked up at them.

"Sorry, we're about to close."

"No, problem," Jenkins said. "We just have a few questions for you."

The man looked at Stan. "You're still alive?"

Stan raised his eyebrows. "Yes. Why do you ask?"

He shrugged. "The way Vincente went out after

you for stealing his beer, I thought he might kill you."

"His name is Vincente?" Jenkins asked.

"Yes. That's what Linda calls him. I assume that's his name."

"What's his last name?" Jenkins asked.

The bartender shrugged. "I don't know. I've never heard her use his last name."

"How long have they been going out?" Stan asked.

"Just a few weeks. He came in one day with an older woman. Linda waited on him, and they hit it off."

"Would the older woman have been Melissa Thornton?"

"Right, now that you mention it."

"Do you know what Vincente's relationship to Melissa Thornton is?"

"Nope. Sorry."

"What do you know about Vincente?" Jenkins asked. "Has he ever got loaded and confided in you?"

"No. He seems to have it all together. He only comes here to see Linda."

"Does he ever bring any friends with him?"

"No. He's always alone, except that one time with Mrs. Thornton. He crashes at Linda's apartment, I think. I don't know what he does during the day."

"Do you think he's a violent person?" Jenkins asked.

"He's got a hot temper and has chased a few customers away. I had to have a talk with Linda about that—can't afford to be running customers off."

"Have you ever seen a weapon on him?"

"He carries a switchblade. He pulled it on a guy once."

"Alright," Stan said, slipping him a fifty-dollar bill. "Don't tell anyone we had this visit, okay?"

"No. I wouldn't chance it anyway. He's too

unpredictable."

They nodded and left. On the way back to the party, Stan wondered about Vincente and worried he might try to find Stan and his family. Jenkins must have been thinking the same thing, as he reminded Stan to be sure and activate his security system.

"I'll file a report on the assault and damage to your car. You'll need it for your insurance. I'll also put an extra patrol on your house for a few days, just in case."

"Thanks," Stan said appreciatively.

They rode in silence the rest of the way back to the Community Center, wondering how Vincente fit into the mystery beginning to swirl around Melissa Thornton. When they arrived back at the party, the crowd was electrified with anticipation. Don Karnes was just stepping to the podium.

"Another precinct is in. The vote for Precinct 107 is Wells 102 and Tenison 171." The crowd screamed their approval. "The total vote with 67 percent of the vote in is Wells 137,200, Tenison 141,302." There was a deafening roar of approval from the crowd.

"This calls for a drink!" Lynn said. "I'm going to find the bar."

Stan nodded, then searched the room for Rebekah. After a few minutes, he found her standing all alone, grinning from ear to ear. He went over to her and put his arm around her. "She's ahead! Can you believe it?"

"I told you she was going to win," Rebekah reminded him. Stan laughed. They embraced and then kissed passionately.

"Where's Kristina? I want to go congratulate her."

"I saw her dancing with Lamar a little while ago."

"Dancing? That sounds good. Let's go."

They waded through the thickening crowd toward

the dance floor. Kristina and Lamar were doing a pretty impressive rumba, and a small crowd had gathered around them to watch. When the dance was over, she rushed over to Stan and embraced him.

"You were right. I am going to win," she whispered in this ear.

"Of course, I always keep my promises."

She let him loose and then looked at Rebekah. "You're a lucky woman. Thanks for sharing your husband with me."

Rebekah gave Kristina a confused look. Stan laughed.

"What are you laughing about?" Rebekah sneered.

"I've been telling you how lucky you are for a long time. Now maybe you'll believe me."

"You can have him," Rebekah teased. "Look at him. He's more trouble than he's worth."

Kristina pondered the offer, and then someone pulled her away to congratulate her.

"Come on," Stan said. "Let's dance."

Rebekah stiffened. "What did she mean, sharing you?"

"She just meant allowing me to be her Campaign Manager."

"That's not what it sounded like. Have you been sleeping with her?"

"No. Don't be silly. She's just talking about the time I've spent with her campaigning."

"Well, you can inform her I didn't consent to it and that you just decided to do it. I didn't have any choice in the matter."

Stan sighed. "Okay. You're right, but now it's over. I don't plan to run for County Chairman again. I'm kind of burnt out frankly."

"Good. You should spend more time with your family."

"I will. I promise."

With each new precinct that reported, Kristina widened her lead, and in the wee hours of the morning it became clear she had defeated the incumbent, Ron Wells, and would be the new state representative for the 67th District. As they drove home, Stan felt exhilarated, for he knew he'd made a difference. He'd been instrumental in unseating a corrupt incumbent legislator and replacing him with an intelligent, capable, and honorable woman. He couldn't help but feel proud.

Chapter 27

The next morning, it had warmed up considerably as a strong wind was blowing from the south. After breakfast, Stan called Agent Rutledge and asked her if he could see her later in the day. She said she had something to do in the morning, but if he came in around noon, they could talk. He left his 11:00 a.m. class a little early and drove downtown to FBI headquarters. He was clutching his evidence bag when he walked into her office.

Agent Rutledge's eyes narrowed. "What happened to your face?"

"That's why I'm here. Some guy has been hanging around Melissa Thornton, and I was trying to figure out what he's up to. He didn't like it much."

Agent Rutledge came over to Stan and carefully examined the lacerations to his face. She shook her head. "Stan, when are you going to learn to leave law enforcement to the professionals? You should have told me about this guy and let us interrogate him."

Stan shrugged.

"What do you have there?" she asked.

"A beer bottle. There are some fingerprints of the guy on it. His name is Vincente. You may want to run them."

"What do you think he wanted with Melissa?"

"I'm not sure. He's either blackmailing her,

threatening bodily harm if she doesn't cut him in on her two-and-a-half-million-dollar life insurance settlement she's about to get, or she's paying him off for something."

"Did you say two-and-a-half million?" Rutledge asked.

"That's what I've been told."

"Why would she be paying him off?"

"I don't know, but this guy is a tough hombre, and since he tried to kill me when he found out I'd taken his beer bottle, he's obviously got something to hide."

Agent Rutledge took the lunch sack and peered inside. "Okay. It will take a couple of days to run the prints."

"That's fine. I'm just worried about Melissa. I'd hate for you to find her dead in a ditch somewhere after she collects the insurance."

"If this Vincente guy turns out to be as bad as you say, I'll see if we can figure out a good reason to bring him in. Would you press charges if we decided that was the way to go?"

"Sure."

"If we have some time, perhaps we can tie him into Silver Springs Ventures."

"Maybe. I don't know what he's into, but whatever it is, I doubt it's legal."

"Where did the altercation happen?" she asked.

"In Plano, at El Chicos."

"Alright. I'll contact the Collin County District Attorney's office and see if they'll help us out."

Stan thanked Agent Rutledge and then went over to his office at Cosmopolitan Life a few blocks away. He had a few applications to turn in, and he wanted to talk to a friend in the claims department about Melissa's insurance claim. His friend's name was Adam Clarkson.

"I don't know how Provincial Life does it, but we

wouldn't pay out that much on a murder victim without an extensive investigation," Adam advised.

"Who would you hire to make such an investigation?" Stan asked.

"We use Sentry Investigations. They're expensive, but they're good. They've saved us millions."

"I wonder if Provincial hired them for this claim."

"There's one way to find out," Adam said. "I can call the Claims Representative on the case and ask him."

"Really?"

"Sure. I'll tell him we've got a policy on the claimant and wondered if they'd found anything negative in their investigation. We share information like that once in a while. It's to everyone's best interest."

"Great. That would be very helpful."

Stan waited impatiently while Adam made the call. He didn't know why he was so anxious about Vincente, but then he realized he was scared. Post-traumatic stress from being nearly killed by the asshole the night before, he guessed.

There was something else bothering him though. He felt like he'd lost something, but he couldn't put a finger on it for a while. Then he realized he'd lost Kristina. Now she'd be caught up in the whirlwind of politics, and she'd be out of his life. He hadn't thought about that when he was pushing her into the state representative race. Now, he almost regretted doing it, but knew in his heart it was the best thing for everybody. Had she not been elected, eventually he might have given in to his feelings for her and ruined both of their lives. Finally, Adam got off the phone.

"Yes, they've got an investigation underway," Adam informed him. "They are expecting to wrap it up this week and send a report to Provincial on Monday."

"Hmm. Anything negative in the report?"

"No, apparently not."

"Did they give you the name of the investigator?'

"Yes, Larry Johnston. I've got his number if you want to talk to him. They can't give you any information on the investigation, but if you have some reason why Mrs. Thornton shouldn't be paid, they'd like to hear it."

"Well, I wouldn't want to torpedo her insurance settlement unless there is a compelling reason."

"Suit yourself, but she'll probably have a check by the end of next week unless something comes up."

"Thanks, Adam. I appreciate your help."

From his office, Stan went back to SMU to study the rest of the day, also in hopes of running into Paula. He needed someone to talk to and someone to brainstorm with about Melissa. He found Paula in a study cubicle on the second floor.

"Hey, there you are," he said.

"Stan, hi. Congratulations on the election!"

"Thanks. What a night, huh?"

"Yeah. Kristina must have been happy."

"She was, definitely. So, what are you studying?"

"Criminal appeals," Paula responded blandly.

"Got a minute to talk about Melissa Thornton?"

"Yeah. What's up with her?"

Stan told her about his encounter with Vincente and his suspicions that he was hanging around to get a cut of her insurance money.

"Have you looked into her family to see if there is someone who might have been kidnapped? Does she have children?"

"I'm sure she does, but they'd be grown. . . .Wait a minute! She took out a life insurance policy, $500,000, and made her daughter Amanda the beneficiary. I think that was her name. I thought it was a bit unusual at the time that she'd be thinking about life insurance when the FBI was all over them."

"She must have known her life was in danger and wanted to be sure she'd be provided for."

"Right. She promised Amanda she'd help her through medical school, and I guess she wasn't sure she'd be alive to do it."

"Okay. You should make sure Amanda is okay," Paula suggested. "It's too bad Melissa won't level with you. It's hard to help someone if they won't tell you what's going on."

"I talked to Agent Rutledge this morning. I'm hoping she'll talk to her. Maybe she can learn more about Vincente and what he's up to."

"Good. I don't know what else you could do," Paula said.

"How are you and Professor Hertel getting along?"

"Oh, that's over," Paula replied sadly.

"What happened?"

"The Dean found out he took me to Mexico and had a fit. He threatened to fire him if we didn't break it off. Apparently, when our dear professor took this job, he promised to keep his hands off the students. I guess his reputation preceded him."

Stan laughed. "What a shame."

"Anyway. I was starting to tire of him. These older men can't always perform all that well in bed. I need to stick with younger men," she noted, slowly licking her lips.

Stan felt uneasy. He stood up. "Uh, well, thanks, Paula. I've got to get home. You were a big help, as always."

"Sure. Anytime you want to study together, we can. We don't have to do it here. We can study at my apartment where we have more privacy."

"Yeah. I'll keep that in mind. Take care."

Stan turned, and with some ambivalence, walked away. As he was walking down the stairs, he fantasized about studying with Paula at her apartment, but each time he ran the daydream through his mind, they ended up in bed. Not a bad outcome for a daydream, but a disaster in real life.

Before he left the building, he stopped at a phone booth and called Agent Rutledge. "Sorry to bother you again, but I just remembered Melissa Thornton has a daughter at A&M. Vincente may have kidnapped her, and the life insurance proceeds could be the ransom. It's just a thought. Hopefully it's a false alarm, but it probably wouldn't hurt to check it out."

"We'll do that. Actually, I'm glad you called. We picked up Vincente and are holding him for the Collin County District Attorney's office. Apparently, you already filed a complaint for assault and battery?"

"Right. Officer Jenkins filed that for me, I think."

"Good. Hopefully we'll get the results back on his prints, and then we'll be able to identify him."

"Thank you."

"If you're not busy, you may want to come down here. We've picked up Melissa Thornton, too, as a witness since she's been seen with Vincente."

"You may want to question Vincente's girlfriend too," Stan suggested. "She works at El Chico. He may have told her something. Her name's Linda."

"Good idea. I'll get someone on it."

"Okay. I'll be at your office in thirty minutes."

"Alright. See you then."

Stan was greatly relieved that Vincente had been picked up since he knew from experience that Vincente was capable of anything. When he got to FBI headquarters, he was escorted to an interrogation viewing room. Agent Adams had just read him his rights.

“So, what’s your full name?”

“Everyone calls me Vincente.”

“I know that much. What’s your last name?”

“Like I said, everyone calls me Vincente.”

“Al right, have it your way. Where are you from, Vincente?”

“I don’t have to answer your questions, right?”

“No, not if you think it might incriminate you. Are you worried about that?”

“I did nothing.”

“So talk to me then. Where are you from?”

“Mexico City, but I live in San Diego.”

“Are you legal?”

“Yes. I have a green card.”

“What do you do for a living?”

He shrugged. “Odds and ends.”

“What kind of odds and ends?”

“Just odds and ends.”

Agent Adams sighed. “Okay, and what brings you to north Texas?”

“I’m visiting a friend.”

“Melissa Thornton?”

“Yes.”

“How do you two know each other?”

“A mutual friend put us together.”

“Why?”

“She needed money, and I make loans from time to time.”

“How much did you lend her?”

“About $200,000.”

Warren’s eyes narrowed. “So, you’re here to collect your money?”

“Yes. She said she’d have it the next week or two,

so I decided to hang around and make sure she didn't disappear without paying me."

"How much does she owe you?"

"Is that important?"

"It could be. The maximum interest rate you can charge in Texas is 10 percent, unless you have a license to charge more."

He shrugged. "I'm not charging interest."

"Who's the mutual friend that referred you to Melissa?"

"I don't remember. I get referrals all the time. I don't bother to keep track of them."

"What did Melissa do with the $200,000 you gave her?"

"That's none of my business."

"True, but didn't she tell you why she needed the money?"

"Something about a foreclosure and money for a lawyer."

"Do you know Carlos Morales?"

"No."

"He wasn't the one who referred you to Melissa, was he?"

"Like I said, I don't know who referred her."

"What about Tony Rubio?"

Vincente shook his head. "No, I don't know him."

Agent Adams got up. "Okay. Give me a minute," he said, leaving the room to confer with Agent Rutledge. He went over to Stan and Agent Rutledge and shook his head. "He's not going to tell us a whole lot," Agent Adams conceded.

"Well, Melissa did need money," Stan noted. "I suppose she could have borrowed it, but it would be pretty stupid to borrow it from a loan shark unless you were pretty sure you were going to collect on the insurance."

"So, you think Melissa knew her husband was going to die?"

Stan took a deep breath. "As much as I hate to suggest it, it kind of looks that way. Did you check on her daughter?"

"Yes. She's okay—nobody has threatened her or anything."

"I was afraid of that. It's possible Melissa may have set this whole thing up."

"You think so?" Agent Rutledge asked. "Why do you say that?"

"Well, think about it. She was on top of the world—big houses, expensive cars, lots of parties, the country club, and dabbling in politics. Then her husband's business fails, and she's devastated. Brad loves her and can't stand to see her so unhappy. She talks about divorce. In desperation, Brad contacts his old buddy from college, Tony Rubio, and asks for help. Rubio needs money laundered, so he tells Brad that if he can come up with something, maybe they can help each other out."

"A plausible theory," Agent Adams agreed. "Go on."

"Okay, so things turn around. Her life is back to normal. She's happy, and then you guys start your investigation and her life turns to crap again. This time, however, money won't fix her problems. Brad could go to jail, and she's in danger of being indicted as well. When she voices her concerns about this, Carlos assures her they have been very careful and the feds won't be able to make a case. They won't be able to find a connection between Rubio and her husband.

"She knows that's not true–there is one person who can link Rubio to Brad, and that's Rob Shepard. Rob knows about Brad's relationship with Rubio in college, and when the feds interrogate Rob, she's petrified he'll cut a deal and turn against them."

"You think Melissa hired someone to kill Rob and his family?" Adams asked.

Stan shrugged. "It's the only thing that makes since. If you remember, someone pulled $50,000 in cash out of one of Silver Springs Ventures accounts just before you froze it. I think she paid the two guys you have in custody to kill Rob and Cindy. They had to kill Cindy because she knew everything Rob knew. I'm not sure if they intended to kill the entire family or if that was something done impromptu in the heat of the moment. It kind of looks like the babysitter had left and then came back and surprised them. I'm not sure exactly how it went down, but they made it to look like a murder-suicide, hoping to conceal the truth.

"Again, everything seemed to be under control until I came into the picture and started nosing around. Melissa couldn't let me stir things up again, so she invited me to her home on the pretext of buying an insurance policy. In reality, she'd hired the same two goons who slaughtered the Shepards to kidnap me."

"But she was kidnapped too," Agent Rutledge reminded him.

"She wanted it to appear that way. She needed to be a victim too. Her plan was for me to die but for her to escape. She wanted it to look like Brad or Morales was trying to kill her so she'd have an easier time cutting a deal with you guys."

"Right," Adams agreed.

"But her plan wasn't totally frustrated when you guys rescued us. It's not a complete catastrophe because she still looks like a victim and is able to cut a deal. Now her problem is with Brad. If he comes home and discovers she's betrayed him, he might figure out what she's done. She can't let that happen, so she figures out how to kill two birds with one stone, so to speak. She convinces me to rescue Brad and then hires someone to kill both of us when we return from Mexico."

"You think Vincente is the assassin?" Agent Rutledge asked.

"He or someone he hired to do it."

Agent Rutledge and Agent Adams looked at each other for a long moment.

"That's a pretty complex scenario," Agent Adams noted. "I'm not saying I don't like it, but I'd hate to have to prove it in court. Maybe I can convince Vincente that Melissa has turned on him—blamed everything on him."

Just then, another agent walked up with a folder. "Here's your fingerprint ID," he said and handed him the folder.

Agent Adams opened the folder. "Okay. Our man in Vincente Perez from Mexico City. He's reportedly a contract hit man. Reports are he's responsible for dozen or more assassinations, but he apparently covers his tracks pretty well, as he's never been charged with any of them. Seven of the assassinations took place in Southern California, the rest in Mexico."

"So, Southern California is his territory. That's why he got the call," Agent Adams reasoned.

"Right," Stan agreed. "And I think you'll eventually discover that Vincente and the two guys you have locked up are connected. He's probably the one paying for their lawyer."

"Okay. I'll tell Melissa that Vincente has given her up and see what she says. Hopefully one of them will be shaken enough to slip up."

"Neither one of them will be easy to crack," Stan worried. "I hope they don't lawyer up on you."

"We've had a little experience at this, Stan. Just watch and learn."

Stan smiled. "That works for me."

Agent Adams went back into the interview room with Vincente's file in his hand. Vincente eyed him warily. He opened the file.

"Vincente Perez of Mexico City," he stated casually. "Let's see… a contract killer for hire. How do you get into that kind of business anyway?"

Vincente swallowed hard. "I've never killed anybody."

"Well, I'm not so sure about that, but I will admit nobody's been able to prove it—until now."

Vincente's eyes narrowed. "What are you talking about? You have nothing on me," he spat.

"I don't know. Mrs. Thornton claims she hired you to kill her husband," Agent Adams lied. "What do you say about that?"

"I say you're lying. I didn't kill anyone, and I know she wouldn't accuse me of something like that."

"So, what's your relationship then?"

"Just a friend."

"How long have you known her?"

"Several years. We met on a fishing trip."

"Really? Where?"

"In San Diego. Hurricane Charters. Check it out."

"I will. So, have you got together since the fishing trip?"

"No. We talk by phone from time to time."

Vincente twisted in his chair and looked away. "I loaned her money. That's it."

"That's not what she says. She says you're the man to call in Southern California if you need someone knocked off. Your file would seem to suggest that's true."

He shook his head but said nothing.

"Why would she call you for money? Do you work at a frickin' bank?"

"No. I have my own resources."

"You mean the fees you get paid for assassinating people?"

"No. I have other business interests."

"Like what."

"My business interests have nothing to do with this case."

"Okay. Who referred her to you? Was it Pablo or Manuel?"

"Who?" Vincente asked with no hint of recognition.

"Pablo or Manuel. You remember them. Aren't you all in the same business—contract killers?"

"I'm not a contract killer, and I don't know these men."

"Why did you hire them a lawyer then?"

"I don't know what you're talking about. I didn't hire any lawyers,"

"I think you're lying. I think you know each other very well."

He shook his head. "No. You're wrong. I don't know them."

"Well, it doesn't matter. Who do you think a jury will believe, an admitted loan shark hanging around to take money from a grieving widow or a pillar of the community like Melissa Thornton?"

Vincente thought about that a moment before he replied. "She has much more to gain from her husband's death than I do."

"Really? How's that?"

"You must know about the insurance money she's about to get."

"I heard something about that. Two-and-a-half

million, right?"

He nodded. "That's why I'm hanging around—to be sure I get paid."

"How much does she owe you?"

"She owes me $500,000. That's what she agreed to pay me."

"To kill her husband?"

"No. Principal and interest on the loan."

"So, $200,000 principal and $300,000 interest?"

"No!"

"Oh, I'm sorry. Was it $200,000 principal and $300,000 to kill her husband and Stan Turner?"

"No. It was a $300,000 bonus."

"Oh! A bonus. I see. Why would she pay you a bonus?"

"It was a risky investment. I declined the request at first until she offered me the bonus."

"Come on!," Agent Adams spat. "Give me a break! It was either interest or hit money. What was it?"

"A bonus."

"A bonus if her husband ended up dead?"

Vincente shook his head in utter frustration. "There's no use talking to you. You're just trying to twist my words. I've said enough. I want a lawyer."

"You sure? You get a lawyer and the US Attorney's not going to offer you a deal."

"What deal? You haven't offered me anything."

"Oh, I didn't tell you. I'm sorry....Well, if you'll level with us and confirm that Mrs. Thornton hired you to kill her husband and Stan Turner, then he won't ask for the death penalty and will recommend leniency to the judge. You'd serve your time in a federal penitentiary and could be out in twenty years with good behavior."

"No guarantees, though, right?" Vincente noted.

"No, but whatever you get will be much better

than what you'll be facing if you don't cooperate."

Vincente shook his head. "Twenty years is a long time."

"True, but life in federal prison isn't so bad—a lot better than if we send you back to California and you end up on death row in San Quentin. You've heard of San Quentin, haven't you? They execute inmates in a gas chamber there."

Vincente rubbed his chin nervously. Warren got up. "Think about it for a minute while I go see how my partner is doing with Mrs. Thornton. Of course, if she confesses on her own, the offer is off the table, and San Quentin it is, Vincente."

"Your offer isn't worth crap!" Vincente spat. "Have you even talked to the US Attorney?"

Adams ignored the question and left the room. He smiled at Stan and Agent Rutledge looking rather pleased with himself.

"So, did I shake him up or what?"

"Yes. He looks pretty pissed," Stan noted.

"We'll let him stew a while Ruth visits with Mrs. Thornton."

Stan nodded and followed Agent Rutledge over to the other interrogation room. She opened the door and entered. Melissa Thornton smiled at her, unsuspecting of what was about to happen to her.

"Hi, Melissa. How have you been?" Agent Rutledge asked warmly.

"Okay, considering everything," Melissa replied with a sigh.

"Well, like I told you on the phone, we picked up your friend Vincente Perez. He tried to kill Stan Turner with a tire iron over at El Chico's the other night."

Melissa frowned. "Yes, that's so terrible. I don't know what got into him."

"I have advised you of your rights in the past. Do you remember what I told you?"

"Yes, I have the right to an attorney, etc., etc… but this isn't about me, is it?"

"I don't know. You tell me. Why has Vincente been hanging around Plano? He doesn't live here, does he?"

"No. He's concerned about me—wants to make sure I'm alright. You know how friends can get overprotective."

"Is he a relative?"

"No. Just a friend."

"Where does he live?"

"In San Diego. We met him on a fishing charter a few years back."

"Just a casual acquaintance then?"

"Well, we've kept in touch."

"How well do you know him? Did you know he is a known contract killer?"

"What? That's nonsense. That couldn't be true."

"What do you think he does for a living then?"

"I truly don't know. He did loan me some money, but it was his own personal funds, I'm sure."

"Yes, he mentioned that. What were the terms of the loan?"

"When I collect the insurance proceeds on Brad, I'm to pay him $500,000."

"Is that how much he loaned you?"

"Well, no, but I was desperate, you know. Nobody would loan me any money, so I had to offer him a premium. I had to get the money or I would have lost all our real estate."

"You mean your home here in Texas and the Maui property?"

"Right. Plus, there were lawyers' fees and

monthly expenses that were way behind."

Agent Rutledge gave Melissa a hard look. "Unfortunately, your stories don't match," she noted.

"What? Don't match? What do you mean?"

"Mr. Perez says part of the $500,000 is his fee for killing your husband," Agent Rutledge lied.

"What? That bastard. That's absurd. He didn't say that, did he?"

"What made you think he'd have that kind of money to lend?" Agent Rutledge asked.

"He mentioned to us—Brad and me—that he makes loans from time to time. He's a very successful businessman."

"Come on, Melissa! Give me a break. This guy is a professional hit man from Southern California. We've got his file. He's no longtime friend. Someone referred you to him—was it Rubicardo or his amigo Pablo?"

"No! He lent me money. That's the truth, and that's all!" Melissa assured her.

"Well, I don't know what to tell you, but Vincente claims you hired him, and you know what that means, don't you?"

"It means he's lying. He must be trying to get you to offer him some kind of deal. You've got to believe me."

"I'd like to, but what he says makes a lot of sense. At any rate, until we can sort this out, I'm going to have to advise the insurance company of the accusation."

Melissa's eyes widened. "No! You can't do that. I need that money," she replied desperately.

"Why? What happens to you if you don't pay Vincente?"

Melissa looked horror stricken. Tears welled in her eyes. "No, please don't do this. Don't contact the insurance company. They promised I'd have the money next week."

"I don't have a choice. The accusation has been made, so I have to contact them and tell them what I know."

"No! He'll kill Amanda."

"Who? Vincente?"

"Yes. If I don't pay him, my daughter is dead."

"Then perhaps you should level with us. We can protect your daughter from him."

Melissa slumped in her chair, the color drained from her face.

"If you tell us the truth, I promise you he'll go to jail for the rest of his life, and neither you nor your daughter will have to worry about him ever again," Agent Rutledge promised.

Tears began streaming down Melissa's cheeks. Agent Rutledge gave her a tissue. She took a deep breath and closed her eyes. When she opened them, anger had overtaken her. "Turner's behind this, isn't he? Is he out there watching?" She gestured toward the window with her middle finger.

"You can't blame Stan for what you've done. He had nothing to do with it."

"He was so worried about clearing Rob's name. Rob was no saint. He should have left it alone."

"So, when did you make the decision to kill Brad?" Agent Rutledge asked. "Was it after you had the Shepards killed?"

Melissa began sobbing again. "Oh, God! I can't believe this is happening!" Agent Rutledge handed her another tissue. "I had no choice. I knew Rob pretty well. He'd cut a deal in a second if it would save his own ass."

"So, you hired Rubicardo and Pablo to do it?"

She nodded. "They weren't supposed to kill the children. It was just supposed to be Rob and Cindy, but I guess the babysitter had forgotten her school book and came back to get it. Then everything went wrong. Their eldest child, Jenny, woke up and saw Pablo kill his mother, so I guess Pablo decided to kill everybody so there wouldn't be any witnesses."

"Tell me about the kidnapping. How was that supposed to work?"

"When Stan Turner started snooping around trying to clear Rob's name, Manuel and Pablo got nervous and wanted me to pay them to kill him. I said I would, but I didn't have any money. That's when the idea came up about killing Brad. I told them about the insurance I had on him. Of course, Brad was in Mexico by then, so that made it impossible. That's when I got the idea to ask Stan to rescue Brad. I couldn't believe it when Stan agreed to it. Finally, I'd caught a break. Manuel and Pablo said they knew a man from San Diego that would kill Stan and Brad, but he was expensive."

"Murder doesn't come cheap, huh?" Agent Rutledge noted.

"No, particularly when the assassin has to wait to get paid. It would have only cost $100,000 had I had the cash up front."

"So, you were going to fund all this with the proceeds from Brad's insurance?"

"Right. The only problem with our plan was that it would seem obvious I was behind the murder. Pablo came up with the idea of kidnapping me and Stan so I wouldn't be a suspect in Brad's death and would seem like a victim. It would have worked perfectly had you not been following us."

"So, tell me about the threats against you and your daughter. That might influence the judge or jury to lessen your sentence."

Melissa took a deep breath. "Well, after we'd negotiated the fee, I asked him what would happen if for some reason the insurance money didn't come through. I was worried about that since I knew they might delay paying the claim on account of the circumstances of his death."

"What did he say?"

"He told me if he didn't get paid, he'd kill me and Amanda."

"And you still went along with the arrangement?"

Melissa shrugged. "The deal had been struck. There was no backing out by that time."

Agent Rutledge nodded. "Okay. Thank you, Melissa. You did the right thing. Now we'll be able to protect you and your daughter and put Vincente away for a very long time."

Melissa looked at her dejectedly. "A lot of good that will do me, but at least Amanda will still have a life."

Agent Rutledge got up and left the interrogation room. She smiled at Stan and Agent Adams.

"Nice work," Agent Adams said. "I guess that wraps it up."

"I guess so," Stan agreed.

"You know, Stan," Rutledge said thoughtfully, "after you graduate from college, you ought to come work for the FBI. You've got great instincts."

"I appreciate the thought, but I'm not very good at taking orders."

"Well, that's true," Agent Rutledge replied.

Stan smiled. "So, I plan to start my own practice."

"So, are you going to be a prosecutor or get rich defending thugs?" Adams asked.

"Neither. Criminal law doesn't interest me that much, but I might take on a little defense work if I think the client is innocent. I'm not one of those purists who thinks you should defend everyone because they all are entitled to the best defense available. I plan to pick and choose my clients."

"Well, that's quite admirable but not very practical, I'm afraid," Agent Rutledge noted. "Anyway, thank you for helping us wrap up all these cases. You did some extraordinary detective work."

"Extraordinarily reckless," Warren interjected, "but effective, I must admit."

Stan shook their hands and left, feeling good about how he'd managed to sort everything out and earn their respect. He knew he should be feeling anger at Melissa Thornton for trying to kill him and for all the deaths she was responsible for, but instead, he felt sorry for her. Her life had spun out of control, and her focus had narrowed to her own self-preservation—not an unusual response for the human species.

He was just relieved it was finally over. It had been a tough year. He hadn't intended to do anything other than make a living and finish law school, but he'd been pulled into the political arena and then faced with Shepard family tragedy by forces beyond his comprehension. He remembered his childhood fortune predicted by the old Univac Computer at the Ventura County Fair. It had foretold of a difficult and perilous life for Stan and, so far, it had been right on the mark. He wondered how long it would be before fate dragged him into yet another impossible situation. When it came he just hoped he'd be ready for it.

Epilogue

In the six months following the November elections, Stan's life settled down considerably. With the election over and his investigations concluded, he focused his attention on law school, his job, and spending time with the family.

Shortly after her confession, Melissa Thornton pled guilty to six counts of capital murder but avoided death row by cooperating in the prosecution of Vincente Perez, Carlos Morales, Manuel Rubicardo, and Pablo Gomez.

Vincente Perez was found guilty in a California court for the murder of Brad Thornton and sentenced to life in prison. He is currently serving his time at San Quentin.

Manuel Rubicardo and Pablo Gomez were tried on five counts of murder in the 299th State District Court of Collin County for the brutal slaying of the Shepard family and found guilty on all counts. They were both given the death penalty and are awaiting execution at Huntsville Prison in Texas.

Shortly after his arrest, Carlos Morales was released on five million dollars bond and is awaiting trial for money laundering and income tax evasion. Due to the complexity of the cases against him and a formidable legal defense team, experts predict his trial could be postponed for years.

Tony Rubio was indicted but never apprehended

and is believed to be living in Costa Rica, but all of the businesses used by the Burilo Cartel in its money laundering operation were seized and the assets forfeited.

Professor Harry Hertel managed to convince the US Attorney not to press for an indictment of Commissioner Barnes, and likewise, no indictment ever came down on Ron Wells. Both agreed to return the profits they'd received from the Silver Springs Ventures to be forfeited, along with the other assets of the venture.

It was May 14, 1977, graduation day at SMU Law School. Rebekah, the kids, and Rebekah's parents sat in the crowd as the graduates paraded across the stage to receive their diplomas. When the ceremony was over, Stan returned to where they were sitting and gave Rebekah a big hug. Then he picked up Marcia and held her in his arms.

"I'm so proud of you," Rebekah said excitedly.

"I'm just glad it's over," Stan replied. "Now, I can finally practice law and make a decent living."

"Where are you going to work while you wait to take the bar exam?" Rebekah's father asked.

"I'm going to stay at Cosmopolitan Life. I'll work there until I get my license and can get some financing for a law practice."

"Daddy. Why don't you stay home with us all day?" Reggie suggested.

"No, no," Rebekah protested. "It's time for your father to support us. I'm quitting my job just as soon as he starts making decent money—which I hope is very soon. Taking care of you monkeys is a full-time job, believe me."

As they were talking, Stan saw Paula. "I'm going to go congratulate a few of my friends and then we can go."

Rebekah nodded. "Okay, but don't be long."

Stan left and went to where Paula was talking with her father and some friends.

"Hey, congratulations, Paula," Stan said as they embraced.

"Likewise," Paula replied. "Can you believe it's over?"

"God, I'm so relieved. What an ordeal, huh?"

"Of course, your extracurricular activities didn't help," Paula said wryly.

Stan smiled. "Actually, I think it made it more bearable. Studying can be so boring."

Paula nodded. "That's true."

"So, have you decided what you're going to do yet?" Stan asked.

"I'm taking the job at the District Attorney's office, I guess."

"Putting away bad guys, huh?"

"At least until I learn the ropes, then I'll switch sides and become a filthy rich defense lawyer."

Stan laughed. "Sounds like a plan. Maybe I'll see you in court."

"I hope so. It's been fun this year. We should stay in touch."

"Yes, definitely," Stan agreed. "Well, I've got to go. The family is waiting to go out for dinner."

They embraced and Stan started back to where Rebekah and everyone was waiting. Before he made it back, however, he ran into Lamar. They congratulated each other, and then Stan asked if he was still going out with Kristina.

"No. I'm afraid not. I saw her a few times after she was elected, but then she got too busy for me."

"Oh, that's too bad," Stan said. "You guys would

have been good together."

"Hasn't she kept in touch with you?" Lamar asked.

Stan shook his head. "No. I haven't talked twice to her since the election."

"Hmm. Well, I heard she was engaged"

"Engaged?" Stan gasped. "That was fast. I didn't even know she was going out with anyone?"

"Yeah, to the son of a wealthy insurance executive, I understand."

"What?" Stan asked in disbelief. "You've got to be kidding."

"No. In fact, her fiancé's father is a lobbyist for the insurance industry."

Stan's heart sank. Could she have sold out already?

Stan said goodbye and rejoined Rebekah and the others. His shock and dismay had turned to anger. Had he been betrayed? Kristina had promised to be independent and challenge the corrupt establishment. Had she been playing him from the start—telling him what she thought he wanted to hear rather than what she believed?

The next day he decided to call her. It took several tries but he finally got through.

"Stan. Sorry I didn't return your call right away, but I've been terribly busy."

"Yes, I can imagine. How are you liking the job?"

"Oh, it's awesome. I love it. It's very demanding, though. I've got so much to learn."

"Hey. I heard you're engaged."

"Oh, yes. I am. How did you hear about that?"

"Lamar told me yesterday at graduation."

"Oh, you've graduated now. Congratulations!"

"Thank you. . . . So, tell me about your fiancé."

"Oh, Mark Branson is his name. He's a grad student at UT."

"What's he studying?"

"He's finishing up his MBA."

"What's he going to do after he graduates?"

"Oh, he's got a job lined up with his father."

"That wouldn't be David Branson, would it?"

Kristina hesitated. "Yes. That's right."

Branson was a notorious insurance company lobbyist who pumped millions of dollars into the campaigns of Texas politicians who were sympathetic to tort reform and laws favorable to big business. His name had come up in Stan and Kristina's conversations in the past.

"I can't believe you'd marry into that family."

"Mark isn't like his father."

"But isn't he about to go into the same business?"

Kristina sighed. "Stan, you're a nice guy, but you're so naive. You shouldn't believe everything people tell you—particularly someone aspiring to be a politician. I'd have done anything, including jumping into bed with you, to get elected.

Stan felt like he been struck by a whip. He tried to keep his composure but couldn't manage it. "So, was it love at first sight or an offer you couldn't refuse?"

There was silence for a moment. "Stan, I owe you a lot. I thought it was going to take me years to get my foot in the door in Austin. Then you offered me my dream on a silver platter. I could hardly refuse it, just like I couldn't refuse what Mark had to offer."

"Of course not," Stan spat. "I trusted you. I believed in you."

"I'm still my own person," Kristina insisted.

Stan laughed. "Keep telling yourself that. Self delusion is a great coping mechanism. I just hope in ten years you'll be able to live with yourself."

He hated it when people lied to him, particularly someone he trusted. It was the last straw for him. He'd had enough of corruption and deceit. When his term as County Chairman was up, he'd be finished with politics forever.

His anger turned to sadness and disappointment as he realized his oldest and most cherished ambition—to be a politician—had been dashed by fate and a sober dose of reality. He had been naive. He should have realized Kristina, like any good politician, would move to strengthen and solidify her position once elected. Marriage was one of the oldest and most effective strategies for doing that. The kings of Europe had been masters at it. Perhaps his outrage was more to do about jealousy than moral outrage. Disappointment that he'd never have Kristina for himself, and the realization that he didn't really like politics now that he understood the ugly reality of it.

He tried to think why he wanted to be a politician in the first place. He couldn't remember. He had told himself it was because a politician could make a difference in the world, but was that really it? Or, was it simply a lust for power and the glamour and riches such a life would bring? Whatever his motivations had been, he knew now he wanted no part of it. Maybe he owed Kristina a debt of gratitude for making him realize it before he was so deeply mired in the mud and slime of politics that he couldn't extricate himself.

"I'm sorry, Stan," Kristina said seeming sincere.

"It's alright. I'm sorry I bit your head off. Congratulations on your engagement."

"Thank you, and don't write me off as a typical politician quite yet. You know I'm full of surprises."

"That's good to hear," Stan said holding back his

tears. "I'll be keeping an eye out for some good things."

"I'm glad. I won't disappoint you."

Stan hung up the phone. He knew it would take a time to get over Kristina and the death of his childhood dream, but he knew he didn't have time for self-pity. He had to try and put aside his disappointment and depression and begin to focus on the road ahead—starting a new law practice.

He couldn't wait to get started—to move on to something new and exciting. There was only one problem—money. He hated having to worry about money, but realistically he'd need a hundred grand to start a law practice. That was a lot of cash, more than he'd made in his entire lifetime, but now that he was a lawyer he figured it wouldn't be a problem.

Then he thought of Tony Rubio. It bothered him that the bastard was probably living a life of luxury in Costa Rica while he organized a new criminal organization to replace the Burilo Cartel. There had to be a way to nail the bastard–some way to exact justice for Rob and his family. Then and idea came to him. He wondered if Rebekah would be up for a vacation to Costa Rica.

BRASH ENDEAVOR

William Manchee
A Stan Turner Mystery
Top Publications, July 1998,
Trade Paperback ISBN # 1-884570-89-5

Step into the shoes of Dallas attorney, Stan Turner, in the late 1970's as he begins the practice of law. Then hang on for the ride of your life as Stan immediately steps into a rattlesnake's nest and has to do some fancy two-steppin' to avoid a lethal strike from his own clients. When Stan's wife, Rebekah, is arrested for murder and a client turns out to be a ghost, Stan turns in his legal pad for a detective's notebook and goes to work to solve these most perplexing mysteries.

Teetering on the brink of bankruptcy, Stan pushes on relentlessly to extricate himself and his family from certain doom. Sex, greed and a lust for power drive this most extraordinary novel to a stunning conclusion.

THE STAN TURNER MYSTERIES

by William Manchee

Undaunted (1997)
Brash Endeavor (1998)
Second Chair (2000)
Cash Call (2002)
Deadly Distractions (2004)
Black Monday (2005)
Cactus Island (2006)
Act Normal (2007)
Disillusioned (2010)
Deadly Defiance (2011)

"...appealing characters and lively dialogue, especially in the courtroom . . . " (*Publisher's Weekly*)

"...plenty of action and adventure . . . " (*Library Journal*)

"...each plot line, in and of itself, can be riveting . . . " (*Foreword Magazine*)

"...a courtroom climax that would make the venerable Perry Mason stand and applaud . . . "
(Crescent Blue)

"...Richly textured with wonderful atmosphere, the novel shows Manchee as a smooth, polished master of the mystery form . . . " (*The Book Reader*)

"...Manchee's stories are suspenseful and most involve lawyers. And he's as proficient as Grisham . . . (*Dallas Observer*)

"...fabulous-a real page turner-I didn't want it to end!" (Allison Robson, CBS Affiliate, *KLBK TV, Ch 13*)